FISH AND DICKS
Case files from the
Digby Neck & Islands
Fish-Gutting Service
& Detective Agency
Jim Prime & Ben Robicheau
Illustrations by Catherine Prime

Cover image and illustrations: Catherine Prime

Editor: Andrew Wetmore

ISBN: 978-1-7772937-0-3
First edition October, 2020

397 Parker Mountain Road
Granville Ferry NS
B0S 1A0

moosehousepress.com
info@moosehousepress.com

We live and work in Mi'kma'ki, the ancestral and unceded territory of the Mi'kmaq People. This territory is covered by the "Treaties of Peace and Friendship" which Mi'kmaq and Wolastoqiyik (Maliseet) People first signed with the British Crown in 1725. The treaties did not deal with surrender of lands and resources but in fact recognized Mi'kmaq and Wolastoqiyik (Maliseet) title and established the rules for what was to be an ongoing relationship between nations. We are all Treaty people.

Acknowledgements

Jim:

Writing these stories with my lifelong friend Ben Robicheau has been an amazing experience. Ben and I share the same sense of humour, which I suspect is the by-product of salt air, comic books, WMEX radio and an excessive amount of fog. Gurrey and Grime are essentially Ben and Jim.

The creation of Gurrey and Grime has given me a small insight into how God must have felt when he came up with Adam and Eve. They are very imperfect creatures but it's their imperfections that make them human and hopefully relatable. We hope you enjoy their misadventures.

Ben:

For something that started out from a typo, Gurrey and Grime have grown far beyond our expectations. As Jim has said, getting to create these stories with your best friend and someone who shares and understands your sense of humour is a special experience.

It is particularly satisfying to see how our characters have resonated with the citizens of the islands where we grew up. We appreciate their support and hope they enjoy the most recent version of our odd adventures.

We'd like to acknowledge the following people for their help with this book:

Jim:

Glenna Prime, for her constant support and for laughing in all the right places.
Catherine Prime, for her wonderful illustrations for the cover and throughout the book, and just for being Catherine.
Ray Rockwell, for being such a generous and vocal advocate of my writing.
Margaret Rockwell for being a constant inspiration to me.
Fin and Sam Canton who both possess the wacky humour gene.

Ben:

Randi Robicheau, for being unfailingly encouraging, even when I'm boring her to death with some ridiculous G & G plot line.

Raymond and Riekie Robicheau, my parents, for demonstrating the importance of storytelling.

Felix, Charlie and Lyla, my grandchildren, for opening my eyes to new adventures every day.

Jim and Ben:

We both thank Aubrey Prime, who generously sponsored the appearance of some of these stories in *Passages*.

Thanks Brenda Thompson for adding this title to her growing list of Moose House publications, and editor Andrew Wetmore for reeling us in only when absolutely necessary.

We dedicate this book to Long and Brier Islands, the people and the places, because both are unique. They shaped our lives in so many ways and gifted us with both a sense of community and a sense of humour. The Islands will forever be "down home" to both of us.

Foreword

Gurrey and Grime are the result of a misprint. In a review of Jim Prime's book *How Hockey Explains Canada*, the reviewer referred to him as Jim Grime. Jim mentioned the faux pas to his friend Ben Robicheau, who said that it sounded like a private detective's name, the kind whose beat might be the "tough streets of Brier Island." A series of emails flew back and forth between the two and the exploits of Gurrey and Grime grew like a toxic fungus.

Prime hails from Freeport on Long Island and Ben from Westport on Brier Island. Their upbringings were shockingly similar. Both are sons of grocers on their respective islands and both share the same sense of humour.

Jim and Ben shared the G and G stories with friends and soon some of them appeared in serialized form in *Passages*, the "*New York Times* of the Tri-Island area."

The result is this book, which includes some brand new adventures.

Disclammer

Hastily edited by Jim Grime and Ben Gurrey on the way across the passage to the printer. Please excuse any spelin errers, incorrect punctuation:;!, accidental repetition, accidental repetition, ungood grammar and bad taste.

Table of contents

Illustrations

1: Funeral Sandwiches

It was Sunday afternoon and Ben Gurrey was sitting in the front row of the small chapel at the Islands Funeral Home and Wax Museum. He was staring at the stainless-steel urn that rested on a low table next to the pulpit.

Suddenly his old friend Jim Grime burst through the door waving a letter in the air. "Gurrey, it's true, it's really true!"

"Grimey, I don't think this is the time or—"

But Grime wasn't listening. He paced back and forth past the urn, reading and re-reading the sheet of paper and chuckling. Finally, he took a deep breath and spoke. "Remember that letter I wrote about a month ago?"

"The one to that Judi Dench? How many times have I gotta tell you she ain't interested in you? That's twelve letters you've written to that poor woman and even Interpol has warned you to cease and desist."

"Dame Dench be damned," said Grime. "This is the letter I sent to that company that traces your ancestry."

"You mean that there Twenty-two Skidoo?"

"Twenty-Two and You. This here's from them. Oh, Gurrey, I'm so excited I could climb a pole. Listen to this:

> *Dear Mr. Grime,*
>
> *Thank you for joining Twenty-Two and You. We have completed the initial stages of our research into your family tree and have discovered the following information—*

"They discover your family tree was a wreath?" Gurrey said.

Grime ignored him and continued reading. "'You come from Franco-English stock, most likely the area then known as Brittany.' Let's see...blah, blah, blah...'family of sheep stealers and sheep shag'...'"

Grime hesitated, then continued, "Blah, blah, blah...'tried for treason'...blah, blah, blah....'placed in the stocks'...blah, blah, blah... 'stowed away on the Mayflower disguised as a nun'...blah, blah,

blah…Oh, here's the good part. 'We have found a match between the DNA sample that you sent us and a sample in our data base. We are certain that you will be excited to learn that we have determined with 85% accuracy that you are a descendant of former Westport, Nova Scotia resident and nautical legend Joshua Slocum. If you wish to learn more about this family connection, please send an additional $149.95 so that we can conduct further research into this amazing discovery.'" Grime looked up from the letter to see his friend's reaction.

"Slocum? I've heard that name before somewhere," Gurrey said, scratching his head with a hymnal. "He the fella used to work down at the fish plant? Got that Hersey girl in the family way then took off?"

"No, no! Joshua Slocum! The greatest man to ever come off these islands! Back in 1895, he was the very first man to sail alone around the world! Wrote a book about it! Can you imagine being a pioneer in circumnavigation, the courage it took? Think you coulda done that?"

"Ain't really given it much thought," Gurrey said, wincing slightly. "I hear tell it's awful painful and at my age I don't see the point. Besides, that ain't a fit subject for a funeral parlour. We oughta be givin' our respects to the recently dear departed."

"Yeah, of course, you're right," Grime said in a more subdued voice. He took a seat alongside his friend. "We'll discuss it later. Poor old Clayton. Some say he was the worst man ever to come off this island."

Seeing the sadness on his friend's face, he realized he'd gone too far and quickly tried to make amends. "Salt of the earth, though, when he weren't liquored up."

An awkward silence followed until Grime eventually asked, "Had he been sick?"

"No, no, he died in excellent health." Gurrey leaned over to whisper into Grime's ear despite the fact that they were the only living people in the room. "Happened while he was on the throne, if you get my drift, attendin' to his toilette. Just finishin' up the paperwork when he took a funny turn."

"That's terrible," Grime said, patting him on the shoulder. "Flushed away in the prime of his life. Poor Bonita."

"You can say that again." Gurrey said haltingly. "Ya see, he was down to Edna Tupper's trailer—you know, that double-wide next to the highway, the trailer I mean, not Edna—when it happened. Bonita sure put up with a lot from that man of hers. You might almost say his passin' was a huge relief."

Grime's face registered little surprise at the news. "Gotta admit, she deserved better."

"Still, it's sad. I've known Clay all my life. Why, we pole-vaulted into puberty together when we wuz 16 or so. Hung out down by the fish plant at Roney's Point trying to pick up the girlies during smoke breaks. You know, Bonita has asked me to deliver the urology."

"Quite an honour. But what do you say about a feller like Old Clay? Laziest man I ever met. Never worked a day in his life if he could help it. Never travelled more than thirty miles from his dinner table. Told me once, 'Travel might broaden the mind, but it sure narrows the wallet.' Cheap!? Clay could squeeze a nickel 'til the beaver squawked. And his womanizing was out of control. Why if even half the stories are true, he was the biggest philanthropist in three counties. Always tendin' up two or three at a time."

"Don't I know it! That's why I'm really struggling to come up with something 'ceptable to say. You know, for Bonita's sake."

Gurrey fished in his back pocket and extracted a crumpled piece of paper, smoothing it out on his pant leg. "I've jotted down a few of them, what you call bon mots, but to tell the truth, it's hard to put him in a good light. You always had a way with words, Grimey. Can you help?"

Grime struggled to control the emotion that was welling up inside him, thrilled that his friend thought so highly of his literary talents. After a brief pause, he answered. "Well, read me what you got. Sometimes it's all in the way you say it."

Gurrey cleared his voice and read. "Clayton Young often visited with area widows until all hours and on two occasions was accused of stealing their welfare checks. He died on the crapper at the home of one of these lady friends."

"No, no, no!" Grime said. "That's no-good a-tall. How 'bout this?" He cleared his throat. "Although he never actually attended church, in his own way Clayton Young was a spiritual man who believed in loving his neighbour, whenever and wherever the opportunity presented itself. He was 'specially concerned with the welfare of the weaker sex. Clay died secure in the knowledge that he had intimately touched many people."

Gurrey stared at Grime with childlike admiration. A smile spread across his face as he quickly scribbled the words in the margins of the lined paper. He resumed reading with enthusiasm. "He fathered countless illegitimate children all over this island," he said, and paused to hear how his simple words would be miraculously transformed by the Shakespeare of the Tri-Island area.

Grime scratched his beard and vigorously explored his left ear with his forefinger before replying. "Let's see here. How about: 'A civic minded man, he worked tirelessly to expand the tax base of Brier Island'?"

Gurrey scribbled furiously, silently mouthing the words he'd just heard. He continued to read. "He was born tired, and laziness set in. Completely bone-idle."

"He was a pioneer in the conservation of energy," said Grime, somewhat smugly.

There was another pause as Gurrey jotted down the words. He took a deep breath and went on. "Clay could not be trusted around your money. He continually lied to your face and always embellished his few accomplishments."

"Pshaw," said Grime, warming to his task. "He had the makings of a fine politician."

Gurrey had to fight the urge to applaud. "Oh, that's good! That's real good!"

"Due to several undiagnosed illnesses that prevented him from exerting any physical effort whatsoever, his money came from welfare and disability cheques, as well as from Bonita's 12-hour shifts at the fish factory, when she wasn't in labour…" For a split second it looked as if Grime had been stymied. He peered upward toward the chapel ceiling as if seeking divine intervention, paused dramatically, and raised a finger.

"The bulk of his income was derived from various high government sources and he was always a firm supporter of women in the workplace."

"Perfect! Just one more Grimey, but it's a tough one. 'His hobbies included, scratchin' lottery tickets, eatin' pork scratchins and plain ol' scratchin'. Also, whittlin', spittin', jackin' deer—and bingo, when his health permitted. His only cultural pursuit was watching *Dating Naked* on the TV…"

Grime improvised a yawn, as if this was too easy. "Clayton Young was a true Renaissance man."

Gurrey copied the words, finishing with a flourish. He wiped a single tear from his eye. "Well done! You shoulda been a lawyer, or maybe a minister or con man of some kind. You got him soundin' practically like a saint. Bonita should be some happy with that."

The mention of the widow seemed to shake Grime. "Er, speaking of Bonita, have you noticed any change in her since his passing?"

"Well, other than looking like she's had a huge burden finally lifted off her shoulders, no, not really. Why?"

"I know this is gonna sound crazy, but I kind of got the feeling that she has the hots for me. She always did sort of give off them vibes, you know, always complimenting me on how I smell and so on. I think it's the mixture of Absorbine Jr and Arrid Extra Dry. Well, I went to the private viewing last night and she was comin' onta me right there in the vestry, while I was munchin' on a funeral sandwich. I think she knows that Clay was cheating on her and wants revenge by sleeping with me."

"Never! Not Bonita!"

Grime was wringing his hands nervously. "Said she don't know how she'll be able to go on alone, now that she's recently become a sexagenarian and all. Sexagenarian! Now ain't that something for a sixty-one-year-old woman to say!?"

"Disgraceful! Er…what exactly is a sexagenarian, Grimey?"

"I ain't 'zactly sure myself, but I think it involves...you know... different positions. Like in that book with the pictures down at Phil's barber shop."

"You mean the Karmann Ghia?"

"That's her!" Grime said. He lowered his voice. "Hey, Ben, what do you think about what they get up to in that 50 Shades of Grey?"

"Perfectly understandable. Vera and me did it in the fog sometimes too. You have to if you live along the coast. Less you wanna stay celebrate all your life."

"No, no, I mean, er, like, did you ever tie Vera up?"

"Why would I do a fool thing like that? She wasn't in any danger of drifting away. But they do say it's good for a marriage to mix things up a bit...er, in what they call the boudoir. What, eh, position do you favour, Grimey?"

Grime raised his eyebrows. "On sex? Oh, I'm all for it, acourse!"

"I assumed that, I mean what position do you favour, you know... in the carnival knowledge sense?"

"Oh, I see. Well, it's been a while, but me and the missus didn't go in for them meringue de trois and such. We only ever had but the one position—the trusty old missionary. Those people do wonderful work. I figure if it's good enough for Mother Theresa it's good enough for Jim Grime. A place for everything and everything in its place. Eyup, never heard a word of complaint from Edna in the 38 years we were married, not a word! Right up to the day she up and walked out the door and never came back. Was spoutin' some nonsense about being unappreciated and unsatisfied. Mumblin' something about me not listening to her or some such foolishness! I'm not really sure, I only heard bits and pieces. I was watching The Wheel at the time. As I recall, somebody was buyin' a vowel."

Gurrey grew wistful. "With me and Vera you could set your watch by it—every Saturday night after the first period of Hockey Night in Canada. When Coach's Corner comes on. That Don Cherry feller is a regular aphrodisiac to Vera. I think it's them suits. You know, the ones that look like seat covers for a 1992 Dodge Dart. The louder the suit the better the... you know. And that 12-minute show is just the perfect time to do our thing, have a cigarette and re-polish the coffee table."

He stuck his chest out proudly. "Yep, over the years, I figure I've scored more often than the Toronto Maple Leafs. Anyways, I'll be glad when the burial is over. It's cold up there to the graveyard. Freeze the you-know-whats off a brass monkey."

"Cold don't bother me," said Grime.

"Why's that?"

"I wear them there Stanfields. Not only was the man a great premier, but he made wonderful long johns. Stanfield's Trap Doors, that's the name. STDs for short. Been wearing 'em for twenty years. Buy 'em by the case every few years up to Digby. Irregulars, but who's gonna tell? Even give 'em as gifts sometimes."

He stood up and stretched. "Excuse me, I gotta go see a man about a horse. Be right back."

Moments after Grime left for the washroom, the chapel door opened and Bonita came in, dabbing her eyes with a tissue. She nodded to Gurrey and sat down beside him.

"Hi Ben."

"Hello, Bon. How you holding up?"

"It ain't easy. I loved Clay, but you know what he was like. Hard to forgive him. He had a wandering eye, you know."

"That's true. He really could've used some corrective surgery."

Bonita gave him an annoyed glance and blew her nose. "I know he was seeing other women. I overheard someone talking about him and it made me so ashamed."

"Oh, Bon..."

"I know you were his oldest friend, Ben Gurrey, but don't try to deny it."

"No better or no worse than most men, I s'pose, Bon."

"I don't believe it. He was the worst man to ever come off these islands! Look at that Jim Grime. Now there's a nice man! Respectful. Clean-livin'. Smells like laundry that's been on the line all day. That's the kind of man I shoulda married. Where is he anyway?"

The words were hardly out of her mouth when she felt a hand on her shoulder.

"Hey, Bonita. Sorry again about Clay," Grime said. He sat down on the other side of Bonita and patted her hand.

Bonita looked at him meaningfully and clutched his hand in hers. "Thanks, Jim. You're a good man. A decent man." She paused, examining his face with concern. "You all right? You're perspiring something terrible."

"Oh, it's nothing, just my STDs. They make me sweat something fierce sometimes. But I tell you, it's worth it! I don't mind putting up with a little sweating and itching. I was just tellin' Gurrey here how I got my first case of STDs twenty years ago from that pretty young red-headed clerk who used to work at the Metropolitan store in Digby."

Bonita put her hand to her mouth, stifling a gasp.

"Yup, then I got my second case from the old lady that mostly worked in Women's Whatnots at Zeller's."

Bonita's eyes grew large and her mouth fell open.

"And the third time it was from that Bruce fella at the Walmart in New Minas, the fella with the Popeye tattoo on his arm. Now it seems I can't hardly go up the Valley without coming back with a new case of STDs. I pass them along to friends, too. It's the gift that keeps on giving."

Aghast, Bonita leaped to her feet and slapped Grime across his face. She moved quickly to the urn, hugged it close to her breast and headed for the door. "I take it all back, Clay," she said to his ashes. "You wasn't the worst man on these here islands. Not by a long shot. Let's go home."

2: The Legacy

It was the morning after Clayton's funeral. A somewhat subdued Ben Gurrey and Jim Grime were slumped on a tattered and stained chesterfield in a weathered old fish shack on the Westport waterfront. Gurrey had a three-week stubble of beard and wore his trusty, crusty red hunting cap with the brim pointing straight up. His shirt was faded green plaid.

Grime's stubble was of similar vintage and his cap was emblazoned with the words *No to Fish Farms*. He also wore plaid, faded blue in colour.

In front of them was a long table piled high with cod fish, haddock and pollock. A crude conveyor belt led to the table through a window facing the open sea. Periodically the slow moving and squeaky contraption dropped more fish into a wooden bin at the head of the table, but the two men ignored their arrival. They were on a self-imposed work break, sipping beer and reading different sections of *The Digby Courier* by the light of a single bare bulb suspended from a dangerously frayed cord above their heads.

"I see here in the Brier Island news that Bertha Haines got married last week," Gurrey said. "I doubt that'll last."

"Why's that Gurrey," Jim said without raising his eyes from his own reading.

Gurrey looked at him. "Well, the feller's from Long Island."

His friend nodded. "Oh, right, I see. A mixed marriage."

"I hope they can overcome it," Gurrey sighed. "He ain't a bad guy."

Suddenly Grime became animated, smacking the newspaper with the back of his hand. "Well, Gurrey my friend, all I can see in this paper is opportunity!"

"How's that, Grimey?"

"Because crime is rampant on these two islands, that's why."

"Like what?"

"Says right here: *Council To Probe Littering*. And here's another: *Man Fined For Faulty Signal Light*. And another: *Local Scofflaw Breaks Streetlight*. And another: *Bootlegger Over-Charges For Beer*.

"And look at this!" Gurrey said. "*Freeport Couple Fined For Smuggling*."

"Actually, that says snuggling, Gurrey. Things get pretty wild down Lover's Lane. But the point is crime is at epidemic levels."

Gurrey nodded in agreement. "It's bad, all right, a regular crime wave. Soon it'll be like downtown Little River on a Saturday night."

"Another Sadam and Gonorrhea, that's what we're looking at."

"But I still don't see how that's an opportunity," Gurrey said.

Grime put down the newspaper and turned to his friend. "Clayton's sad passing and somewhat dubious legacy has given me pause to think. Do we wanna end up like Clay, or do we wanna be remembered like my close personal relative Josh Slocum? Heroes or zeroes, that's the choice. Up 'til now we've been fish-gutters, and darn good ones too, but we can see it's a dyin' industry. In a few more years it'll be gone altogether and then what will *our* legacy be? What will we be remembered for? I say it's time we got diversified."

"Well now, Grimey, I never was much for religion, not since the last pastor took off with the undertaker's wife and the Sunday School collection."

"Diversified, Gurrey! Diversified! We need a business that's recession-proof and, more importantly, will guarantee that our names live on in infamy long after we're both takin' our own permanent dirt-naps. And I know exactly what business will do it! What two things go together more naturally than fish and crime?"

"Well, I can think of quite a f—"

"Exactly! It's a perfect match! When our detective work slows down, we can fall back on fish-gutting, and versa visa. The factory can't handle all the fish, and the nearest Mountie is two ferries and forty miles of bad road away...it's a natural. Supply and demand. Fish and dicks."

"Do you really think it'd work?" Gurrey's voice reflected his growing interest.

"I've put an ad in this very paper and made some changes to the sign out front," Grime said triumphantly, rubbing his hands together. "We are now the Digby Neck & Islands Fish-Gutting Service & Detective Agency. Catchy, ain't it? Now we just wait for the clients to line up. Take a look outside and see if anyone's lined up yet."

With some effort, Gurrey extricated himself from the sagging couch, went to the door and opened it. He squinted his eyes and stared out into the grey murk.

"Well, the fog's pretty thick but I don't see no one."

"Matter of time," Grime said. "Matter of time. Soon the DN&IF-GS&DA will be on everyone's lips.

The words were scarcely out of his mouth when the door burst open and a shapely shadow fell across the office desk/gutting table. Looking up, Grime flashed a gap-toothed grin at the leggy dame who had insinuated her way through the door.

She was a tall drink of water with gams that went on till next Tuesday and big blonde hair that appeared to have come straight from a peroxide bottle. She appeared to be in her mid-fifties and wore makeup that looked as if it had been applied with a spatula. Her skirt was short and she wore fishnet stockings with more runs in them than a weekend track meet. An unfiltered Export A cigarette dangled from her lips.

She peered around the interior, adjusting her bloodshot eyes to the dim light, and then sashayed to the centre of the room. A disparaging look was fixed on her face, a cross between contempt and *rigor mortis*, as she looked them up and down.

"She's a hot dame," Grime thought. "Oh, maybe not surface-of-the-sun hot. More like defective-hot-plate hot—but still hot. Or at least lukewarm."

Grime looked her up and down, from arse to teakettle. It was obvious that she'd been around the block more times than a newly hired FedEx driver. She had more curves than the Bear River Road. She had hills and valleys and peaks and plains and rich fertile bottom land. In short, she was a geographer's dream.

The unlit cigarette dangled provocatively from her luscious lips. "Gotta match?" she purred seductively.

Grime leapt to his feet and fished a book of matches from his pocket. His hand shook as he struck a match and lit her cigarette. She inhaled deeply and blew a perfect smoke ring that momentarily framed his face before dissipating.

"Your lungs do you credit, if I may say so, miss," he said. "And your teeth aren't nearly as yellow as one might expect from a tobacco enthusiast such as yourself." He smiled, thankful to have been blessed with such a smooth way with the girlies.

Ignoring Grime's clumsy attempt to be charming, the woman cast a critical eye around the newly-established detective agency. "It looks like Dante's Inferno in here."

Gurrey smiled. "You mean that new pizza place in Weymouth? Thanks! We think it has a certain ambulance."

"I think you mean ambience," the woman said.

"You obviously haven't tried their pizza."

The woman rolled her eyes and placed both hands on the table. "Are you two the dicks I've been readin' about?"

Grime looked at her with undisguised admiration. He smiled and assumed his most professional air. "We certainly are, madam. What can we do for you?"

"Depends. You any good?"

Gurrey bit off a chaw of chewing tobacco. "You lookin' for detective work or fish-guttin'?"

The woman shot him a withering look. "Do you see any codfish?"

Gurrey aimed a stream of tobacco juice toward a Maxwell House coffee can on the floor. "Well, those fishnet stockings look like they might have snagged a few in their time."

Sensing trouble, the always diplomatic Grime quickly intervened. "You'll have to excuse my partner. His sense of humour was lost at sea. You are our first official client, although we have done some pro boney work in the past. Most recently, we brought the Westport bingo cartel to its knees. They were using dummy dobbers—dobbers with invisible ink so they wouldn't have to pay up. Caught 'em red-handed, so to speak... although the red soon disappeared." He realized he was babbling and stopped abruptly.

"Don't forget the cold case," Gurrey said.

"It's in the fridge, Gurrey, but I hardly think this is the time or place—"

"Not the case of Moosehead, Grimey! I'm talking about that case from five years back—"

"Probably skunky by now."

"The *cold* case, Grime, the cold case that we solved, the break-in at the Syst place. Old Sebaceous was a Syst on his father's side, you see, miss, and—."

The woman held up her hand. "All right, all right! What about an extramarital affair?"

Grime sprang from his seat. "Not sure about Gurrey, here, but I'd be up for one."

"You idiot," the woman said. "Have you two even heard of a paternity suit?"

Once again, Gurrey took offence. "Well, if the way we're dressed offends you, perhaps you should take your business elsewhere."

Grime hurried to the rescue. "Sure, sure! Certainly! We know the ways of the world. Affairs, paternity suits. What do you need us to do?"

The woman let out a deep sigh and spoke resignedly. "Well, I guess you two are as good as I'm gonna find in this god-forsaken hell hole."

Grime blushed at the compliment. "Thank you miss. We're flattered."

The woman scanned the room for a place to sit. Spotting an upturned bait barrel, she slunk across the small room, nudged it nearer the table and sat down with as much dignity as the situation allowed. She leaned her elbows on the desk/gutting table behind which the newly-minted dicks were seated, partially obscured by the pile of fish. Her ample bosom strained against its fragile restraints, threatening to spill forth and breach the twin levees of her triple D bra.

The cleavage caused Grime to fidget in his seat. He tried manfully but unsuccessfully to avert his eyes.

"What are you staring at?"

"Oh…er…nothin', Miss, I was just thinkin' about the new breastwork they're buildin' down the road where the tide broke through during the August blow. Government project. Federal erection…er…election comin'. For some reason, your what you call, decoupilage reminded me of the drainage ditch they had to dig to let 'er drain."

She looked at him blankly for a full ten seconds before continuing. "My name is Lucy Dulsé, accent acute on the 'e.' You might have heard of me. I used to be known as Lucy the Floozy. Sure, I slept around a bit, but who didn't in those decadent days of the 60s?" She paused. "70s." Pause. "80s." Long pause. "And 90s!" she concluded defiantly. "Let she who hasn't spent a long weekend with the Grand Manan dragger fleet cast the first stone!"

Grime was visibly shocked. "Are you saying that you were fast and easy?"

Lucy flicked her cigarette ash on the floor. "Like Kraft Dinner, honey."

Ben stared at her intently as if struggling to remember something. "So, what's the problem, miss…Dulse, is it?" he said.

"Accent acute, yes. I want you to find the father of my child… well, he's hardly a child any more…36 years old, God bless him. I fell for a devilishly handsome young fisherman many years ago and got pregnant. Met him at a dance in Meteghan River. He doesn't even know he has a son. We were ships passing in the night." She chuckled. "Although in some ways he was more of a dingy, if you get my drift."

"What were you, a tramp steamer?" Gurrey said under his breath.

Lucy Dulsé ignored him. "All I know is that he's about my age, medium height and weight and brown hair. He wasn't the sharpest hook on the trawl line, but he had a good heart. First name was Ben and he had a tattoo of his boat on his chest. I think he's from one of these islands."

"We're at your disposal 24/7," Grime assured her, "As long as I'm home by 9:00 to watch *Housewives of New Jersey*."

She rose from her seat and moved toward the door.

"Oh, and Miss Dulsé, I'm afraid we'll require a retainer. Uh, is $15.00 too steep?"

"I guess I don't have much choice," she said. She fumbled in her purse and threw two rumpled bills on the table. "I'm staying at the Tide's Inn B & B in Freeport. I want you two dicks to keep me informed." She moved to the door and opened it.

"Richards," Gurrey said

Lucy spun around to face him. "What?"

Gurrey was casually examining his finger nails. "Dicks is such a common term, don't you think? We prefer the term Richards. A very cute accent on the 'chard'."

Lucy slammed the door as she left, causing the lone light to flicker momentarily.

Grime stared into the near distance, obviously love-struck. "Now that was one hot dame. Bet she doesn't have to pay for her own liquor at the bootlegger's." He shook his head in admiration. "Anyways, looks like we need to make a trip overseas to make some inquiries."

"You mean Freeport?" Gurrey said. "No need for that."

"Why not?"

"I'm the one we're looking for!"

"You mean—?"

"Yes, I am that devilishly handsome young fisherman."

At just that moment the door burst open and Lucy Dulsé re-entered the shack. "Forgot my purse," she said.

As she moved to retrieve it from where it lay on the floor near the bait barrel, Gurrey struggled awkwardly to rise from the chesterfield. He moved to face her, feet apart and shoulders back, and ripped open his shirt, sending a barrage of buttons shooting past Dulsé's head.

There on his hairy chest was the tattoo of a boat that appeared to be in distress, riding atop a rather large swell that was in fact his ample belly.

"Lucy, it's me. Ben. They call me Gurrey now." He hesitated. "I'm the father of your child."

Lucy Dulsé's mouth fell open. She looked him up and down and then moved closer and examined him once again. She slowly closed her mouth, opened it as if to speak, then quickly closed it again. She tried once more but words still failed her.

Finally, a shudder passed through her body and she managed a deep, shuddering sigh. "Never mind," she said. "Keep the retainer."

Grabbing her purse, she rushed out the door and was immediately swallowed up by the thick fog.

Gurrey dropped back onto the chesterfield, a wistful look on his face.

"Well don't just sit there!" Grime said. "Go after her!"

"No, no," Gurrey said, popping the cap off a bottle of lukewarm Ten Penny Old Stock Ale. "Let her go, it's the kindest thing to do."

"What in the world are you talking about?"

"Didn't you see? It was so obvious! I knew her when she was slim and young and beautiful. When she realized who I was, when she saw that I hadn't aged a bit in all those years, physically, emotionally—or mentally, I might add—she couldn't handle it. She knew she couldn't compare; she was embarrassed by how the years had changed her and left me unscathed. We've grown apart in two different worlds, Grimey. No, it's better that she go, go away to dream and wonder at what might have been."

He gestured grandly around the fish shack. "If fate had only been kinder, all this could have been hers."

Grime put his hand gently on his friend's shoulder. "You're right, old pal, the kindest thing you could possibly do for that woman is to let her get as far away from here as possible."

Figure 1: Headquarters

3: Purloined Periwinkles

It was a moonless night on Brier Island. The fog-shrouded street-lights cast misty, pale pools upon the empty street, and the Peters Island foghorn moaned morosely in the background.

Gurrey and Grime, influenced by this melancholy scene, were reminiscing over past events and rehashing more recent decisions.

"I can't believe it took so long for me to come up with the detective agency idea," Grime said "We already earned a cool $15 working the Lucy case!"

"Except we didn't really do any work," Gurrey replied. "I feel kind of bad taking her money."

"Don't. If you think about it, we've been doing this kind of work for years. We just haven't been getting paid for it."

"That's true. Everyone around here has thought of us as a couple of dicks for a long time now. I've overheard people saying that exact thing. Makes me kind of proud to know they think of us that way. I guess there's no harm in calling ourselves professional dicks and making a little money from it."

"It's not like we're inexperienced, we've pulled a lot of dick moves in the past. There was the Bingo Case and the Cold Case we mentioned to Lucy—"

"And the Mace Face Case," Gurrey interrupted. "Remember? When you tried to break up the turkey bacon riot down at the Fireman's breakfast. You tried to mace them, but had the can wrong-way round and sprayed yourself right in the face. Broke up the riot, though! Everyone was laughing so hard they forgot why they were upset...at least until they found out about the tofu sausages, then it all started up again!"

"That wasn't so funny! My eyesight is still fuzzy, and I haven't been able to smell anything since. Besides, we've actually solved some serious cases. Remember the P. Jack Case? We were the ones who found out who was luring the youth of the town into being mugged."

Several years previously, teen-aged boys began turning up on Southern Point, unconscious, with the chains on their trucker's wallets cut and the wallets stolen. At first the town elders pretty much ignored the situation; after all, who knows what crazy shenanigans those teens get up to! But then it was rumoured that a couple of married men had fallen victim to the same mysterious predator.

At this point Gurrey and Grime were asked to look into the situation. They quickly ascertained that each of the victims had received a seductive note inviting him to meet by the Joshua Slocum monument for what was classily described as "A roll in the hay you'll never forget."

Grime and Gurrey decided to set up a stake-out to work the tough lower east side of Brier Island where Southern Point was located. Through the wind-blown wisps of fog and by the intermittent flashes of illumination provided by the Peters Island lighthouse they could just make out the dark form of a shapely dame leaning provocatively against the Joshua Slocum cairn, twirling her beaded handbag and smoking an unfiltered Export A.

"Want me to take you boys around the world?" she hissed between her luscious, inviting lips.

She was the kind of dame whom desperate lonely men conjure up when they have been at sea far too long and the sea creatures began to look like women. Except in this case, the woman actually did resemble a sea creature, perhaps a walrus or a seal of some kind.

Frantically digging in his pocket for loose change, Grime approached the dame. Obviously, he was about to take her up on her alluring offer.

At the last moment Gurrey held back his naïve and unsophisticated partner. "That ain't no dame. And that ain't no beaded handbag. It's a baitbag full of rocks."

The Southern Point seductress was in reality none other than a cleverly disguised P. Jack, the evil nemesis of the two brave detectives. The sharp-as-a-tack gumshoes soon put two and two together and came up with a number not too far removed from four. Sure, the foggy figure was wearing sexy attire but there was something very fishy about her, and not just the smell. On closer inspection, it was obvious that her fishnet stockings still had some herring caught in them and it was clear that they'd been there for some time. Her translucent bodice was stretched across two well-placed fluorescent traffic cones, most likely stolen from the Department of Highways garage in Tiverton.

Grime recoiled. Gurrey retched. Hoping to take advantage of their weak stomachs, P. advanced, swinging the bag of rocks at them.

The two detectives retreated as the deadly baitbag whistled over their heads and around their ears, until they found themselves backed up to the very edge of a cliff. Before them advanced the dastardly P. Jack, determinedly swinging his lethal weapon; behind them was a twenty-foot drop into the swiftly flowing and ice-cold waters of Grand Passage.

As Grime and Gurrey assessed their chances of surviving a plunge into the salty deep, a piercing scream rent the air, and Jack disappeared in a swirling tornado of black and white feathers. The Peter's Island seagulls, attracted to the unusual activity on the rocks, had suddenly caught scent of the rotting sea life in Jack's fishnet stockings and had attacked *en masse*.

In an instant, Jack was fighting for his life against a thousand sharp-beaked attackers. He took a few desperate but futile swings and then ran for it. Unfortunately—his vision blocked by the vast cloud of birds—he ran straight off the cliff, bobbed once, and disappeared forever under the frigid and unforgiving waves.

Gurrey turned to Grime to check that he was all right. Over Grime's shoulder he saw the majestic cliffs of Long Island and, just beyond, the enchanting community of Freeport nestled snugly to her bosom.

"If only I could get a transfer there," he had thought to himself. "Like they say, 'If you can make it there, you can make it anywhere.'"

~

The phone rang, jolting the two detectives from their reverie.

Gurrey Ben, being younger and more agile, reached the phone first. "Gurrey here. What?...what?...what? Okay, we'll be right over."

He slammed the phone down and turned to Jim Grime. "Looks like we got our first big case, Grimey! A break-and-enter over to the fish factory in Freeport."

"What'd they take?"

"Looks like some purloined periwinkles, snatched sea snails—misappropriated molluscs, if you prefer."

Grime pounded his fist on the desk. "We'll teach them to loot our *Littorina littorea*," he said learnedly, despite being livid.

"Also someone has rustled some mussels, nabbed some crabs, and scrammed with some clams. Looks to me like a repeat of the old clam scam of 1962. Fits the MO of one of the most dastardly villains ever to set foot on these islands —old Clamface himself."

The two dicks rose as one from their seats beside the oil barrel wood stove that provided the sole source of heat for their office/fish shed. Grabbing their fedoras off the rack of antlers that was tastefully mounted on the wall by the door, they headed out to the company car.

The official vehicle of the DN&IF-GS&DA was a well-worn 1964 Buick Skylark sedan which had been converted into a reasonable facsimile of a truck by hacking off the back seat and trunk area and replacing it with a wooden box. The two detectives found that the bastardized Buick made a good surveillance vehicle since it blended in well with the other Island modes of transportation, and if things happened to go a little slack in the detecting/fish-gutting business, they could always bring in a bit of extra money hauling gravel for the Department of Highways.

Gurrey untied the rope that held the door closed and helped his more senior partner into the passenger seat, thoughtfully tucking a blanket around his arthritic knees to protect him from the drafts that would soon be coming up through the rust holes in the floor. As he easily leaped over the driver's door and slid his buff form in behind the wheel, Gurrey reached under the dash for the two frayed wires that replaced the long-gone ignition switch. After a few minutes of Gurrey cranking the starter, pumping the gas and ignoring unasked-for advice from Grime about not flooding the engine, the big V-8 roared to life in a cloud of blue oil smoke and a cacophony of clattering tappets.

"Someday we're going to actually get paid for one of these cases," Gurrey yelled, "and then I'm going to buy a muffler for this thing".

A few seconds later they were noisily idling in the boarding line for the ferry to Freeport. Grime turned to Gurrey and, shouting over the clamour emanating from under the hood, asked, "Does this mean...?"

"Yes. We're going overseas for this one. Everyone knows that if you are in possession of pilfered periwinkles, have lifted a load of lobsters or scammed some scallops, the only person around here who is low down enough to take them is Clamface, so we're heading right into his sanctuary of stolen seafood, located in that den of thieves, that wasteland of West Nova, that hellhole known as...Central Grove."

"Do you like being a dick, Gurrey?" said Grime, apropos of nothing, as he was apt to do. "I mean, I had to really work hard at becoming one, but to you it comes so naturally. It's like you've been a dick your entire life. I look at you and you have dick written all over your face. People are always telling me what a dick you are."

Gurrey blushed bright red at the compliment. "Thanks Grimey. Now watch your back. Them Central Grovers are vicious and are almost certainly guarding the hideout. Why do they call him Clamface anyway? Is it because he clams up—you know, doesn't talk much?"

"Use your powers of observation," Grime snapped. "It's that bivalve growing out of his cheek. He got teased a lot when he was a lad. Kids can be cruel when you resemble a clam. That's what drove him to a life of crustaceous crime."

Grime noticed the hurt look on his friend's face. "Sorry I raised my voice. The pressure of this damn case is getting to me. You're a great detective, one of the best in the Tri-Island area. I had no right to snap at you like that. I've always thought that if you and I—from totally different backgrounds and cultures on Long and Brier Islands—can get along and work together...well, damn it, there's hope for the Muslims and Jews, the Protestants and Catholics, the Pro fish farmers and the Antis..." He choked up briefly, but recovered. "Anyway, let's go make us some Clam chowder, if you know what I mean."

"I have no idea," Gurrey replied, scratching his liver-spotted head. Recently he had begun to worry about the mental stability of his partner. It seemed that every conversation over the past few months had eventually devolved into a long-winded and semi-coherent rant involving the problems with various religions and the comparative differences between Muslims and Jews and Long and Brier Islanders.

Gurrey suspected that due to his advanced age, Grime was no longer able to keep up with the multi-ethnic, fast-moving, hustle-bustle urban lifestyle of downtown Westport; his deteriorating, Ten-Penny-soaked brain was starting to yearn for the simple-minded, deathly-boring, unsophisticated, almost cartoon-like pleasures of his boyhood home in Freeport.

Still, Gurrey had to admit that when he could get Grime to focus on a case there was no one better. If growing up on Long Island had done nothing else for him—and Lord knows that it hadn't—it had at least given him an uncanny ability to tell when someone was being less than truthful. All those Saturday nights during his otherwise wasted youth spent hanging out in front of Lloyd's Dance Hall observing people pretending to be sober and listening to guys deny being the baby's father had helped him develop an unerring ear for a lie.

After taking a brief detour to fly the Buick over the bump in the road known locally as 'Thrill Hill'; Gurrey headed down Flour Cove Road toward the well-fortified lair of the notorious Clamface. As they clunked and rattled down the dusty, rutted road, Gurrey turned to Grime and said, "Okay, partner, this is it, we're going in there and we're coming out with our pockets packed with periwinkles...or we're not coming out of there at all!"

Nearing the end of the dirt road, they left the car and continued on foot, tracking Clamface and his gang through dense underbrush to his secret hideout. As they drew nearer, they encountered signs nailed to trees that said: *2 miles to Clamface's secret hideout*, *This way to*

Clamface's place and so on. Perhaps their foe wasn't the evil genius they had thought he was. Evil, sure, but genius, no, probably not.

Finally, they spotted the hideout, although with the fluorescent orange paint and large arrows, it was relatively hard to miss. The shack was fashioned from driftwood and the focs'l of the old Tiverton ferry, circa 1975.

Not wanting to make any noise, Grime patted his partner to get his attention, quickly realizing, to his embarrassment, that he had tapped the prosthetic left leg. Luckily, Gurrey hadn't noticed so Grime signalled with his hand, making sure that the signal was within sight of Gurrey's one good eye. 'Shhhh," he motioned, then whispered. "You limp in and I'll be right behind you."

Moving cautiously to preserve the advantage of surprise, Gurrey was creeping stealthily up to the imposing barricade constructed from old lobster crates and decommissioned fish flakes when he was startled by a loud clanging sound behind him, followed by a dull thud.

"Help me, Gurrey! Officer down, officer down!" Grime gasped.

Gurrey turned to see his aged partner sprawled in the middle of the road, his feet hopelessly tangled in the hose to the oxygen bottles that he always dragged behind him. Grime had been insisting for years that switching his two-pack-a-day habit to 'menthols' was clearing up his emphysema, but Gurrey was beginning to have his doubts.

After helping his partner back to his feet and dusting the road-dirt off the spittle-stained front of his sadly out-of-date paisley-print Nehru jacket, Gurrey resumed his advance upon Clamface's hideout. Judging by the laboured gasping and wheezing, Grime was right behind him.

The two dicks slipped warily past the fortress gates, fully prepared to be viciously repelled at any moment by Clamface's henchmen, but were surprised to find the enclosure eerily quiet. To the right they spied what they had come for, piles and piles of the pinched periwinkles, as well as heaps of heisted haddock, cases of confiscated clams and tonnes of illicitly taken tuna.

As they advanced, Gurrey became gradually aware of a ghastly and eerie sound drifting across the compound, a sound that made his hair stand on end. Grime's hair would have also stood on end had he only had any.

Looking to the left, they spied two large pots boiling over an open fire. On the ground around the fire lay Clamface and his crew, moaning and groaning in agony, clutching their stomachs, their faces sickly shades of green. Some had traces of pink on their lips, a telltale sign that Pepto Bizmol has been consumed.

Gurrey took in the scene in one all-encompassing glance and with his finely-honed detective's mind, immediately understood what was taking place.

"What's going on here Gurrey?" whispered a confused and bewildered Grime, "Do they have the vapours...or consumption? It's not contagious is it? You know I shouldn't be around sick people with my delicate condition!"

"Not to worry, Grimey. What they've got isn't catching. See all those lobster and clam shells lying about and all those empty Digby Dairy milk bottles? Clamface tried to set himself up as a big man in the hot seafood business, the foremost fence of fraudulent fillets. But he foolishly forgot about those unbreakable tenets that have been the downfall of so many who have tried to play fast and loose with this tough mistress we call the fresh seafood game: The Rule of the Three Gs: Greed, Gluttony, and Grandma."

He held up three gnarled fingers to illustrate the lesson. "First, Clamface got greedy. He couldn't be satisfied with stealing just *some* of the area's seafood, no, he let his ego run away with him and let him think he could achieve total control of *all* of the black market in missing mackerel, heisted herring, codged cod, grabbed crab and all the other alliterated sea life. He thereby attracted unwanted attention in the form of the long arm of the law in the Tri-Island area, us! Second, he let gluttony get the better of his henchmen, allowing them to recklessly gorge themselves on their ill-gotten but delicious bounty, eating and drinking to the point of utter incapacity. And third, and this is probably his most grievous error, he forgot, or worse yet, ignored, the two golden rules that every grandma that ever boiled a lobster or steamed a clam lives by: don't drink milk with lobster and never eat shellfish in a month with no R."

Having tried and failed to snap his fingers in a classy way, Gurrey concluded, "So, thanks to the human stomach's natural revulsion to the combination of seafood and dairy products, as well as the algae-infested shellfish caused by this July's toxic red tide, we're able to just waltz in here and apprehend this poor passel of puking perps."

With Clamface and his men too weak to put up much resistance, Gurrey and Grime soon had them trussed up with lengths of cod-line they found lying conveniently near-by. After a quick call to Alton Nealey, the ambulance driver/undertaker-taxi driver/prisoner deliverer, the periwinkles purloiners were soon on their way to the Digby hoosegow in the ambulance/hearse/taxi/paddy-wagon.

With Clamface's last words ringing in his ears—colourful and unsettlingly specific advice on where best to insert a swordfish in the human anatomy—Gurrey turned with satisfaction to his partner. "Well, Grimey, looks like we've wrapped up another one,"

Grime smiled tolerantly at his old friend. His razor-sharp mind had already deduced that July was a month without an "R" in it and, "ipso fatso," as he later explained, the purloined periwinkles were poison!

He thought back to a day in elementary school when old Mrs. Tibert was teaching the months of the year. She had enunciated each name slowly and clearly, using the very latest phonetic approach. "Jan-u-ary, February, March, April, May, June...,"she intoned, as she wrote each month on the blackboard.

At that moment, six-year-old Delbert Titus, later to become the arch villain Clamface, put up his hand and frantically waved it about. When he finally got Mrs. Tibert's attention, he requested permission to visit the washroom, having consumed four Nesbitt Oranges and a Mountain Dew during recess. If not for that happy stroke of fate of leaving when Delbert was only halfway through the months, Clamface would have known that July does not contain an R. Now, some fifty years later, his weak bladder, coupled with the fact that he had never been properly hooked on phonics, had come back to foil his evil plans.

Grime turned to his flatulent friend, who he suspected was unsure of what month or indeed year it was and didn't know his R's from a hole in the ground, and intoned, "Case closed!"

Gurrey looked at him, confused. Grime moved to his other side and shouted, "Case closed!" into Gurrey's functional ear.

"And not a minute too soon," ejaculated Gurrey. "I have to get home to watch Corrie. Isn't that Tracey a bitch?"

Grime smiled tolerantly. The fact was that Grime loved his lifelong friend, warts and all, although the wart at the end of his bulbous nose was a tad off-putting. "Yes. Yes, she is, Gurrey. But I wouldn't kick her out of bed for eating Betty's hotpot, if you know what I mean."

"I have no idea," Gurrey said.

Soon the two dicks were motoring past the bright lights of Freeport toward the lone bright light of Westport—the one that flickered at the end of the ferry wharf—satisfied that, at least for now, the citizens of the Tri-Island area could sleep safely.

4: The Bingo Cartel

Having successfully resolved what they considered their first official case, Gurrey and Grime were celebrating by lazing around their detective agency office/fish-gutting service watching re-runs of *Car 54 Where Are You?* on their black and white Emerson TV.

"Remind me to go up on the roof to turn the antenna," Gurrey said as he gutted another cod and threw it on the pile. "Reception's pretty bad. Someday I predict they'll have some kind of cable or even a satellite to bring us a clearer picture."

Not wanting to burst his friend's bubble, Grime decided not to tell him that his home town of Freeport had had such a system for two weeks.

Suddenly the ancient wooden door to the fish house burst open and there stood Owen Otley, all 5'4", 365 pounds of him. Because of their advancing ages, the two detectives had hired Otley as their leg man whenever speed and agility were required. So far it hadn't worked out all that well. Just the week before, Horace Perly, a 95-year old shoplifter with a walker, had managed, very slowly, to escape Otley's pursuit.

"Trouble at the bingo hall," a red-faced Otley wheezed between gasps of air, "Big trouble!"

The bingo hall was owned by the powerful Robichini family which, in truth, owned most everything on the island: the all-night shepherd service, the shoe cobbler's place, the belt stretcher, the bootlegger's, the Brier Island Stock Exchange (where islanders exchanged cows for bulls), and, of course, the dry cleaning establishment, which was used to launder money, a very popular service since many locals worked in the fish business and their cash often reeked of fish guts and lobster bait. Then there was the fake whale watch which used inflated plastic whales to dupe naive American tourists out of their 'Yanqui dollars'.

The Robichinis controlled the bingo cartel through their head honcho, Wallman "The Wall" Robichini, and this wasn't the first time that something had smelled fishy in the tiny village of Westport. The problem was that Grime knew that his partner had connections to the Robichini family. Would he be able to dispense justice impartially, or would he be just another wart on the festering buttocks of Brier Island? Only time would tell.

Gurrey seemed to take forever to strap on his prosthetic leg, wash the fish guts from his hands, and grab his dobber, which he always carried with him in a specially fashioned holster "just in case."

While Grime waited, he made small talk about the weather and various points of interest on the island. The two old friends were always reminiscing. "I remember the time I got lucky down at Beautiful Cove in the back seat of my 1965 Valiant."

Intrigued, Gurrey turned up his hearing aid. "Give me some details."

Grime stuck out his chest. "Yup: found $1.25 in the back seat, stuck down in the crack. Talk about getting lucky!"

Gurrey turned away from Grime in disgust and focused on the red-faced and perspiration-drenched Otley, who was still standing in the doorway."What's happening over to the bingo hall?"

The weathered timbers of the old building gave out a tortured groan as Owen leaned his full weight against the door-frame. "Give me a minute to catch my breath," he wheezed. "I just beat my own personal best time running over here from the hall. Four hundred yards in just under twenty minutes."

Gurrey thought that Otley may have even puffed out his chest a little when he said that, but couldn't really tell since his chest looked puffed out all the time anyway.

Still struggling to catch his breath, Otley dug some makin's out of his shirt pocket, and, despite his sausage-like fingers, quickly and expertly rolled himself a reasonable facsimile of a cigarette. After sucking it down to a smouldering stub with one long drag, and gasping and hacking through a coughing spell that went on for several minutes; he finally said, "That's better," and launched into his story.

According to Otley, the problem at the Bingo Hall started when the organizers of Freeport's weekly Saturday night tea party had to cancel on short notice after someone misplaced the teabag. Casting about for some way to alleviate the drudgery of their miserable existence, the Teabaggers, as they called themselves, were drawn to the shiny lights and exotic sounds reflecting off the water from the glittering metropolis across the Passage; in particular, it was the huge blinking neon "Bingo" sign that caught their attention...then lost it...then caught it...then lost it...then caught it again.

Eventually the Teabaggers were able to break the hypnotic spell of this mesmerizing sight and decided to take a walk on the wild side and try out this exotic high-stakes game they had heard so much about.

When the large group of gawking Freeporters shuffled timidly through the ornate doors of the Westport Bingo Hall, a buzz went around the room. Fortunately, Westporters are a naturally-peaceful people, accepting of even the most unfortunate members of humanity, and all was relatively quiet until the game actually got under way.

The first few numbers of the evening were called with no trouble, but when "G-23" was shouted out, suddenly all the Teabaggers were staring at their cards with stunned and puzzled looks on their faces. In a frenzy, they began to tear off first their own, and then their neighbour's socks and shoes and began 'cipherin' on all available fingers and toes.

This was the first number over 20 to be called and the Freeporters found themselves to be out of their depth: all that is except for Six-Digit Darryl, who was considered 'gifted' by the Long Islanders due to his ability to count all the way up to 24.

The Teabaggers quickly realized that they were at a distinct disadvantage in this game, so they demanded that no numbers higher than 20 be called. Of course the Westporters objected.

"And it all went rapidly downhill from there," Otley said. "The Long Islanders thought that this was some kind of a plot against them, a way to show off the natural superiority of the Brier Island educational system. Things got out of hand and it all ended up with the Bingo caller being kidnapped and held for ransom."

Otley shot an apprehensive look in Grime's direction before continuing with an almost apologetic air, "The Bingo caller tonight was Rikilini Robichini."

Grime, who had appeared to be dozing off in his chair during most of Otley's story, came to with a loud snort and was suddenly teetering unsteadily on his feet.

"They can't do that!" he shouted, "That's terrible, I won't stand for it...I...I...I...!" Grime began to gag and choke and finally spat his poorly-fitted false teeth out onto the top of the splitting table, where they skittered across the slimy surface like some errant Halloween decoration and sank out of sight in the murky water of the splitting tub. "Lasht time I buy teeth at the Dollarshtore," he said.

"Take it easy there, Grimey," Gurrey cautioned. "You don't want to blow the fuse in your pacemaker again. Remember the last time that happened? It was just sheer luck that we happened to have a set of jumper cables in the car!"

It was well known throughout the Tri-Island area that Grime and Rikilini, the eldest and tallest of the seven Robichini sisters, had once had a brief, torrid affair. It had ended almost as soon as it had begun, and no one knew why: were the differences too many, was the Westport / Freeport cultural gap too vast to bridge, was the social stigma of a mixed marriage too much to contemplate, were the constant ferry trips too tedious and taxing to take?

Even after all these years, Rikilini still refused to acknowledge the tenuous connection between the two, and although Grime also was reticent to speak of that extremely brief period in the otherwise unremarkable history of his mediocre love life, Gurrey suspected that somewhere, deep in Grime's erratically beating heart, he still harboured feelings for the fair Rikilini.

Grimey knew that "Six-Digit Darryl" could actually count to 25, but not without dropping his pants. His natural modesty had cost Freeport the Bingo bragging rights. Sure, Grime had been distracted by Rikilini, the beautiful Amazon who appeared so out of place on this island of dwarfish people. She stood out like Dolly Parton at a Twiggy look-alike contest. The mere mention of her name had sent Grime's easily-addled mind a spinning. Long-repressed memories suddenly came flooding back...

Long hair flowing out the open window of his Volkswagen bug, Grimey's friend Gurrey had been a man about town in his youth, courting what he insisted on calling "the girlies." Only the women of Freeport, much more urbane and cultured, were able to see through his shallow façade of pseudo-suaveness. Sure, he wore only his best hip-boots to the dances, and sure, he cut them off at just the right jaunty angle, and sure, his wallet had the fanciest chain on it, and, okay, his collection of plastic anchors on his car dash was the largest on either island. But substance, that's what the real women wanted, and Grimey had that up the old wazoo.

Coincidentally, Grimey and Gurrey had enjoyed almost identical upbringings. Both were the sons of grocery magnates on their respective islands and both were heirs to the kind of vast fortunes that only small-town grocery sales can produce. Gurrey had frittered his money away, sinking every last penny into TV antennae and phone booth stock. Grime had invested in a chain of boot-legging establishments that had not worked out. In truth Gurrey had tiptoed into puberty a few months prior to his friend but Grime had pole-vaulted past him in no time. Besotted women often sang of his charms around campfires on the spectacular cliffs of the glorious Freeport mountain range known far and wide by the descriptive but gender-confused name of Aunt Tony, the Rockies of the Tri-Island area.

Gurrey had noticed lately that Grime seemed to be spending more and more time living in the past—and, oddly, it didn't appear to be his own past he was living in! He would happily waste countless hours bending the ear of any unfortunate who happened along, bragging about his so-called "glory days." Grime apparently still fancied himself quite the ladies' man and could go on in colourful but nauseating detail about his imaginary accomplishments as what he coyly and crudely called a "pole vaulter."

It just so happened that Gurrey knew the unvarnished truth: that, even as a young man, Grime rarely if ever was able to "clear the bar", and that for the last several decades even the advent of a certain little blue pill had not been able to get Grime's "pole" back in the game.

Still, blithely ignoring the overwhelming mountain of evidence to the contrary, Grime clung tenaciously to the image he had built up in his own fevered mind; that he was "a chick magnet." He even had it printed on his business cards:

Jim Grime
Private Dick - Fish-Gutter - Chick Magnet

Grime also liked to go on *ad nauseam* about having 'substance', and Gurrey suspected that this may well be the source of Grime's slow but steady downhill slide into unrequited decrepitude. It wasn't actually 'substance' that was the problem so much as it was 'substance abuse'.

Oh, it had started out innocently enough. Many, many, many years earlier, when Grime was still a youngish man, he had abandoned his boyhood home and struck out to seek fame and fortune in the traffic-congested, mall-dominated, fast-food-infected Valley town of New Minas. Here, against all odds, he somehow managed to publish several books about an obscure Boston sports team and become a minor celebrity.

Unfortunately for the unsophisticated, naive, youngish man from the wrong side of the ferry, he was about to learn that celebrity on the mean streets of New Minas came at a high price.

Grime soon found himself caught up in a dizzying whirlwind of New Minas's most prestigious social events. It was the bowling alley one night, the curling rink the next, followed by a non-stop blitz of the forty-seven Frenchy's used clothing outlets in town. Blinded by the glamour and bright lights that comprised the day-to-day life of the New Minas *glitterati*, Grime soon found himself being introduced to "the substance." At first, he only partook of this trendy stimulant because all of his new "friends" were doing it, but in short order he developed an insatiable craving for the substance and subsequently found himself lining up with all the other addicts to get his daily fix.

When the common street variety lost its kick for him—when he started noticing he was getting lethargic and irritable without regular infusions—he sought out a specialty supplier and started experimenting with exotic blends from mysterious, far-away places like Colombia and Bolivia. Then he finally graduated to "designer items" with exotic names like latte and cappuccino.

When he over-indulged one reckless night and woke up the next morning with a burly tattooed longshoreman in a silk teddy on one side of him and a strangely-alluring sheep on the other, Grime finally had to admit that he was under the thrall of the dreaded bean; his caffeine habit was totally out of control. In a rare moment of clarity, he decided that the only way to break this vicious cycle of dependency was to return to the safety of his boyhood home, far from big-town temptations.

Sadly, upon his less-than-triumphant return, Grime found himself spurned by his former friends and neighbours. They had heard of his off-Island exploits, and although they had absolutely no problem with him now being a desperate and degenerate addict, the feeling throughout the community was that since he had published a book he would most likely be, as they said, "All high and mighty with his fancy readin' 'n' writin.'"

Despondent, Grime found himself seriously contemplating a life-ending leap from Rony's Point one desperate night when he happened to raise his eyes up to see an array of beautifully glimmering lights reach out to him like the arms of an angel from across the water. As the foghorns sang like a chorus of heavenly voices in the background, the Mecca across the harbour emerged like a glorious mirage out of the parting fog.

Suddenly, Grime was struck as if by a thunderbolt with the realization that before him, like a vision from Heaven itself, lay the only community in the Tri-Island area that had a library. As hard as it was to accept, Grime came to the reluctant realization that he might fit better into that literate, sophisticated, urbane world across the water, that a whole new future lay before him just on the other side of the harbour.

As he stood there trying to absorb the reality that he was no longer wanted or appreciated on his beloved home island, Grime's mind drifted to the only positive that he could find in his up-coming self-exile to Brier Island: his long and enduring relationship with his pal, Gurrey.

Not that there hadn't been the occasional "bump in the road" during their decades-long friendship. Grime had noticed over the years that this mainly solid friendship would sporadically be tested by rampant jealousy.

In fairness, Gurrey had not had an easy life. Like most Brier Islanders of his time, in his youth he had been forced to subsist on a diet of grubs, berries and field mice, and often there wasn't enough to go around in his massive, massive family where babies appeared with the frequency of power outages. In fact, the two were doubtless connected. There was little to do but fish and fornicate and Gurrey's father hated fishing.

Sure, the missionaries from Freeport occasionally brought provisions, including what Westporters called 'store-bought' clothes, but their proud nature prevented them from accepting too many such hand-outs.

After an excellent education in Freeport's finest institution of higher education, Gurrey had accepted a position as a 'trainee' at the Metropolitan Store in Digby and it looked like he was on his way to respectability. Unfortunately, fate intervened as he was accused of unseemly behaviour in the 'Women's Whatnots' section of the store and he was subsequently thrown out on his ear. He began to hang around with the wrong crowd in Digby, holding séances in graveyards and impregnating so many local girls that today most Digby people over 25 look exactly the same.

But Grime still had a fondness for Gurrey. The two had been in Cub Scouts together and had learned many ancient secrets of the forest—like how to cook frozen wieners over an open fire, and how to clean up the puke left on the floor of the church vestry by the scoutmaster's humongous Newfoundland hell hounds. Due to the inconsistent Westport transit system Gurrey even stayed overnight at Grime's home on Cubs night. There he learned such rudimentary social skills as sitting at a table and using utensils instead of the pointy stick that he employed at home to 'stab the little critters.' On one occasion Grime stayed at Gurrey's home, where he was shocked to discover that he had to put his own milk on the cereal and, so as not to embarrass Gurrey's lovely, long-suffering mother, he ate it dry. He was, not to put too fine a point on it, a saint in every conceivable way.

This natural rivalry between the two islands resulted in an on-going, good-natured war of one-upmanship between the two friends. Recently, the two dicks had spent so much time trying to cast the ultimate insult toward each other's hometown that they had been neglecting their detective agency/fish-gutting service. The result was that crime had been running rampant in the Tri-Island area and local restaurants were forced to resort to serving ungutted fish, convincing customers to perform that task at their tables 'as part of a culinary experience'.

With a start, Gurrey realized that he and Grime had slipped into one of their all-too-frequent reveries. He turned to his semi-comatose partner and gave him a shake, "Come on, buddy. I need you to be sharp. You're the only one who can negotiate for Rikilini's freedom. You grew up with most of those kidnappers; you understand their unusual version of the English language, their fractured phrases and twisted idioms; you actually 'get' most of their obscure references. I can't do it; I'm not even sure what the accepted response is to the traditional Freeport greeting of 'Gettin' any?', and I'm even further stymied when asked, 'How's it hangin'?', but you have a natural flair for that sort of conversation."

Grime's mind had finally cleared somewhat. He planted both hands on the arms of his chair and with a groan and a resounding fart, pushed himself to his feet. "I'll do it", he announced. "But first I'll need to get out of these clothes."

Gesturing to his usual outfit of hip-rubber boots, fish-gut covered rubber apron known locally as a barvel, and a tattered Frenchy's tee-shirt proclaiming 'Baby On Board!' above a downward pointing arrow, Grime explained, "This get-up might be okay for socializing on any other night of the week, but this is a Saturday night. Everyone in town has had their weekly bath, scoffed down a charge of beans, and put on their best Sunday-go-to-meetin' clothes. If I'm going to slip into that bingo hall without attracting a lot of unwanted attention, I've got to fit in."

With that, he strode to the back wall of the office/fish-gutting parlour and entered a door near the overflowing liver barrels. Several minutes later he returned, transformed in a purple, crushed-velvet Nehru jacket worn over a white dickey and adorned with a heavy imitation gold chain linked to a large peace symbol. His colourfully-striped bell bottoms were held up by a wide, white pleather belt that matched his funky six-inch-heeled platform shoes.

"This should get me in the door without drawing any undue attention." he said, adjusting the rose-coloured lenses of his wire-rimmed granny glasses.

On his way out the door, Grime beckoned to Otley, "Come on, Owen. I'm going to need your help." In response to Otley's distressed look, he said, "You don't have to walk. We'll take the Buick over to the Hall."

With a look of relief, Otley turned sideways and after a brief struggle, managed to squeeze his globular form through the doorway and follow Grime out to the car.

The bingo hall parking lot was full, so Grime pulled into the adjacent Westport Volunteer Fire Department lot and stopped in front of a garage door marked *Emergency Vehicles Only: Do Not Block*.

"Well, if this isn't an emergency, then I don't know the meaning of the word," Grime said, exiting the car. Otley struggled to keep up.

They approached the hall and slipped quietly through the open door. Immediately every eye in the place was on them.

"See that, Owen?" Grime whispered. "This is why I put so much thought into my disguises. They're thinking, 'Oh it's just another well-dressed hippie with a 5'4", 365-pound man coming to play some bingo.' It's almost as if we're invisible."

Ignoring the guffaws and calls of "Shouldn't you be at Woodstock?" Grime began to mingle, his steel trap mind taking in every seemingly minor detail. He circled the room twice, snapping his fingers to the Mantovani record playing in the background and greeting everyone with "Groovy" and "Far out!" and "Hey man, what it is!" His disguise was working perfectly. He was blending in so well that people were ignoring him as if their very lives depended on it.

Finally he had seen enough. "Go and watch the door, my pudgy little friend. We don't want any escapes."

Otley did as he was told, wedging himself into the door frame and rendering it hermetically sealed.

The Freeporters were sitting together at a long table, grumbling. He approached them and flashed his ID card. "You the Teabaggers from Freeport?" he said.

"Might be. What's it to you, Sonny Bono?" said a man, obviously the leader.

Grime blanched at the sound of the snarling voice. His usual pallor, the result of long hours in the dimly-lit fish-gutting shed, turned several shades paler, bordering on transparency.

The leader of the Teabaggers was none other than Freeport's infamous eighty-seven year-old town bully, Stanley "Soda" Crocker. Crocker suffered from a genetic calcium deficiency that caused him to have abnormally brittle bones, bones that would snap like the saltine that gave him his nickname.

A lifetime of broken, weakened bones resulted in him being extremely short-statured, bow-legged, scrawny and hump-backed. Despite this, Crocker used his physical condition to his advantage by challenging anyone who disagreed with him to a fistfight. Since everyone in the Tri-Island area was fully aware of his delicate condition and no one wanted to be responsible for one more possibly fatal broken bone, he was able to claim victory when his opponent would invariably back down.

Over the years the diminutive Crocker had "won" fights with every man, woman and child on the islands.

Despite unexpectedly coming face-to-face with this formidable foe, Grime managed to remain cool, the kind of cool that only a man dressed as a hippie in a room full of grey-haired seniors can manage. "What seems to be the problem?"

"We want our money back," Crocker replied. "This here thing is fixed. Three times we yelled out BINGO and three times they told us it didn't count!"

Grime instantly knew the problem. "As a fellow Freeporter, I can understand your frustration," he said. "Back home in Freeport, the Athens of the Tri-Island area, you would of course be right. Unfortunately, spelling is not the strong suit of the average Westporter. They spell it BIGNO over here. I've tried to explain it to them but they won't listen. Let me have a word with the proprietor."

He went to a smoky back office and found the manager, Pete Peters, a grey little man with a receding hairline that seemed to have taken refuge in his nostrils and ears.

"Look," Grime said, "We can argue all day about the BINGO vs BIGNO, but let's compromise."

Peters started to protest. "But they don't know their numbers, either."

Grime held up his hand. "I don't want to have to bring up the dummy dobber incident. One more infraction and you could be closed down."

"They want a full refund," Peters said. "I can't help it if they can't count."

"This is where compromise comes in," said Grime, the Henry Kissinger of the Tri-Island area. "Westporters can't read and Freeporters can't count. It all evens out, doesn't it?"

Peters reluctantly conceded that Grime had a valid point and agreed to the refund, but an impasse was reached when at the very last minute, the hostage-takers also decided that as compensation for mental anguish they would demand two trays of those delicious little egg-salad sandwiches that the Super Seniors sell at the Bingo Hall canteen. It's common knowledge that the Super Seniors can be a feisty bunch, and they stubbornly refused to give in to the demands of the kidnappers; saying something about how living through the depression and fighting a world war earned them the right to control who they gave sandwiches to.

It took some tough negotiating, but in the end, Grime got all parties to agree to a refund; half in cash, half in Canadian Tire money; plus a tray of day-old olive and cream-cheese sandwiches and some of that left-over Jell-O salad with those little multi-coloured marshmallows in it.

Grime couldn't wait to report his success back to Gurrey.

"Sorry we took so long," he said as they entered the office/fish house. "Owen here got stuck in the door to the hall and we had to borrow the Jaws of Life from the fire department to get him out. And then the fire chief gave us a half-hour lecture about parking in front of their garage." He took a breath. "But we did it. It was one man against the odds. Well, I guess with Owen along, more like two-and-a-half men, but you get my drift. The point is that Rikilini has now been safely returned to the bosom of her family and everybody has gone home happy."

Gurrey was excited. "BIGNO! Just like that: another case closed. Now, what are we going to do about that Balancing Rock situation in Tiverton?"

"What??" Grime said dreamily, "Oh, sorry, I was just thinking of Rikilini and bosoms."

Figure 2: Grab your dobber and get ready to play!

5: Bad Day at Balancing Rock

Times were tough in Tiverton; terribly, terribly, tough. Things had been slowly sliding from bad to worse for years, starting way back when negotiations to bring the PGA golf tour to town fell through after they discovered that the Tiverton Golf Course operated out of a barn, had only three holes, and was mostly built on the side of a hill so that even the greens were slanted at a 30-degree angle. Attempts to re-purpose the course into an elaborate outdoor Whack-a-Mole arcade and amusement park were short-lived when the local chapter of the SPCA got wind of the idea and were not amused.

Then the decline in the fisheries caused the shutdown of the fish plants and over time the neglected old buildings slowly crumbled and disappeared, to be replaced by gaping spaces that left the waterfront looking like Gump Worsley's post-game grin.

Oh sure, there had been attempts to develop new industries. Several of the locals decided that since wild fish were becoming scarce, they would go into business growing their own. Having heard about the multitude of environmental problems involved with raising fish in ocean-going pens, the group decided the land-based method made much more sense. They purchased property, built infrastructure and ordered several tanker-trucks full of baby fish.

The day the trucks finally arrived was an exciting one for the citizens of Tiverton; a long-awaited new future was about to begin. Unfortunately, excitement quickly turned to despair when all the fish died within hours of being offloaded.

The company manager, Ozzie Owdows, announced, after several days of intensive investigation, that they had narrowed the disaster down to one of two causes. Either they had planted the fish too deep or they had used the wrong kind of fertilizer. Either way, that was the end of fish farming in Tiverton.

There were several more attempts to rev up Tiverton's sputtering economic engine over the ensuing years. A concerted effort was made to get in on the current trend for wind generation, but despite the entire village subsisting on a diet of nothing but cabbage and beans for several months, they couldn't quite generate enough wind to make it worthwhile; and besides, they never did figure out exactly what they were supposed to do with the wind they did manage to generate.

Things continued to deteriorate rapidly. Despite their best efforts, the finest minds in Tiverton were unable to stop the relentless downward spiral. Then—just as the situation appeared to be at its bleakest—a rock came to the rescue.

This was not just any rock. Located on the craggy shore of St. Mary's Bay, this was a natural phenomenon that made the Grand Canyon look like just another hole in the ground and Niagara Falls resemble a leaky faucet. The narrow, 20-foot, vertical column of basalt stood precariously on the edge of a rock platform, defying gravity, as if a perching seagull could bring it tumbling down.

For years, islanders had taken the rock for granted, and some for granite, although they did take some satisfaction in the fact it appeared to be making a rude gesture to the mainland. And then a visiting tourism official from Halifax saw it and the secret was out.

Once the general public learned about it, The finger of stone quickly became the darling of the Provincial tourist industry, appearing on glossy covers and in salacious stories in the tourism gossip magazines. Suddenly, politicians wanted to be photographed with it, geologists wanted to study it, and snotty-nosed kids wanted to stick their gum on it. Thanks to this newfound celebrity, Tiverton was once again thriving.

But just when things were going well, there was a problem. Tourists were coming back from Balancing Rock ashen-faced. Too stunned to talk, they immediately left the Island. Even locals who trekked down the trail refused to speak of what they had seen there. Word was spreading that something was terribly wrong: Tiverton's fragile one-note tourist industry was starting to crumble.

"This...is...where...we come in," Gurrey gasped. He and Grime were huffing and puffing their way along the woods trail leading to the rocky St. Mary's Bay shoreline where the now-famous column stood like a sentry, guarding the island from all and sundry threats. "Now that we've handled the bigno situation we have time to take a look at this thing, figure out the problem and set it to rights again."

"Bingo," Grime corrected, but nodded in agreement. They were nearing the end of the trail and working their way down the long flights of sometimes-slippery stairs that led to the viewing platform.

Gurrey, who was slightly in the lead, turned the last corner and immediately fell back into the closely-following Grime. "Great Caesar's ghost," he exclaimed, "I can't believe what I'm seeing; this can't be possible."

Grime, with the grace of the ballet dancer he had once been, pirouetted lightly around his partner, took one look at the scene before him, and fainted dead away.

There before them stood the biggest erection they had ever seen...and just beyond this newly-erected building was what used to be Balancing Rock. But instead of the beautiful, precariously perched rock formation that had graced more brochure covers than the giant blueberry of Oxford, NS or the mythical ship known as the Yarmouth-Bar Harbor ferry —but still fewer than Peggy's Cove lighthouse—and captured the imagination of dozens of visitors, was a statue, apparently chiselled from the rock.

The likeness was uncanny. It was an exact replica of New York City's Statue of Liberty, but with the added adornment of a revolving restaurant on top.

Gurrey and Grime stared up at the revolving bar/restaurant. "Holy liftin' siftin'!" Gurrey exclaimed.

Visible through the windows that wrapped entirely around the garish establishment were women in low-cut black dresses and men in tuxedos. They appeared to be sipping cocktails and laughing in that casual, devil-may-care way that rich folks are wont to do.

"The fog's pretty thick," Gurrey said. "Can you tell who's up there? Is it the island's literati and social elite out at another one of their fancy bean suppers?"

"Don't think so," Grime replied, squinting to see through the swirling mists. "Usually at the bean suppers the windows are fogged up on the inside. This is something even more elaborate."

Just then Rikilini Robichini, wearing a mini-skirt and high heels, wiggled into sight in that seductive way that had driven men from Grand Manan to Bear River East wild. With only the merest acknowledgement of their presence, she turned and started scaling the erstwhile rock, her finely-tuned body taut and yet soft at the same time. Grime noticed a tattoo of an obviously diseased salmon on her upper arm.

"What are you doing?" he stammered., looking upward at the ascending, Amazon-like goddess.

"I'm going to see who's up there."

Grime turned to his partner who was leafing through his tattered notebook. "What are *you* doing, Gurrey?"

"If she falls, we may have to notify her next of kin. I'm looking up her address."

Glancing skyward appreciatively, Grime muttered, "Me too."

"Not dress, you idiot," Gurrey said. "Ad-dress, ad-dress! Keep your mind on the job at hand."

From her vantage point high on the side of the statue, Rikilini—or Riki, as her friends called her—could clearly hear every word of the juvenile conversation being carried on below. She quickly rappelled back to the ground, adjusted her miniskirt, and strode up to the detectives.

"What are you dicks doing here, anyway?" she demanded.

"We're on a case," Grime said. "We heard that something strange was going on, so we're looking into it. We're investigators so we're investigating, that's what we do, investigate. It's our job to look into things...I mean, we're trying to keep abreast...we hope to rise to the occasion and...that is, as you noted, we're a couple of dicks, so we're just doing what dicks do, that's all, I swear."

Aware that he had become flustered by Riki's unexpected mere presence and drop-dead gorgeous appearance, Grime fell silent and consoled himself by noting how the red glow from his face enhanced Rikilini's soft-yet-firm, ever-so-sexy skin.

"That's what *we're* doing here," Gurrey said, trying to ignore the disturbingly sensual moans and groans coming from his partner, "but what are *you* doing here? Where did these erections come from, who are those people, what happened to Balancing Rock and why were you climbing that statue?"

Riki eyed the two detectives as if trying to decide if she should trust them. Finally she appeared to reach a decision. "I'll start at the beginning," she said. "Try to keep up. What's happening here has come as a big surprise to most people, but I've been keeping my eye on this gang for a while. What we have here, gentlemen, is a collaboration between two of the most reprehensible groups of people known to mankind."

"Liberals and Conservatives?" Grime asked.

"No," Riki said.

"I know! I know!" Gurrey waved his arm in the air, "Time-share salesmen and TV evangelists!"

"Even worse," Riki said. "Theme park operators and fish farmers! I suppose you're aware of the theme park that opened recently on the mainland?"

"Sure," Grime said, "Six Flags Over Tiddville, I went there right after it opened to try out the Freddie Tidd Memorial Bumper Car ride."

"Well," Riki said, "that place has been losing money since it opened. They thought Tiddville was a good location because it gets a lot of traffic, but the cars don't stop. I mean, who in their right mind would, when

Digby Neck is just the colour cartoon before the main feature? They just rush right through to catch the ferry to our island paradises. When they realized that people were passing by their so-called attraction to go see Balancing Rock, the park operators secured a lease on the land that the rock stands on. They decided that if all those people would come to see a balancing rock, even more would come to see a balancing Statue of Liberty. Because of possible copyright issues and the fact that the lease is limited to three years, they've called it The Statuette of Limitations."

Gurrey and Grime noticed for the first time that, unlike the monument in New York Harbour, this statue was balanced on one leg; one foot solidly planted on the ledge that the Balancing Rock had formerly occupied and the other foot hovering in mid-air. There was another difference. The New York Harbour colossus featured a plaque which said in part:

> *Give me your tired, your poor,*
> *Your huddled masses yearning to breathe free,*
> *The wretched refuse of your teeming shore.*
> *Send these, the homeless, tempest-tossed to me,*
> *I lift my lamp beside the golden door!*

The plaque at the base of this statue said:

> *We'll charge you $20 for the tour,*
> *You muddled asses, earning to pay the fee for,*
> *The wretched refuse we hawk in our gift store.*
> *Send these, the wealthy tourists, to me.*
> *To the rest, I lift my finger and show the door!*

"They thought they could improve on Mother Nature's creation," Riki said, "but, true to form, that turned out to be another bad decision. The people who come here want to see what is left of the rapidly-diminishing natural world, not some cheap replica of an American icon. They were on the point of going broke again until the fish-farm people approached them with an offer. Fish-farming has been getting a lot of bad PR lately, so they wanted to join forces with a company that has a better image and develop a fish farm theme park; you know, trained salmon performing tricks for the crowd, bumper boats in the fish cages, fish petting area, a games midway where you can bet on how many fish can survive being crammed into a cage, Slip & Slide in the greasy scum the fish waste leaves on the shoreline, that sort of thing. They think it will improve their image. Tonight they're holding a gala ball to celebrate the signing of an agreement between the two companies. I was climbing the statue in protest and to put up this sign."

With a flourish, she unfurled a large banner that read:

Let Our Lobsters Live - No Fish Farm in St. Mary's Bay

Suddenly Riki pushed the two detectives into the bushes.

"Easy there, girl." Grime said, "If you want to go grassin', just say so. No need to be so rough!"

"Quiet, you old fool. Someone's coming."

A large salmon appeared, walking down the trail.

"What the hell's that?" Grime whispered.

"That's the park's new mascot, Sammy the Spaced-Out Salmon. We call him that because of all the drugs in his system."

"I thought the park mascot was a leprechaun," Gurrey said.

"They got rid of that when the Tiverton Irish community complained it was demeaning," Riki replied.

"Tiverton has an Irish Community?" Grime asked.

"Of course," Riki said. "Everybody knows the O'ssinger clan, and the O'uthouses, of course."

Suddenly a group of island protesters calling themselves Occupy Tiverton surrounded the mascot. They began singing protest songs to keep their spirits up, beginning with *I Am A Rock*, moving on to *Like a Rock*, and ending with *Rock of Ages*. They were what you might call a rock group.

Meanwhile, Rikilini was getting her groove on—gyrating suggestively in front of the giant salmon mascot.

It was a bizarre scene of chaos and the people in the penthouse of the Statuette of Limitations formerly known as Balancing Rock rushed to the windows to watch. Unfortunately, the weight of so many people on one side of the structure proved too much to bear.

The Occupy Tiverton group had just finished *Rock Me Gently* and were launching into *Rock Around The Clock* when they noticed that the shoddily-built edifice towering over them was about to collapse.

Quickly assessing the situation, they abandoned their repertoire of rock songs and, with little thought for their own safety, rushed directly into a rousing rendition of *I Fall To Pieces*.

Meanwhile, Sammy the Spaced-Out Salmon, through his chemical-induced haze, hallucinated that the Statuette of Limitations had come to life and was walking toward him.

"Far out man," he mumbled, "that's so trippy."

Gurrey and Grime jostled Sammy aside as they rushed toward the teetering tower.

"Hey dudes, be cool, don't bring me down man, you're harshing my mellow, man!" Sammy shouted after them.

As they neared the structure, the two detectives realized that the statue wasn't actually falling. Instead it appeared to be collapsing in very slow motion.

"What's going on here?" Gurrey said.

"It's so obvious," Grime replied. "The only logical explanation is that we have somehow slipped through a portal in the space-time continuum and entered another dimension where everything moves v-e-r-y s-l-o-w-l-y, like in Sandy Cove or Ottawa."

"No, you idiot, you're unfortunately still in this dimension." Riki had walked up behind the two dicks. "Remember who we're dealing with: theme park and fish farm operators. They both deal in misinformation, make their living by producing a poor imitation of the real thing, and are good at putting up false fronts. When I climbed this statue earlier I noticed that it was made of some unusual but strangely familiar material. I just now figured it out. This structure is constructed entirely of papier-mâché."

"I suppose that does make more sense than my alternate dimension hypothesis" Grime admitted. Then he added, "Your front isn't false, is it, Rikilini?"

Gurrey tried to ignore his drooling partner's suave pick-up line but made a mental note to try it himself sometime. "And it explains what's happening now," he said. "The unofficial Eighth Natural Wonder of the World, our famous Bay of Fundy fog, has softened the papier-mâché, causing it to slowly lose its shape."

"Exactly", Riki said. "The same fog that has destroyed the firmest of perms on thousands of well-coiffed Island women over the years. But right now we have to figure out what to do about those unfortunate people up there. Their tin-foil stairway has collapsed and cut off the escape route."

Just then the statue gave a shudder and slumped a bit further. From above they could hear the screams of frightened party-goers.

"That restaurant will soon fall, and when it does, it will land right on the rocks," Gurrey said, "We don't want to have to sing *It's Raining Men*, although it is a hell of a song by a hell of a singer. What we need is a soft landing for them. Come on, I've got an idea!"

They dashed around to the water side of the statue, and found Riki's climbing ropes still attached to the structure. Floating just offshore were the fish cages with their protective net canopies.

Gurrey grabbed a rope and yelled, "C'mon, pull!"

The protesters had been bravely doing the only thing they could think of to prevent the tower's imminent collapse, an a capella version of *Don't Bring Me Down,* but quickly realized that if they could actually assist in changing the direction of the tower's lean, there was a chance the restaurant would safely fall right into the fish cage nets.

They rushed to help, and with a resounding chorus of *Haul Away Boys*, put their weight to the task. Even Sammy the Salmon joined in, although he had a bit of trouble getting a grip on the rope with his fins.

Bit by bit, as it continued to slump and sag, the tower slowly changed direction. Just as the team on the ropes reached their limit, the papier-mâché Statue of Liberty lost its hold on the rock ledge, and with a sound reminiscent of a wad of wet paper towel hitting the floor, fell.

As the statue toppled, the circular restaurant separated; flew through the air, skipped once off the water, and, like a Sydney Crosby slap shot, landed perfectly in the back of a net.

~

Three days later, Gurrey, Grime and Rikilini were the guests of honour at a luncheon at Lavena's Cafe. After the dust settled—they hadn't had time to sweep the floor yet that day—it was clear that the world-famous Balancing Rock was still in its rightful place. The statue had just been constructed around it. The Statuette of Limitations was up, by which we mean down.

For their heroic efforts in saving the iconic Rock as well as the people in the rotating bar/restaurant, the three heroes were allowed to pick whatever they wanted from the menu and received passes for a free ferry ride.

To the surprise of everyone present, the theme park/fish farm operators rose and announced that their near-death experience had taught them not to fool with Mother Nature and so they were henceforth getting out of the fish farm business and turning all their theme parks into wildlife refuges. "We'll model ourselves on that Tiger King guy," said one operator. "What could go wrong?"

As the gala evening drew to a close, Rikilini turned to Gurrey and Grime and said, "Well, boys, looks like you closed another case. You've helped return our greatest natural wonder to its pristine state. I'm almost starting to respect you."

"Thanks, Rikilini!" Grime gushed. "Those phony rich folks would do anything for a quick buck. You have to respect tradition."

They all shook their heads at the follies of big capitalists. Then Grime said, "Is now a good time to tell you about our plan to put a fast food restaurant on top of the Rock and call it the Leaning Tower of Pizza?"

Figure 3: The Balancing Rock Revolving Restaurant

6: Food Feud

Gurrey and Grime were sitting around their combined detective office and fish shack discussing philosophy and taking the odd call from a client as they gutted the few remaining pollack.

"We've only had one fine day all summer and they called it a weather breeder," Gurrey said.

"Your arse is sucking wind," Grime countered, wiping entrails from his final report on the Balancing Rock affair. "We had that other day...late August, I think it was."

Having exhausted the subject of weather, they turned their attention to the other topic that occupied their downtime.

"Getting any?" posited Gurrey.

"Naww, and I'm as horny as a three-peckered owl."

"You mean you're as raspy as a file?"

"Whatever," Grime said. "The point is a man like me has needs, needs that must be met, damn it. I was voted Sexiest Man in Freeport four consecutive years 1967-70 inclusive."

"Listen," Gurrey said, "That don't amount to the square root of..."

The phone rang, interrupting the discourse. Grime grabbed it and barked a hello.

"Okay. Okay. Okay. Okay. Okay. Okay. Okay, we'll be right over." He slammed the phone down, creating a brief flurry of fish scales.

"What's up?" Gurrey said.

"It's that chick Virginia from the Briar Island Lodge. Claims that Levena from Levena's has been bad-mouthing her clams. That's the third call this week. Last week it was Levena claiming that Virginia was defaming her dulse. This restaurant war has got to stop, damn it!"

He pounded his fist on the desk, striking a small herring that had been inside a rather large gutted codfish. The fish exploded all over Gurrey who wiped his face off nonchalantly as if this was an everyday occurrence, which it was.

"What are we going to do?" Grime said. "These are both fine eating establishments. We've got to make them see that there's room for everyone in this all-inclusive Tri-Island paradise of ours."

"I think it's time to go undercover," Gurrey said.

The two eyed each other, Grime through the beautiful green peepers that had rendered the knees of island women weak just a few short years prior, and Gurrey through his lone, still-functional bloodshot bulging orb.

"Great idea, Gurrey!" Grime said. "It'll give us a chance to try out those new disguises we bought at Dollarama in New Minas, the Fifth Avenue of the Valley. This is definitely better than a kick in the ass with a frozen boot."

Twenty minutes later they were hardly recognizable to each other, let alone the general public. Grime wore a tuxedo complete with top hat and silver-knobbed cane, and sported an elegant handlebar moustache and monocle. Gurrey was his date. He wore a knee-length pleated dress, circa 1968, and a simple white pullover sweater. His shoulder-length hair was made of frayed yellow polypropylene rope. He had stuffed bait bags in his chest area to approximate his fading memory of what women's breasts look like.

Grime looked him up and down and declared: "The last time I saw legs like that they had a message attached."

"Never mind all that," Gurrey said. "I'll just throw on some makeup and lippy and we'll go check these places out." He had never before felt so lovely.

Grime and Gurrey decided to make Lavena's their first stop. They jumped into the Buick and caught the ferry. The old car had no heater and its rusted-out body was no match for the cold wind blowing off the North Atlantic. Grime was shivering. "How do you stay so warm?" he inquired of his partner, who had removed his coat and was fanning himself.

"I hate to admit it but it's the male menopause," Gurrey said sheepishly.

"Men don't have menopause," Grime said.

"That's what I thought until I went to the dentist. Besides, it's right in the name. MENopause?"

"The dentist told you you have male menopause?"

"No, he told me I needed three crowns and a bridge. It was the magazine in his waiting room that told me I have the menopause."

"Oh, I see. Medical journal, was it?"

"*Chatelaine* I think. It said that the male menopause increases your body fat, gives you boobs, ruins your concentration, saps your energy, destroys your motivation and reduces your vibrato."

"Libido," Grime corrected.

"Oh, you have it too?"

"No, I—"

"Also selective hearing, ear hair, nose hair, loss of head hair, and excessive flatulence."

"Flatulence?"

"Yeah. It said in the article that flatulence was the male version of hot flashes. That's why I never let one go in the woods when the forest fire index is high. Don't wanna start no brush fires."

"*Chatelaine* said all this?"

"I think so. Might've been *Cosmo*. Wait, I think I have another hot flash coming on." He rolled down the window.

Outside, within earshot and enjoying the ocean breeze were two attractive middle-aged women whom both men had had their eyes on (three eyes in all, as earlier indicated). The women suddenly looked up, startled, at the sound of a loud report.

"Hot flash," Gurrey said by way of explanation and smiled, showing lipstick-stained teeth.

The women turned away in disgust.

"Playing hard to get," Gurrey said with a wink of his good eye.

~

"What is it we're doing again?" Grime asked for the third time in as many minutes.

As the ferry approached the Freeport slip, Gurrey patiently went over the plan one more time for his nearly senile partner. "We're going undercover to observe the goings-on at Lavena's. The key to this operation is to not attract attention. We've got to fly under the radar on this one, we don't want people to know who we are or even notice that we're there."

With that, Gurrey started the big Buick V-8, floored the gas, and with the unmufflered engine roaring and rear wheels spinning in the wet seaweed, fishtailed up the ferry slip.

Sliding into Lavena's parking lot in a spray of gravel, with the 8-track blasting Iron Butterfly's "Inna-Gadda-Da-Vida," the partners quickly found a parking space and then nonchalantly sauntered over to the restaurant.

"Hi guys, what's with the get-ups?" Lavena greeted them as soon as they stepped through the door.

"I'm sorry, you must have us confused with some other high-society couple." Grime said, "My date and I are complete strangers here and are just looking for a good place to get a meal."

Lavena shrugged. "Whatever you say." She showed them to a table.

When they were seated, she said, "What do you think of our new menus?" and handed them a pair of leather-bound folders with gold-leaf lettering that spelled out *"Lavena's Catch: Where the Elite who Eat More than Meat Meet to Eat.- Have a Seat."*

"I think our slogan needs a little fine tuning," she said. "It doesn't sound quite as catchy as I had imagined."

After perusing the menu, Grime declared in what he perceived to be a cultured, upper-crust tone of voice, "My guts are in an uproar today, I think I'll just have a pine float."

"I don't see that on the menu," Gurrey said. "What's a pine float?"

"It's a toothpick in a glass of water."

"Cheap bugger," Gurrey muttered. "I think I'll have my usual, Chicken Chow Mein and a grilled cheese sandwich."

As they waited for their order to come, the two dicks surreptitiously observed the activity in the cafe. Despite being interrupted every few minutes by people greeting them by name, they were still able to overhear a conversation between Lavena and her chef.

"We're out of flounder," the chef said flatly.

"I hate to do it in light of what's been happening lately," Lavena replied reluctantly, "but send the new girl over to the Lodge again and see if they can loan us some."

She pulled a bag of lobster meat from the freezer. "Tell her to take this. I know they need it for tonight's chowder."

As they left the Cafe to a chorus of good-byes from both staff and patrons, Grime astutely observed, "I'm not sure, but I think our undercover personas may have been compromised."

"I think you might be right.," Gurrey said. "Our car is too well known. It must have blown our cover. Before we go any farther with this, we need to change vehicles."

Owen Otley was just finishing up a lazy mid-afternoon breakfast of cold finnan haddie, rappie pie and an extra-large pepperoni and anchovy pizza when a knock came on his door.

"We need to borrow your car, Owen," Grime said. "We need something that won't attract as much attention as the Dickmobile."

"Okay," Otley said, "but I need it back by tonight. I've got a hot date."

"Yeah, right, a date with a deep-fried cheesecake," Gurrey muttered.

"What was that about cheesecake?" Otley said, suddenly alert. "Are you taking the car to get cheesecake?"

"No," Gurrey said. "There's no cheesecake, what I said was, um, 'this fog makes my knees ache.' Yeah, that was it!"

"I could have sworn you said cheesecake," Otley said, turning dejectedly back to his table.

Otley's vehicle was a 1970 Dodge van with chrome reverse wheels, chrome exhaust side-pipes and a fancy paint job that included an air-brushed portrait of an overly-endowed scarcely-clad woman reclining seductively below the scripted words, "Shaggin' Wagon". The interior featured a waterbed in the back, purple shag carpeting on the walls and dash, three pairs of never-worn women's panties hanging from the rear-view mirror, and black-lights.

Gurrey and Grime climbed into the diamond-pleated, faux-leather front bucket seats. Gurrey reached for the white rabbit's foot hanging from the ignition and turned the key. Suddenly the deeply melodious, intimate voice of Barry White filled the cabin.

"The longer we make love...The closer I want to be...I just can't get enough...I love the way you freak me."

Otley's twelve-speaker high-end sound system made it feel like Barry White was standing right behind them, whispering the words in their ears.

"Don't think...just feel it...Ooooh... just do it"

Gurrey suddenly became acutely aware that he was still wearing his undercover disguise and was dressed as a woman. An incredibly attractive woman! After a few seconds of exchanging uncomfortable glances with Grime, and before Barry could sing another verse, Gurrey snatched the cassette out of the player and flung it out the window. "I think we can do without that," he said in a deep, masculine voice.

"Yeah, for sure." Grime replied awkwardly. "So, how about them Red Sox?"

~

The deviously disguised dicks decided to return to Westport to visit the restaurant at the Briar Island Lodge. Grime thought he had the germ of an idea about what might be causing bad feelings between the proprietors of the two magnificent eateries. Using his superior intelligence and razor-sharp deductive powers, he had deduced that something didn't smell right. In fact it stank. It stank bad. It stank real bad.

"Something stinks," he finally said out loud.

"Sorry about that," Gurrey said. "It wasn't another hot flash. I had some leftover chili for breakfast."

"Not that," Grime said, "although that is incredibly foul. No, it's the 'new girl' who stinks, and I mean that in a metaphoric rather than an olfactory way if you take my meaning."

"I do," Gurrey said.

"I recognized her right away, of course," Grime said. "Sure she's changed in the 40 years since we saw her last—put on 70 or 80 pounds, had a face-transplant, butt-lift, fixed her bow-legs—but I'd recognize those ear lobes anywhere. Besides, how could you forget the most fiendishly talented mime to ever come out of the Tri-Island area?"

"You mean—?" Gurrey blurted.

"Yes: Rubella Perry-Outhouse-Thurber-Cann, the thrice-married Countess of Mimicry. She could impersonate anyone, living or dead or anyplace in between. The 'girl of a thousand voices,' they called her. She once packed the finest venues with people clamouring to see her act. The IOOF Hall in Freeport one night, the IOOF Hall in Tiverton the next. Those were heady days for Rubella, until she decided to use her unique powers for evil."

"I remember now," Gurrey said. "She was sent for a long stretch in prison for trying to rob the bank by impersonating Elsie at the phone office so that she could intercept calls and get the inside scoop on when the bankroll was coming to Westport for the weekly bank day. Luckily that was the day we decided to try out our idea for the drive-through gutting service and traffic was held up long enough for the cops to get her. High five!"

The two dicks exchanged high fives, congratulating themselves for their role in solving that crime.

"Why would she be working at Lavena's?" Grime wondered out loud.

"Come to think of it, she's working part time at the Lodge too," Gurrey said. "I saw her there at the Swift bar mitzvah."

"Okay, Gurrey, let's put the pieces of this puzzle together: Piece One – she can imitate any voice. Piece Two – Complaints have come in from Virginia and Lavena, even though they were always very friendly. Piece Three – Rubella works at both restaurants. Piece Four – The last I heard of her, she was training as a cook while she was inside.

"Conclusion: She's trying to drive both businesses under and start her own."

"Your perspicacity amazes me Grimey," Gurrey said, adjusting his knee-length nylons.

As they careened onto the ferry, striking the car ahead and causing a chain reaction that left the front car hanging precariously over the bow,

Grime began to think of what a great pal Gurrey had been to him all these years. He suddenly recalled that the drive-through fish-gutting service had been Gurrey's idea, and a damn good one too. It was called Gut 'N' Go (their motto was: 'If you got fish, we'll gut 'em') and it was so successful in Westport that they had opened outlets in Tiverton and Freeport. Soon franchises sprang up all over the Tri-Island and Digby Neck region. They were making money faster than they could spend it, which was pretty fast. Soon the fast money led to fast women, fast cars and fast celebrity.

Unfortunately, they went bust when they overextended themselves by putting all their money into a trendy Barrington Street fish-gutting boutique. Surprisingly, it turned out to be a total disaster. Not only was there a shockingly low demand for fish-gutting from the Halifax populace, but the other franchises were irrevocably damaged by the downturn in the fishery. Soon their outlets were taken over for failure to pay taxes and became drive-through psychology clinics, run, coincidentally, by Gurrey's main squeeze at the time, Randi.

"Randi by name, randy by nature," Gurrey used to boast before the two split up over who got to deworm the cats.

Nevertheless, life for a while had been good for Gurrey and Grime and now Grime remembered that it was all down to his friend. He began to regret some of the things he had said about him. It was all true of course, but he regretted it nonetheless.

The ferry ride to Westport seemed to take forever and the talk turned to their former wives and children. "How's the family, Gurrey?" Grime said.

"Well, Peter is in detox. Rita runs a convenience store with Norris. Tracey just got out of prison and is sleeping around. Chesney got his girlfriend pregnant and Sally is thinking of getting back with her husband Kevin who had a baby with another woman who died in a trolley crash. How about your family?"

Grime's life-long addiction to British soap operas had reached the point where his addled brain was no longer able to distinguish the difference between real life and working-class Limey fantasy. As a result, Gurrey was forced to humour his slowly dementing partner by presenting plot-line reviews from the telly as real events in an attempt to spice up Grime's otherwise uninteresting life. Grime, for his part, had started to notice lately that he always zoned out on the ferry, he put it down to the radar interfering with the plate in his head; he found that his mind wandered a lot recently and it seemed to take him longer than usual to find it and bring it back.

Luckily for Gurrey's sanity, the inane conversation was cut short by the scow thumping the wharf as it slid onto the Westport ferry slip, causing the Shaggin' Wagon to sway abruptly and jostling Grime back into the real world.

A few short minutes later the two dicks were cruising the gritty streets of downtown Westport.

"These streets sure are gritty." Grime said.

"It's all the rain washing the gravel from the driveways onto the street."

"Too bad we're tied up with this case. We could be up to the gravel pit right now, loading up the Dickmobile. At five dollars a load, we could be making some sweet bread, mister man."

By now the detectives had left the Lowertown part of the Westport metropolis and were wending their way up the majestic peak known as The High Knoll. Presently they pulled up in front of The Brier Island Lodge, and after checking that their undercover disguises were still intact, walked up to the reception desk.

"Hi, guys," Virginia said, eyeing Grime's moth-eaten tuxedo and Gurrey's Christian Dior gown and flowing yellow polypropylene hair. "If you're looking for a room, I'm sorry, but we're all booked up, and besides, we don't rent them out by the hour."

"No, no," Grime said, " my lovely fiancée and myself are planning on tying the knot, a bit of a shotgun wedding affair, if you catch my drift, and we're checking out places to hold the reception. Could you show us the features offered by your fine establishment?"

"Okay," Virginia said, "I'll play along. Just step this way and you'll notice our dining room with its large picture windows and magnificent view. The architect that designed this building positioned it in such a way that every seat has a wonderful panoramic view of the harbour and a perfect vantage point from which to appreciate the many glorious features of the village of Westport, while at the same time being shielded from any direct view of Freeport. That is one of our most popular features here. We have patrons who come back year after year just to enjoy the view, many of them from Long Island."

"Fine, fine," Grime said, "but this will be one of the biggest social events of the year, second only to the Super Seniors Annual Skip-Bo Tournament. I'd like to see if your kitchen can handle a crowd that big."

"We're just starting to prepare this evening's meal," Virginia said, "but I suppose we can take a quick look."

Stepping through the double swinging doors, Gurrey noticed a familiar figure preparing to dump something into a large pot. Suddenly, Grime roared out, "DROP THAT MEAT."

Over in the corner by the sink, a pimply-faced teenager looked up and in an embarrassed voice whined, "I wasn't doing nothin'! Honest! I was just jigging around in my pocket looking for a breath mint!"

"I didn't mean you," Grime said, turning from the dishwasher to the figure at the pot. "I meant you, Rubella!"

At the sound of her name, Rubella Perry-Outhouse-Thurber-Cann, for indeed it was she, dropped the package of lobster meat and ran for the door.

Thinking quickly for a change, or possibly just as a spontaneous response to one of his many nervous tics, Grime reached out with the walking stick he was carrying as part of his disguise and tripped her as she dashed by.

Rubella went sprawling across the floor and ended up under the sink, almost knocking over the dishwasher, who apparently was still busy looking for that breath mint.

"Rubella!?" Virginia gasped in surprise, "She told me her name was Rosacea Titus-Welch-McDormand-Graham."

"Yes, well, she is a master of disguise and impersonation. I wouldn't have recognized her myself if I didn't have such intimate knowledge of her earlobes, her damned tiny, perfect, irresistible earlobes."

Grime's voice broke with emotion at the mention of earlobes and Gurrey noticed a certain wistful tone in his quavering voice and a far-away look in his rheumy eyes.

Recognizing that his partner was about to slip into one of his all-too-frequent reminiscences, Gurrey stepped up and slapped Grime smartly across the face. "Shape up here, buddy. "You're on a case; not parked at the end of Lovers' Lane."

Coming back with a start, Grime looked around the room to orient himself, and then fixed his glaucoma-blurred gaze upon Rubella. "Okay, girl, you've got some explaining to do."

"Oh, Grimey, can't we go out back and discuss this just between the two of us?"

"You fooled me once...no wait, you fooled me twice...actually, you fooled me three times with that ploy, but you won't fool me again. I've removed thoughts of your luscious lobes from my mind. You might say I've had a lobeotomy."

With what Gurrey took to be a pout, Rubella began her tale:

"I used to be so happy. I was born to be an entertainer and I had found my niche in the world of show business. By combining the usually distinct disciplines of mime and mimicry, I had carved out a career that saw me selling out halls from one end of Long Island to the other. I was the only talking mime in show business. If only I could have been satisfied with that, but no, I had to reach for that impossible dream that all in this business desire; to appear on Westport's Great Off-White Way. A venue was booked; the venerable and highly regarded Fire hall. Tickets were offered, it was a sell-out, and my big night finally arrived. Now I was really on my way.

"The whole thing turned out to be an unmitigated disaster! Unfortunately, unlike the hayseed Long Islanders, the more sophisticated audience of Brier Island knew the difference between a mime and a mimic. Half the audience didn't want to see a mime who spoke, even if it was in the voices of long-dead or near-dead celebrities, and the other half didn't want to see a mimic in whiteface and white gloves pretending to be Robert DeNiro trapped in an invisible box. To make matters worse, the Actor's Union heard about my act. The mimes sent two guys over to pantomime kicking me out of the group, and the mimics left me a phone message in the voice of Jack Nicholson telling me I couldn't handle the truth about being expelled."

She wiped a phantom tear from one eye. "Left with no other option, I turned my talents to crime and ended up being sent up the river for attempted bank robbery and impersonation. While I was inside the Big House I decided to turn my life around by becoming a writer, I figured it can't be that hard, any idiot can write a book, right? Anyway, I managed to publish several books under the pen-name of Margaret Aintwood. They were fairly successful, but I wanted more. I missed the adulation that I had gotten on stage so I entered every literary competition I could find. I tried for The Giller Prize, The Booker Prize, The Stephen Leacock Medal for Humour, even the Pulitzer Prize, but with no luck. They all rejected me.."

"All that work," Gurrey said, "and you had no luck at all?"

"I did manage to get a book on CBC Radio's Canada Reads competition, but it was read on the air by Don Cherry, I knew I didn't have a chance when Don assured me that he would do a good job and pay close attention to the pronunciation "an' everythink like dat".

"I don't see da problem," the dishwasher said.

"I was feeling dejected, rejected and even a tiny bit neglected when it was brought to my attention that I could reduce my time in the pokey by taking a retraining course. I decided to take cooking and found that not only did I have a talent for it, I loved being in front of the stove even more than on the stage. I started winning awards for my culinary masterpieces, I took the Griller Prize and the Cooker Prize, I won the Stephen Leacock-a-Doodle-Do award for my roast rooster, and a chicken dish I created, Pullet Surprise, came in first at the Canada Feeds Competition. I was feeling appreciated for my talents again. The only problem was that the kitchen at the hoosegow for some reason only served fowl."

"Are you saying the food was foul?,"Grime said.

"Yes, that's what I said, it was all fowl."

"They fed you foul food?"

"Exactly! We were fed fowl frequently."

"So you were forced to feed on foul food?"

"I wouldn't say forced, in fact I found I favoured fowl."

"Wow," Grime said, "doing time in the slammer is worse than I thought."

With a confused look, Rubella continued her story. "The day I was freed from my unfortunate incarceration, I determined that I would follow my new calling by opening my own restaurant. Since all I had learned to cook during my time in the jug was various bird dishes, I decided to name my bird-based bistro 'The Perch' and bought what I thought was an appropriate location on the aptly-named Gull Rock. In retrospect, this might have been a less than astute business decision. It was bad enough when it turned out that my restaurant was located on a ledge that was underwater for several hours every day, but the real problem was that most of the tourists who come to these islands are looking for authentic down-home seafood, the kind served by Lavena's and at The Lodge."

"What's wrong with our food?" Virginia demanded, hands on hips.

"Nothing! It's fine. People love it. That's my point: why would they go to a new restaurant with a new kind of food? Faced with the prospect of losing my chance at a new start, I decided the only logical way to improve my prospects was to drive my competition out of business, so I decided to undermine both restaurants. You know, try to start a feud between them. With them out of business I'd have the most successful restaurant in the Tri-Island area—at low tide anyway. I placed those calls, it was me, me, I tell you, me."

At this juncture, she broke down sobbing, perhaps realizing what she had done. "Thank god you stopped me before I grilled again!"

As the unfortunate ex-con was being driven onto the ferry in the back seat of an RCMP cruiser, Gurrey and Grime sat on the wharf and watched in silence.

Eventually Grime was the first to break the silence. And after the resoundingly flatulent outburst that caused small ripples on the water below, he spoke. "Well, I guess we brought that case to a successful conclusion. In fact, I guess you might say we put a lid on that stew...we cooked her goose...she got her just desserts..."

Unable to understand the brilliant wordplay being tossed his way, Gurrey simply sat there, mesmerized by a piece of loose string he'd found on his skirt. Grime sighed loudly.

"One thing is certain, Gurrey. It would be wrong for us to profit from solving this case."

Gurrey scratched his dandruff-laden head. "What do you mean Grimey?"

"Well," Grime said. "Some people might expect some kind of thank-you gift from Lavena and Virginia next time they were in those fine eateries. That would be wrong. We solved this case not to get a large slice of Lavena's ridiculously delicious peanut butter pie or Virginia's amazing cheesecake, but because we are good cops, dammit! Damn good cops. Sure, their food is incomparable—nothing like it in the Tri-Island area or anywhere in Nova Scotia, Canada or the world for that matter—and sure we saved their businesses at great risk to our own safety, but that doesn't matter, We are cops and the only reward we need is justice, justice, dammit. Sure, the fish and chips at both places is mouth-watering and sure the chowder is sublime, but taking a single morsel of those foods would be like taking a bribe—and that would be wrong, dammit!! Can't you see, Gurrey, you poor, simple, lovable, incontinent sap?! We'd be undermining all that is great about the Canadian judicial system to accept such largesse, dammit!!"

Grime smacked his right fist into the palm of his left hand in frustration, and then spent a couple of moments waggling his right hand until the pain subsided. When he could speak again, he said, "Certainly they are grateful and they should be—damn grateful, dammit! But does that mean they have to treat us to what admittedly for them is just a small, even insignificant, bit of their larder of delicious food while to us would mean so much? No, dammit! As I have reiterated, and I hope forcefully, that would be wrong—wrong, damn it all to hell."

Gurrey, drooling uncontrollably and his stomach emitting sounds like those produced by a 1965 Valiant with an underpowered slant six engine going up MacIntyre's Hill in dead low gear, finally spoke, albeit weakly. "Wrong," he muttered. "Right, it would be wrong, Grimesey…even though we haven't been paid for any of our last five cases, and I personally haven't eaten in a week, it would be wrong. Wrong, wrong, wrong."

"I'm proud of you, Gurrey. I just know those breathtakingly beautiful, generous, intelligent, talented women who own those establishments—well worthy of a sixth star from the Michelin Guide, if you ask me—will continue to produce fine dining for islanders and visitors alike long after you and I have shucked off this mortal coil. Though, the way I'm feeling, that won't be long. I'm already faint from lack of food."

"But you still say that taking a piece of their pie would be wrong?" Gurrey said as he chewed on the bait bag that was protruding provocatively from his bodice.

"So wrong, Gurrey. So very wrong. Dammit."

Gurrey looked at his friend. "Perhaps some day some talented writers will write stories about our cases, Grimesey. Maybe someday they'll go into Lavena's or the Lodge. Would it be okay for them to take this...what did you call it, Grimesey...largesse?"

"Entirely different scenario, Gurrey my boy," Grime said. "That would be absolutely fine, dammit."

Figure 4: Ample parking in the downtown business area

7: Struggling with Smuggling

Gurrey and Grime were now famous. They had just solved their fifth consecutive case and as a result had been written up in the *Crime and Punishment* section of *Passages*, the *New York Times* of the Tri-Island area.

Gurrey and Grime now lived together in a bachelor pad in the fashionable "Low Water Mark Towers", a one-and-a-half-storey building offering a spectacular view of Freeport and the looming majesty of Roney's Point, the local equivalent of the White Cliffs of Dover. Both dicks were single. Gurrey's third marriage was a story of lost love that was so common it had practically become a cliché on the islands: Man places ad in the *Digby Courier* asking for a live-in housekeeper to do some "light housekeeping." Woman arrives to discover that it was actually 'lighthouse keeping' and that she was expected to clean the lighthouse top to bottom, with special attention to the windows that surrounded the warning beacon that flashed on and off sixty feet above the razor-sharp rocks and churning sea below.

Gurrey dearly wanted to help but suffered from selective vertigo and sadly could only wash the inside of the windows and do some light dusting. Despite his fear of heights and her loss of hearing from being blasted in the face by a 120-decibel foghorn whenever she was cleaning the windows, they fell in love and married.

As time passed, his wife found it increasingly difficult to shimmy up the sides of the lighthouse, especially when pregnant. She left him after three years, taking their four children, three cats and a rescue seagull with her.

After a number of failed marriages, Grime had finally decided to live the remainder of his life as a bachelor. His marriages had imploded so completely and spectacularly that padding out this paragraph with further details would only depress the reader. Suffice it to say that when Grime was a fisherman, his Cape Islander had X-ed out women's names that extended from the rail to just below the water line: The Betty S, the Heather M, the Susan D, the Penny P, the Judy T—well, you get the picture.

He and Gurrey were living the life of swinging singles, always on the go, looking to be seen at the most happening places in the two communities. One night they might be boogieing on down at Disco David's Disco and Take Out Pizza in midtown and the next night at Studio

55, an abandoned scallop dragger that you entered through a gaping hole in the starboard side. It was parties here, receptions there, fancy dress balls, fêtes, costume parties, afternoon teas and those combination orgies and crokinole competitions that had become the latest fad with the desperate housewives of the Tri-Island area.

Their lives had become a whirlwind of fame, with paparazzi hounding them at every stop. Hardly a day went by that their pictures weren't to be found in the society pages of scandal sheets such as the *Digby Courier*, *Passages* and the R.E. Robicheau *Shoppers Weekly*. There were pictures of Gurrey with local celebrity and former go-go dancer Frisky Larue, shots of Grime dancing up a storm with socialite and post office mistress Penny Arcade. And of course, there was the unfortunate X-rated photo of Gurrey getting out of his car after a Robbie Burns celebration with his pleated kilt hiked high enough to leave nothing to the imagination.

The debauchery didn't end there. It was becoming alarmingly common to see a strange white powdery residue under Gurrey's nose the result of snorting pixie sticks. And Grime had also flirted with the drug sub-culture of the Islands, a group of shady characters who had been running their nefarious operation out of an abandoned submarine. They had recently got hold of some bad weed and as a result Grime suffered dandelion wine poisoning.

The two debauched dicks woke up one Sunday morning in their bachelor pad with its disco ball, mood lamps, lava lamps, circular revolving Murphy beds, shag carpets, Chianti bottles with candles in them—in short everything that made the "girlies" weak in the knees. They had it all and they knew it. And yet, they weren't happy. They were looking for another challenge. Truth be known, they were both vying for the coveted Dick of the Year Award.

"You can't be dick of the year by just wearing the latest bell bottom trousers and platform shoes with a live mackerel in the heel," Gurrey said sagely.

Grime looked up from the debris of another raucous party with the islands' extremely desperate housewives. "Very wise, Gurrey," he agreed. "We need to get back to work."

Just then the phone rang loudly. Gurrey picked it up on the second ring. The conversation was short. "We'll be right there," said the dick before hanging up.

"I think we've got smugglers using these islands to bring in their stuff, and you'll never guess what that stuff is."

"Do tell, Gurrey. Do tell."

"Actually," Gurrey said, "I'm not sure I want to tell you about this case. It looks like it could be a dangerous one. These are hard-core professional smugglers. They might be out of our league."

"Pshaw!" Grime scoffed, covering his partner with a fine spray of chewing tobacco juice. "We've dealt with smugglers before. Remember the counterfeit belly button ring ring? We easily pierced that operation. And then there were the Mexicans who nearly ruined the local hat business by trying to bring in embargoed sombreros. We soon put a lid on that!"

"True, true," Gurrey mused, wiping the spittle-soaked remnants of Grime's plug of 'chaw' from his face, hair and shoes, "but this is something new. These people are smuggling coke. It looks like they have a whole system set up. We'll have to contend not just with the smugglers, but with their dealers and the end users. You know how those coke-heads are. If they don't get their regular fix, they go crazy. And it looks like it's a big operation. They're not just bringing in coke, but Pepsi and Dr. Pepper, too." His voice dropped. "Even Mountain Dew," he whispered.

"For the love of God, no!" Grime said, almost choking on his chaw.

The phone call had been from Wallman "The Wall" Robichini, owner of the Tri-Islands' largest grocery conglomerate. He had just returned from the annual meeting of the South-West Nova Groceteria and Markette Owners' Association where he learned that every store in the area had suffered a recent and calamitous drop in the sale of soft drinks.

"Apparently," Gurrey said, "someone recently found several cans of pop in Pond Cove. The fact they were unopened was not that unusual, but what was really strange was that there was absolutely no French on the label. At first it was thought it was just some defective cans discarded because of a printing error, but in light of the decline in sales of legitimate soft drinks "The Wall" suspects that someone is bringing in cheap sodas from Stateside, and landing them in Pond Cove."

"Well," Grime said, "we'd better go get ourselves some STDs, boy. It looks like we're going to be spending a long, cold night staked out at Pond Cove."

Midnight found the two dicks on the crest of a dune overlooking the cove. Grime was lying in the sand amongst the sparse bushes, surveying the moonlit horizon with a pair of G. I. Joe binoculars that he had acquired on his 12th birthday. Gurrey, who had been making a quick reconnaissance of the area, approached stealthily and lay down in the sand beside his partner.

"See anything?" he said.

"Nothing so far."

Casting a glance in Grime's direction, Gurrey said, "You look worried. What's the problem, prostate acting up again? If you need to take yet another leak, go in those bushes over there. I'll keep an eye on the beach."

"No, it's nothing like that. Besides, I just took a leak in the sand right there where you're laying."

After quickly moving a couple of feet to the right, Gurrey said, "I know something's bothering you. What is it?"

"I'm trying to decide if I should tell you something. It's of a personal nature and I don't want you to think less of me because of it."

"Believe me, Grimey, there is no way I could possibly think less of you than I already do."

In an emotion-choked voice Grime replied, "That's real nice of you to say so, Gurrey, old pal. I should have known I could depend on you." Grime blew his nose loudly and discreetly wiped a tear from his eye, the one that tended to always look to the side.

Using his uncanny powers of observation, Gurrey noticed that his friend's eyes were moist. "Your eyes look rheumy," he said gently.

"Roomy enough for two pupils and a coupla cornea," Grime said, taken aback by the strange comment. "Anyways, when I found out we were going to be doing this stake-out, I asked Owen Otley to keep an ear to the ground for information on who was running hot cold drinks over the border. When you're 5' 4" and 365 pounds, keeping your ear to the ground is not easy, but I must say that Owen came up with the goods. If his information is reliable, and I have no reason to doubt it, sometime tonight we should be coming face-to-face with a notorious smuggler by the name of Percival 'Pearly' Prime."

"Okay," Gurrey said. "I still don't see what there is to be embarrassed about. So you used Owen to get some information; that's nothing. Usual stipend? Three lemon meringue pies and a McCain's Deep and Delicious? I've got him to do way worse things than that for a large order of fries."

"No, no, that's not the embarrassing thing. The embarrassing thing is that I'm directly related to this outlaw."

"How can that be? Your names are completely different. Yours is Grime, his is Prime, totally different."

"I've never told this to another living soul, but our family name used to be Prime. Generations ago, back when the land was still new and wild, the Prime family came to this country, seeking to make a fresh start free of the constrictions, creditors and paternity payments of the Old World.

Unfortunately, times were tough and some of the family turned to crime, mostly penny-ante stuff, rolling old ladies for their petticoats, high-jacking people's penny-farthings. It was all minor crime and overlooked by the authorities until one particularly bad apple, Parsimony Prime, was caught rustling fish from the weir at Seawall Hill."

"That's pretty nasty."

"This was still in the time of the Wild West-Nova. Fish rustling was one of the most heinous crimes a man could commit. Justice was usually swift and brutal and retribution was found at the end of a rope slung over the nearest weir pole. The local frontier paper, *Ye Olde Digby Courier*, sent a reporter down to interview some of the residents. One of the people he talked to was my ancestor, Pulchritudinous Prime. When the story came out they had misspelled his last name as Grime."

"Not much has changed, eh?"

Grime nodded. "Since he was on the law-abiding side of the family, Pulchritudinous took the opportunity to disassociate himself from the criminal element and our branch of the family has been known as Grime ever since. Now I'm about to meet and most likely arrest one of my long-lost relatives. 'Pearly' Prime. He got that nickname because of his brilliantly white teeth that he flashes at all the girlies."

Grime grinned despite himself. "That 'chick-magnet' thing runs in the family I guess. I can't believe how nervous I am. Do you think he will like me, Gurrey?"

"What?, Gurrey said distractedly. "Sorry, old bean, I haven't been listening. I've been busy watching that boat and those people wading ashore."

Sure enough, down below, clearly visible in the glow of the full moon, several burly men were struggling ashore with heavy sacks slung over their backs.

Grime spotted Pearly immediately, the moon reflecting off his brilliant white teeth. "Handsome bastard," he muttered under his breath. Handsomeness and humility had always been the twin curses of the Prime/Grime family.

"I'm torn, Gurrey," he said earnestly, looking his friend in his good eye. "I mean, blood is thicker than water. How can I be expected to arrest one of my own? With his incredible good looks he would be easy pickings in the slammer, if you know what I mean. And yet I represent the law. It's my duty to see that justice is done—and justice is blind, even blinder than you Gurrey, if that's possible...I'm over here Gurrey, that's a fence post you're gazing at."

Following the sound of his friend's voice, Gurrey finally looked in his direction. "I understand your dilemma, my friend," he said. "For years we've also been trying to live down our own shameful past. You know me as Gurrey Ben, but actually my full name is Gurrey Ben-Gurion Robicheau, part of the Robichini grocery cartel. Wallman "The Wall" Robichini is my second cousin once removed on my Dutch-Italian-Israeli mother's side. My father was French Canadian. Ricolini is my sister! So I too have a vested interest in the outcome of this case. Wallman has been putting pressure on me to solve it so that he can continue to be the exclusive Coke King of the Tri-Island area. It's the same old story: French Canadian man meets Dutch-Italian-Israeli girl, marries her, changes the family name to Robichini for no apparent reason, opens a successful grocery store and monopolizes all the Coke in the Tri-Island area. If I've heard it once, I've heard it a thousand times. We once tried to trace our family tree but apparently it was full of dry rot. So, you are really a Prime, and I'm really a Robicheau. And it took this sordid case of smuggling carbonated contraband to make it all fizz to the surface."

The smugglers were making their way slowly up the slope and it was becoming apparent that they would pass within a matter of feet of the concealed dicks. They lay motionless, save for the irritating twitches and facial tics that had dogged Gurrey since a troubled youth spent living in the penthouse apartment that housed the Western Light foghorn.

The smugglers were winded from the steep climb and paused to catch their breath near the prone positions of Gurrey and Grimes. Pearly Prime was the first to speak. "Well, the hardest part is done. Now all we have to do is load these into the hidden truck and drive them to the 'fence.'"

"Why would we drive them to a fence?" an eerily familiar voice gasped.

"Not a fence fence, you fool," Pearly snapped. "A fence."

"Barbed or electric?" the confused smuggler said, hands on his knees as he struggled to breath.

"Neither, you fool!" Pearly said. "A fence!! A guy who accepts and distributes stolen goods is a fence!"

"That doesn't sound right," the high-pitched accomplice wheezed. "I hope you don't take offence, but a fence is a fence and when you say we're driving the Coke to a fence, it doesn't make much sense. Perhaps I'm too tense."

"Too dense, more like it," Prime growled. "Unless it's just pretense."

All of a sudden the two dicks realized who owned the second voice. It was their leg man, Owen Otley, all 5'4" and 365 pounds of him.

"That dirty traitor," Grimes whispered.

By this point the smugglers had their second wind, all except Owen who hadn't recovered his first. "You go on ahead," he said, unable to move. "I'll wait here until you get back."

With a final look of disgust, Pearly and the rest of his pack of thieves disappeared into the underbrush.

When they were sure that the gang was indeed gone, Gurrey and Grime sprang upon their duplicitous detective junior grade, who had pulled a turkey leg from his left pants pocket and was attacking it with gusto.

"Why, you dirty—" Gurrey sputtered.

"Of all the—" Grime added.

Otley looked up at them and smiled broadly.

"Well boys, I hope this gets me that promotion I've been after: full partnership in the DN&IF-GS&DA. Against all odds, I've managed to infiltrate the most diabolical smuggling ring in the Tri-Island area. Look at me! I'm a mole!"

The two seasoned dicks were gob-smacked by this completely unforeseen development. Otley had never shown any interest in moving up the detective food chain, although in retrospect he had always been shockingly interested in the food chain itself.

Was he a rat or a mole? His physical appearance showed elements of both. His face was indeed rodent-like as was his brain capacity. Grime imagined him running through a maze in some laboratory in search of a piece of cheese, or more likely, cheesecake.

"But why didn't you tell us about your plans to infiltrate the smugglers?" Gurrey asked..

"Because I knew you wouldn't let me do it," Otley said. "I'm known for my physical prowess, my speed, my agility, my ability to outrun the villains of the Tri-Island area. That's why I'm your legman. You forget that my brain power is almost as good as my physical wherewithal." He paused to dip his turkey leg into his right trouser pocket, which apparently contained gravy. "I keep my brain sharp by doing Lexicon in the *Herald* every day."

The two dicks decided to believe him. "What were you able to find out?" Grime said.

"Oh, I found out a lot," Otley said, motioning for the dicks to move in closer and lowering his voice. "For instance, did you know that it's not a good idea to keep gravy in your pants pocket? Sure, it feels kind of nice running down your leg, and you can't beat that warm, squishy sensation as it pools in your shoe, but in the end it ruins the flavour of the gravy."

"Nothing is worse than shoe gravy!" Grime nodded in agreement. "At first it seems to taste okay, but then you start getting that subtle undertone of sweaty sock combined with a strong hint of Odor-eaters."

"If you two gourmands are finished," Gurrey said, "I'd like to hear if Owen has any news that isn't gravy related."

"Well," Otley said, "I did find out that this operation is a lot bigger than we thought. In addition to being Coke smugglers, these guys are gum runners. They've got a whole arsenal of machine gums, you know, the kind of gum you get out of those coin machines at the mall. But actually, the soda and gum is just a side-line. Their main business is in the drug trade!"

Gurrey and Grime looked aghast as Otley continued.

"And it's a vile, evil drug, too. I'm ashamed to say that I tried this drug a few years ago and it almost killed me. I must have overdosed, I was as sick as a dog and couldn't eat for almost an hour, I thought I'd die."

"What was it Owen? Heroin, meth, crack cocaine?"

"Worse! Much worse. It was cod liver oil."

"They're bringing in contraband cod liver oil?"

"No, they're smuggling it out in exchange for the Coke."

"But the production of cod liver oil is highly regulated! Where are they getting it?"

"They make it themselves."

"But how? It requires expensive and complicated equipment, where would they get that?"

"Remember the old Westport Cod Liver Oil Factory?" Otley said.

"The one in the Cod Liver Oil district? Sure," Grime replied, "but that was destroyed years ago, washed away in the Groundhog Day storm of '76."

"That's right," Gurrey said, "I saw it with my own eye. The first tidal wave swept the building off its posts and the second wave carried it out into the harbour. The last I saw of it, it was floating out through the passage."

"And it kept right on floating," Otley said, "finally drifting ashore in the worst possible place, that pirate's lair, that den of iniquity, that no-man's-land for decent folks, that hell-hole we call Central Grove!"

Otley paused to get his emotions back under control and to let his wildly-racing heart drop back to its normal rate of 160 beats per minute.

"Are you saying...?" Grime started.

After waiting several minutes in vain for Grime to complete the sentence, Otley decided to do so himself, "That's right, Prime and his gang salvaged the equipment and set up a lab where they cook up batches of this vile liquid. Apparently, they're pretty good at it, too. The stuff they turn out is pure and potent. They've built up quite a clientele, cod-heads they're called, and it seems they can't get enough of it."

"I don't understand the attraction myself," Otley continued, dipping his well-chewed turkey leg in the shoe gravy. "How can people eat that disgusting stuff?"

Gurrey and Grime looked at their leg man with expressions of, if not quite respect, then at least a lot less derision than before. "That's surprisingly good work Owen," Grime said. "Maybe you do have the makings of a mole after all."

"I'm the one who first pointed out that resemblance." Gurrey said proudly.

"Well, I've got even more news for you," Otley mumbled around his mouthful of turkey and gravy. "Prime has fallen into his own trap, he's become hooked on the oil. They say he drinks the stuff by the gallon. Those shiny teeth of his? The result of rubbing cod oil on his gums every night. Did you happen to notice his thick, gleaming hair?"

"I did." Grime said, unconsciously running his hand over his own hairless dome.

"That duck's ass hairdo that he has would require a half tube of Brylcreem to keep in place for a normal person, but his hair is so naturally greasy from all the oil that no one has ever seen so much as a single strand go astray."

"Cod liver oil does that, does it?" Grime muttered absently, his head gleaming like a melon in the moonlight.

"But now his addiction to the accursed cod is starting to cause problems. He's trying to force all his men to become cod-heads too. Some of them have jumped ship and he's having trouble raising a crew. That was how I could infiltrate his gang so easily. He's even taken to carrying a big barrel of oil on deck and all the crew have to line up for their 'ration'. To avoid suspicion, I was able to secrete my portion right here." Otley patted his upper chest area drawing the two dicks' attention to a dark, oily stain that spread from Otley's shirt pocket down to his ample belt line.

"Some of the crew refused the oil outright and tried to mutiny, but Prime is so greasy now that they couldn't get a grip on him and he was easily able to slip from their grasp and fight off the attempted insurrection."

"Well," Grime said, "this all makes my decision a lot easier. If I arrest him, I will actually be doing him a favour. This will be his chance to break free of the vicious hold that the oil has on him. I know that when I was in the throes of my terrible caffeine addiction, I would have welcomed someone willing to help me with my problem," Grime threw an accusatory glance in Gurrey's direction, "instead of asking me twenty times a day, 'I'm going to Timmy's, want something?"

"It's nice that you want to help him," Otley said, shoving the well-gnawed remnants of the turkey leg into his back pocket. "But how?"

With a gleam in his eye that was either a spark of inspiration or the beginning of an aneurysm, Grime replied, "I might have a plan, Owen, I just might have a plan."

One thing was certain. They had to put an end to this smuggling ring and that meant entering the dead zone known locally as Central Grove.

On the ferry trip from Westport to the pearl of the Tri-Islands area that was Freeport, Gurrey and Grime were discussing their newly-arrived business cards.

"It just seems wrong somehow," Gurrey said.

"But it's exactly what you wanted," Grime countered. "I remember our conversation distinctly. You said that you weren't getting enough credit for your leadership abilities within the detective agency."

"I remember that, but—' Gurrey stuttered.

"You said that you deserved to head up our organization, isn't that right?"

"Well, yes, but I—"

"And I, Jim Grime, agreed, did I not? Does this card not state quite unequivocally that you are the head detective, even though in reality we are really equals?"

"Still—" Gurrey said.

"No, no, no. You can't have it both ways."

"Well, okay," Gurrey said with a sigh. "But somehow *Gurrey Ben, Dickhead* just sounds wrong."

"Pish posh," Grime said. "Besides, they made a couple of small mistakes on my cards, too." He thrust a new card at his partner that read:

Jim Grime - Private Dick, Fishgutter, Chick Maggot.

Just then the ferry docked and the Dickmobile, as it had come to be known by a grateful populace, fishtailed up the slip, causing two elderly foot passengers to jump into the water to escape. "Old people," Gurrey said from behind the wheel. "They always bring a smile to my face."

Just then the ancient CB radio crackled to life: "This is the Legman. Over." True to his reputation as a man of action, Owen had caught an earlier ferry.

"This is Dick Mobile," Gurrey answered. "What's your 20? Where are you, Legman?"

"I'm roundin' Suicide on two wheels and heading for the Grove," came the static-muffled reply. "What's your position Gurrey? Over."

"I'm the Dick Head. Over."

Grimes interrupted. "I think he means what's your geographical position, not your position within the Agency."

"Oh. Sorry, Legman. We're just leaving Freeport and cruisin' toward the Grove. Over."

"Meet you there. Over and out."

Minutes later the three intrepid detectives were conferring in the weed-covered parking lot of the now-defunct Tiny Tattler Restaurant.

Central Grove was a kind of no man's land, a desolate strip inhabited by squirrels, rabbits and a few simple village folk. Amidst the despair and desolation that passed for daily life, their main joy was standing at the side of the road and waving at the cars whizzing past en route to the exotic towns of Freeport and Tiverton and, to a much lesser extent, Westport.

"This place gives me the creeps," Gurrey said. "Let's get the job done and get the hell out of here." He periodically looked over his shoulder in anticipation of a sneak attack by villagers who wanted to learn the ways of the outside world.

Central Grovers would often kidnap wayward passers-by, hold them captive and try to extract information about the place that they called "Out There."

"What's it like Out There?" they would ask. "Is Freeport just a mythical place—like Camelot—or does it actually exist? The legends say that the people there are god-like. Is it true that another island exists to the west of Freeport, a place continually enshrouded in fog where the people embrace strange practices such as sun worship and philately? Is it true that the people there resemble the birds that they have so long worshipped? Is it true that Freeport has a place where people can dance and such—and places where they teach all manner of things? Is there really a conveyance to the east that carries people to another shore, one with no water surrounding it? Is Tiddville really a place or are you guys just shittin' us? And what of Halifax? Is it true they worship cats?"

They would throw an abundance of questions at those unfortunate enough to be waylaid. The Central Grovers never harmed a soul, fearing reprisals from Out There, but the experience was nonetheless unnerving, to say the least.

Otley again glanced nervously over his shoulder as he approached the two detectives across the parking lot, or at least he would have glanced over his shoulder if it wasn't for the rolls of fat on his neck preventing him from turning his head that far. "This place creeps me out." he said. "There is nothing sadder than a restaurant that isn't open. What are we doing here? Back at Pond Cove you said you had a plan. Is this it? Why didn't we arrest Prime when we had a chance?"

"That was all part of my master plan," Grime replied. "Back on the beach, Prime had his crew with him, so we were outnumbered. Also, as private dicks we have a responsibility to keep the public safe. Pond Cove is the Daytona Beach of the Tri-Island area, with a constant flow of tourists and sightseers. We couldn't take the chance of involving innocent citizens in our set-to, our fracas, our foo-fa-ra, our argy-bargy, our kerfuffle. By letting him get away then, we can capture him now while he is alone in his secret drug lab. Yes, my flawless plan worked flawlessly...except for one small flaw."

With a sense of dread, Gurrey inquired, "And what would that one small flaw be, pray tell?"

"I have absolutely no idea where his secret lab is."

"Hence my previous question," Otley said. "Why are we here?"

"This is the most obvious spot," Grime replied. "We are in the geographic centre of this hell-hole we call Central Grove. It sits in the middle of this island like a thorn between two other thorns, it is sparsely populated with insular, uninquisitive people who spend all their time clustered by the highway watching cars whiz by. This is the perfect place to hide a secret drug lab and smuggling headquarters. If only we had some way of figuring out exactly where it is."

At this Otley spoke up. "I was looking at some of your old back issues of *Dick Weekly* and I read that some P. I.s have their own canine units. Maybe we need something like that."

"Good idea, Owen," Grime said. "A drug-sniffing dog could find that drug lab in a second, but since we rarely get paid for any of our cases, we can't really afford a highly-trained dog like that."

"Maybe we don't need to spend a lot of money." Gurrey said. He walked over to the Dickmobile, reached into a cardboard box in the back, and lifted out a small, grey, lump of fur.

"What is that? It sure isn't a drug-sniffing dog."

"No it isn't, maybe we don't have a canine unit, but we could have a feline unit. This is my cat Lucky. She's kind of old and slow now, she's gone deaf and her eyesight isn't so good anymore, but her sniffer works better than ever. Open a can of tuna or a tin of sardines anywhere in the neighbourhood, and she's there like a shot. If there's anyone made for the job of sniffing out Prime in his counterfeit cod liver oil lab, it's Lucky."

"I don't know", the Otley said. "If word gets out that we have a drug-sniffing cat, we could become the laughing-stock of the private dick business."

"Give her a chance." Gurrey said, placing the little cat on the ground. Lucky promptly sat down in the middle of the parking lot and took a leisurely minute or two to scratch her chin with her hind leg and make sure all her fur was licked down into its proper place.

Then she lifted her head and sniffed the air. Suddenly she was on her feet, making a bee-line across the lot with the three dicks following behind. As they neared the edge of the parking area, a faint trail into the woods became visible.

After nearly an hour on the trail, the last forty minutes of which Gurrey had to listen to constant complaining from Grime about how he strained his hernia pulling Otley out of the last two bog holes, Lucky abruptly stopped and peered into the dense undergrowth, her tail twitching back and forth. Through the dense brush, the dicks could just make out the faint outline of what had to be Prime's hidden lair.

Quietly approaching an open door, the trio peered inside to see walls lined with cases of smuggled soft drinks, boxes of machine gums, and, sunken into the floor, the huge vat from the old Westport Cod Liver Oil Factory. Standing beside the vat was none other than Pearly Prime himself, totally absorbed in sampling the latest batch of his cod-livery brew.

"Drop the oil, Prime, we're here to rescue you from that stuff." Grime shouted.

Startled, Prime dropped his sampling ladle and dashed to the door in an attempt to slam it closed before the intrepid dicks could enter.

Lucky, attracted by the spilled cod liver oil on the floor, darted in through the door and ran under the smuggler's feet, knocking him off balance. Flailing about in an attempt to regain equilibrium, Prime knocked over one of the boxes, blanketing the floor in rolling gumballs.

His arms windmilling wildly, his legs bicycling as his feet skated on the errant gum balls, Prime staggered backwards until he reached the vat where the edge struck him behind the knees. Despite one last desperate effort to save himself, Pearly Prime flipped neatly backward and disappeared below the glassy surface of the oil-filled cauldron.

Gurrey, Grime and Otley rushed over to the vat, but could not locate Prime through the murky oil.

Suddenly, just as they were about to give up hope, a faint gleam pierced the oily gloom. Pearley's shiny teeth had saved the day again.

After several failed attempts, due to the difficulty of keeping a grip on the oil-saturated Prime, the trio of dicks succeeded in pulling the choking and gasping smuggler out of the vat. As he sat on the floor recovering while Lucky licked cod liver oil out of his pant cuff, Prime declared, "That was the closest to death I ever want to be, boys. It was the slowest type of drowning possible."

He shook his head, spraying oil on one and all. "I have seen the error of my ways. I never want to get near another drop of that rancid fish oil,"

Prime subsequently abandoned smuggling and the sea, took up organic farming and made a fortune producing chemical-free oils such as sunflower, peanut, olive, corn, canola, and palm. He formed an organization called Oil Products Except Cod to market his products—OPEC for short.

Gurrey, Grime and Otley finally made it to The Dick of The Year Awards, where Owen Otley won for his larger-than-life role as Best Supporting Dick.

Despite being the only fully registered detectives on the islands, Gurrey and Grime lost the coveted Dick of the Year Award to Lardy, Otley's morbidly obese bloodhound. Three months earlier, Lardy had been dozing in the mid-morning sun outside the corner store when young Gordie Thomas ran out with a shoplifted Cherry Blossom and three bags of Twizzlers, two red and one black. In his haste to escape, he tripped over Lardy, who promptly shuffled over and sat on the petty thief until the grateful shopkeeper could carry out a citizen's arrest.

But the star of the evening turned out to be Lucky, whose exemplary olfactory skills won her the ground-breaking honour of becoming the first non-canine to win first place in the canine division.

Gurrey and Grime were disappointed but still proud to finish tied for second in a one-person category. "At least we closed another case," Gurrey said.

"Oil drink to that," Grime said.

Figure 5: Elegant Digby Neck and Islands architecture

8: The Christmas Mackerel

The snow was lightly falling upon the dark waters of Grand Passage, large, fluffy, flakes of snow, just thick enough to obscure Long Island from sight as Mother Nature's temporary gift to Brier Islanders. It was Christmas Eve at the Digby Neck And Islands Fish-Gutting Service And Detective Agency and not even a mouse was stirring.

However, Atticus, the wharf rat that lived in the attic of the DN&IFGS&DA was about to become very active indeed. The large rodent had become a kind of mascot for Gurrey and Grime, the two peerless dicks who were the founders and brains behind the highly successful crime prevention and fish cleaning operation.

Atticus lived on scraps of food left by the two dicks and as a result his cholesterol level and blood pressure were alarmingly high. In fact, a diet of potato chips, Cheesies, Beef Jerky sticks, bologna, and stale beer had rendered him all but immobile. It was hard to say who was more lethargic, Atticus or the other rodent-like creature who hung out at the office on stilts, their legman and dick-in-training, Owen Otley.

Despite Lucky the tracking cat's award-winning performance in hunting down the illegal cod liver oil lab, it turned out that she much preferred basking in the sun and licking her nether regions to police work. Owen Otley's dog Lardy, on the other hand, was always more than eager to go for a ride with Gurrey and Grime in the Dickmobile but within a matter of seconds his near-lethal flatulence would have the two dicks gasping for air. The sight of the two mangy creatures—three if you include Lardo—speeding past, with their heads out the windows, tongues lolling in the breeze, did not instill confidence in the local populace.

The absence of a reliable police animal to assist them in their quest for justice had been rectified when the two dicks returned home one night to discover Atticus, a huge rat, sitting on their kitchen table, helping himself to their digestive crackers. With the help of the crackers and other tempting snacks, Gurrey and Grime had trained Atticus to assist them on cases where man's best friend would usually be used. They soon discovered that Atticus could follow a trail as well as any canine and before long he had brought many a criminal to bay.

This Christmas Eve, Atticus was eating the last of the Cheese Whiz that Gurrey had given him as a holiday treat. The two dicks sat dozing at the desk/gutting table in an overstuffed stupor, having consumed two small turkeys with all the trimmings, a large ham with pineapple sauce, a pumpkin pie, and a figgy pudding each.

Suddenly the phone jangled. It was RE Robicheau's store.

"Sorry to bother you on Christmas Eve, fellas, but I don't know who else to call," Wally 'The Wall Man' Robichini said. He was the Islands' grocery magnate and sometime smuggler. "We recently got a new kitten and now it's gone missing and…well, it's snowing out there and…well….can you help?'

Since entering the private dick game, Gurrey and Grime had fancied themselves in the "Sam Spade" model of rough and tough gumshoes. The truth was that, despite the hard-boiled exterior they affected, anyone who knew them could tell you they both had soft spots. "Soft in the head" was a commonly-heard phrase in reference to the detecting duo.

But tonight Wallman's story touched another soft spot, the one in their hearts. "We'll get right on it," Gurrey said. "We'll bring our tracking rat. Atticus will find that pussycat."

The two detectives hauled themselves to their feet, expelled a pair of invigorating belches, bundled up in two layers of flannel shirts, and ventured forth into the worsening snowstorm, Atticus ghosting faithfully at their heels. When they reached the store, Wally was impatiently pacing back and forth.

"Do you have an article of clothing that the kitty was wearing at the time of his or her disappearance?" Gurrey said. "Also height and weight and any discernible scars or tattoos."

Grime gave him the kind of look that suggested his partner needed help, and said,"What he means is, do you know what he ate last? Atticus can follow scents really well. We just need a sample smell to put him on the trail."

"Why yes," Wally said. "His Christmas dinner was ground-up mackerel. The little guy loves it." Wally momentarily broke down in tears before recovering. "Here's his dish."

"Perfect," Gurrey said.

He took Atticus to the dish and had him smell the mackerel remnants while Grime fumbled in his pocket and took out a small pill bottle, one of many that he kept on his person at all times. He emptied the contents into his pocket and filled the vial with milk from the kitten's drinking dish. He asked Wally for some masking tape from the well-stocked store shelves and fashioned a loose collar that he hung around Atticus's neck with the pill bottle attached.

"What are you doing?" Gurrey said.

"I've seen it in the movies," Grime said. "St. Bernards have them to help avalanche victims."

"Atticus is a rat, not a St. Bernard."

"A rescue rodent," Grime corrected. "The same principle applies."

The two detectives led Atticus out into the bitter night and turned him loose. "Go get him boy! Go get that kitty!"

Atticus scurried off into the softly-falling snow with the two dicks scurrying awkwardly along behind him. Within minutes the rodent was scratching at the front door of a nearby house.

The owner was surprised on this frigid night to find an obese rat and two half-stiff dicks standing on his doorstep but, in the spirit of Christmas Eve, he invited them in.

Atticus appeared to be hot on the trail of the wayward kitten, but after thoroughly scouring the house, turned up nothing.

Gurrey and Grime, cups of Yuletide eggnog in hand, were just getting comfortable next to the roaring kitchen stove when Atticus squeaked insistently and moved to the door. They soon found themselves back out in the cold, following their intrepid rodent to the next house. Again, despite seeming to have caught his scent, Atticus could not find the wayward kitten.

This scene—roaring fires, half-finished cups of eggnog—repeated over and over throughout the long night at house after house. Hopes rose and fell, rose and fell with each new search.

Finally, as the eastern sky began to gradually lighten on a clear, cold Christmas morning, a frost-covered and eggnog-saturated Grime turned to Gurrey and through chattering teeth, confessed his doubts about the skills of their tracking rat. He did so with a vehemence that made Atticus flinch. "I hate to say it, but I'm beginning to lose faith in that rat's nose.. In fact, I'm on the verge of becoming rabid and saying, 'Boo, ratley, you've failed in your mission.' We've scoured every house on the Island but are still no closer to finding that kitten. This whole thing has been a useless trial. I'm about to give up and go home. It's cold enough out here to kill a mockingbird."

"Not so fast, oh ye of little faith", Gurrey responded. "As usual, you've overlooked some obvious clues. First of all, we haven't been to every house on the Island. The houses Atticus has taken us to all have something in common. Do you know what it is?"

Grime untied the strings to his ear flaps and removed the insulated deerstalker that he had taken to wearing after seeing an episode of *Sherlock Holmes* on BBC Canada. He gave his head a scratch as the snow settled on it like flakes in a crystal globe, and a light finally began to dawn behind his watery, near-sighted eyes.

"Well, now that you mention it, every one of those houses had a cat, and I did think it rather odd that under each tree there was a fresh mackerel, I just assumed it was some strange Brier Island tradition that I didn't know about. Do you think those might be clues?"

Before Gurrey could enlighten his befuddled partner, there was a loud jingling sound overhead and a brilliant red streak blazed an arc across the morning sky, appearing to land at the low water mark on the sandy beach near the store.

The two detectives grabbed Atticus and jumped into the Dickmobile and, with bald tires spinning, the dynamic duo slid and slued through the slushy, pre-dawn streets of the still-deserted Westport commercial district.

As they skidded to a stop on the road next to the beach, they once again heard the sound of jingling bells and caught another glimpse of the streak, this time receding rapidly away from the beach.

"What was that?"Grime gasped. "The last time I saw something move that fast it was going around Suicide on two wheels, heading to the bootleggers in Tiverton."

"I don't want to say what I think it was just yet," Gurrey said, "but I do think we better check out the area where it landed. Careful there, Grimey, you don't want to break another hip. You've already broken two."

Tentatively making their way over the slippery snow and seaweed-covered rocks, Atticus and the two dicks reached the part of the beach where the clam beds were exposed by the now-low tide. There, perched on a dry mound of sand, sat the missing kitten. Atticus nuzzled the tiny feline and it responded with a loud purring sound. Grime gently removed the pill bottle from the rat's neck and the thirsty kitten eagerly lapped up the milk.

A woefully weary Wally, worn and wan from weeping and worrying all night, was ecstatic to see his kitten again. "Where was he? What was he doing all night?"

"Well," Gurrey said, "we're not exactly sure, but it appears that your little kitten spent the night travelling from house to house making sure that every cat on the Island was left a Christmas present under the tree."

"But that makes no sense. He's just a little cat, how could he do that by himself?"

"Let's just say it was a night of Christmas mackerels," Grime said with a reverential note of awe in his voice.

"And we believe that he was not alone," Gurrey added. "Our professional and expert examination of the marks and tracks we found on the beach leads us to confidently speculate that this kitten's dirty feet are not the only evidence of the presence of sandy claws tonight."

As the two tired dicks made their weary way back to their office/fish-gutting shack with their faithful rat following close behind, Gurrey turned to Grime and said, "Well, buddy, I'm not quite sure what happened here this Christmas night, but I think we can safely say we've closed another case. Merry Christmas, Grimey, ol' pal."

"And merry Christmas to you, Atticus!" they said in unison. "We couldn't have done it without you."

Gurrey scooped the rescue rodent from the snow and placed him on his shoulder where he stayed until they were back in the warmth of his adopted home.

Figure 6: Atticus

9: The Blackmailing of Lucy the Floozy

Jim Grime was absorbed in wrestling the backbone out of a thirty-pound codfish at the Digby Neck & Islands Fish-Gutting Service & Detective Agency's office/fish shack when a seductive and somehow familiar shadow fell across his desk/splitting table. The smell of Dollarama perfume reached his nostrils, causing him to look up. Even in the dim light Grime could tell she was the kind of sophisticated dame who drank her wine from a glass.

Gurrey Ben eyed her warily from his place in the corner where he was gutting a small cusk. He was having a case of deja vu, and not for the first time.

She slunk across the room and perched her well-travelled posterior on the edge of Grime's desk. "It's me, Lucy Dulsé, accent acute on the 'e'. I never thought I'd have to say this again, but I need your help."

Grime began to speak but Ms Dulsé held up a hand to silence him. "I've been living a quiet life in Digby since I last saw you two dicks. I married a nice respectable dentist. We have two kids, a dog, four cats, and a pelican. Just your ordinary, hard-working middle-class family. And then this letter arrives out of the blue and suddenly my life's been torn ass-under."

"Asunder," Grime corrected.

Lucy ignored him. She handed Grime the letter and broke down in sobs that racked her entire body, once again drawing his attention to her still-adorable arse and tremendous teakettle.

"Well, read it, for Pete's sake," Gurrey said from across the room.

Reluctantly returning his attention to the matter literally at hand, Grime adjusted his bi-focals and began to read, his lips silently and painstakingly forming the words. "Out loud, Grimey!"

Grime haltingly read the letter aloud:

> *Der Loocy the floozy,*
> *Member me? We had a gud tyme won nite behand the post orfice and agin in a punt. Send me sum monee or I'll be ritten to that rich dental husbind of yurs.*
> *Leaf it in a waterpruf bag tied to rownd rock in Freeport by nun tomoro. Don't contak polis or yule be sory.*
> *Best wishes,*
> *A-nonny-mouse.*

"What do you make of it, Gurrey?" Grime said.

Gurrey rose slowly from his stool and walked into the better lit part of the office. "Hello, Lucy," he said. "I knew you'd be back."

"Believe me, I would have been entirely happy to see the back of you two, but I need the help of someone who is closely acquainted with my past, someone who can keep a secret. In addition to your notoriety as professional dicks, it seems you also have a reputation for being discreet."

Being known as the local dicks by all and sundry was now old hat to the duo, but they both preened slightly at being praised for their ability to keep information private, conveniently overlooking the fact that it came more from their faltering memories than from any deliberate adherence to a professional code of conduct.

"I'm so sorry Lucy," Gurrey said. "I'd really love to help you, but I'm afraid that in this case I have to accuse myself."

Lucy did one of those double takes that would have made Abbott and Costello do a double take.

Grime was obviously puzzled by this development. "What the holy heck are you talking about, Gurrey? Accuse yourself of what?"

"I'm too personally connected to this client, so ethically I shouldn't be involved. Surely you remember that Lucy and I carried on a torrid love affair off and on for the better part of a long weekend. I was her stud muffin, her love toy, her fancy boy, her main squeeze, her Romeo, her—"

"All right, I get it!" Grime said. "You were the lobster to her well-baited trap. And the word you're looking for is *recuse*, not *accuse*."

"Exactly!" Gurrey said, once again wishing that he had been blessed with the facility for language possessed by the Bard of the Tri-Island area. "I didn't know this until years later, but Lucy got pregnant after our romantic liaison in the backseat of my 1965 Valiant and once more in the hay field behind the Meteghan legion. For a while I'm sure Lucy must have been a scorned woman. Like Hester Prynne, forced to wear the scarlet letter, only in this case it was a scarlet S for skank. Later it was probably H for harpy, then S again, this time for strumpet, then...well you get the picture."

"I can hear you, you know," Lucy said.

"Oh, right!" Gurrey said. "Just let me finish this bit of exposition for my partner."

He cleared his throat and continued, "Instead of a punishment, Lucy saw it as a kind of badge of honour and worked hard to live up to her reputation. She won skank of the year honours five years running. I mean she was faster than a 1962 Buick Wildcat with the governors taken off 'er. All the married women hated her because they had to settle for someone who wasn't yours truly and the single ones despised her because she had robbed me of my virginity, several times! She also robbed me of eight dollars in small change and a quantity of Canadian Tire money. All of that trauma resulted in a trail of broken hearts that stretched from Mink Cove to Western Light. Remember that, Grimey?"

"Of course I remember," said Grime, who didn't remember at all.

"I don't have a problem with you working my case" Lucy said. "I prefer someone who knows me intimately, my past history, all of my foibles and faults, someone who will give me the personal attention that I require."

"What exactly is it you would like from us, Lucy?" Gurrey asked expectantly, as he plucked the ransom note from the palsied fingers of his partner.

Lucy sashayed around the table, her curvaceous hip bumping the splitting tub in passing and sloshing the red-tinged water onto the office/fish-house floor. "As I said, I need your help." Her breathy voice set Grime's imagination—and other parts of him—on fire. "I can't go to the police so I asked around about private detectives and everyone assured me that you guys were still the biggest dicks in town."

"As many times as we've had that shouted at us from passing cars, I never tire of it," Grime said, welling up. "Just tell me what you want and I'll try my very hardest to do it to, er, *for* you."

"How many times have I heard that?" Lucy murmured into Grime's ear, "I hope you're not going to disappoint me like so many others have done." She paused and drew back slightly. "Is that a codfish in your pocket or are you just happy to see me?"

"Codfish," Grime said. "But I *am* happy to see you."

"Back off, Lucy! Look at what you're doing to the drooling old fart." Gurrey was immune to Lucy's well-developed attractions. Their long-ago affair had inoculated him against the wanton fever that she seemed to be able to kindle at will in the hearts and minds of lesser men.

Grime was a prime example of her power over those men who were unsophisticated in the ways of the world. Clutching the edge of the table, his face flushed with perspiration, Grime was trembling all over and seemed to have temporarily lost the power of speech.

Lucy straightened up and looked at Gurrey, "I'm sorry. Old habits die hard. This is how I'm used to getting things done. I guess it's second nature to me now. I don't even realize I'm doing it."

"Enough with your powers of sedition! We're willing to investigate this for you, but it won't help matters any if you give Grimey another stroke. They say the fifth one does the most damage, you know."

"Okay, okay, I'll tone it down. Do you really think you can find out who sent that terrible letter?"

"That depends," Gurrey replied. "Did the events mentioned here actually take place? Do you remember who was there at the time?"

"Oh, they took place all right, but it was a long time ago and I'm sure it happened more than once. Even if I could remember all those times and all those involved, it would still leave us with several dozen suspects."

Holding the letter up to the bare, fly-specked light bulb that hung from a frayed cord in the centre of the room, Gurrey stared intently at the single sheet. "This page was torn from a Hilroy narrow-ruled, spiral-bound, hard-cover scribbler and the watermark indicates that the paper is more than four decades old."

Glancing over at Grime, who appeared to be slowly recovering his faculties, Gurrey said smugly, "Still think that three-year Dick Tracy Junior Detective correspondence course on document identification was a waste of time and money?"

"I'm impressed by your little trick," Grime said, sounding not at all impressed, "but we still don't know who wrote the letter."

"I'm not done yet. There are faint indentations on the paper, as if someone wrote on the page on top of this one. I just need something to bring out the writing and make it visible."

Glancing around the room, Gurrey noticed the bucket that Grime used as a spittoon for the chewing tobacco that he liked to indulge in while splitting fish of a summer's day. Dipping his hand into the bucket, Gurrey smeared some of the tobacco expectorant onto the page and then held it up close to the light. As the heat from the bulb dried the tobacco juice, words slowly appeared.

"Wow," Grime said, "this time I really am impressed—and more than a little nauseated. Can you make out what it says?"

Squinting at the barely legible lettering, Gurrey read out, "Homework for Monday: Explain why the Battle of Lundy's Lane was a pivotal event in the War of 1812."

"Okay, I'm unimpressed again, We're trying to find a blackmailer and all you can come up with is a fifty-year old homework assignment?"

"Actually, Grimey, old pal, this fifty-year old homework assignment just might lead us right to the blackmailer. You'll notice that there are distinct similarities in the handwriting in both of these notes, the old and the new, so most likely they were both written by the same person. Secondly, with his numerous spelling errors, sloppy syntax and disjointed sentence structure, one would naturally assume the blackmailer was brought up in the inferior Freeport education system and is a Long Islander. But this was just a clever ruse. We can see from the writing in the older note that he was in fact properly educated and therefore must be a Westporter."

A sudden light dawned on Gurrey's rugged yet handsome face. "I know exactly when and where this homework note was written...and you do, too, Lucy! Do you remember Mrs. Hooper's Canadian History class?"

"Remember it? I wish I could forget it!" Lucy said. "That was the year the new Islands Consolidated opened in Freeport. It was also the summer I finally developed. Looking at me now you probably wouldn't believe it, but I was a late bloomer. Then the big change happened, and when I walked into that classroom, the boys were all over me like a rash, which I later developed."

"I would have been, too," Gurrey said, "but there was such a crowd around you all the time..."

"In the beginning I thought it was kind of sweet. They all seemed to be real concerned that I was in prime physical shape to use the new gym, always wanting to see how many jumping jacks I could do and testing my flexibility by seeing if I could touch my elbows behind my back. I soon caught on to what they were doing. After all, boys would come running from all over the schoolyard and stand there with their tongues hanging out and their eyes popping. They thought they were being so smart, tricking me into giving them a show and a cheap thrill, but in the end, the trick was on *them*. I kept on giving them the thrills but they weren't so cheap any more. They had to do my homework for me, carry my books and buy me snacks at the student council canteen.

"Some of the boys resented that I wasn't giving it away for free anymore and the girls hated me because they thought I was stealing their guys. They started spreading nasty rumours about me and calling me names. One of the worst was P. Jack, which was surprising because I thought at first he really liked me, he used to call me 'Juicy Lucy', which I thought was cute. That all changed after the first dance in the new gym. It was a big deal. They even had a live band, The Purple Candle Secret, all the way from Digby. P. asked me to go with him but I turned him down, to go with you, Gursey, as I recall."

"That's right," Gurrey said, reacting to the long-forgotten pet-name with a kind of dreamy look. "That was a wonderful, magical evening."

"Yes, it was." Lucy said, "until P. made that awful scene, called me all those names and declared that he would forever be your evil nemesis."

"It's interesting that you would mention him, Lucy." Gurrey motioned her in closer and turned the page so his partner could also see. He revealed a faint design that had appeared on the blackmailer's note. There, made visible by the drying tobacco juice, was a drawing of a heart pierced with an arrow and containing the inscription 'P loves L'.

Grime studied the paper with a puzzled look and a furrowed brow; the furrow, being unimpeded by hair, rippled like a wave on the open ocean all the way to the back of his head. "What does this mean, Gurrey?"

"Is that intermittent Alzheimer's kicking in again?" Gurrey asked. He knew that his partner had a disdain for evidence; a distinct liability in the detective game. Grime preferred to 'listen to his gut.' Unfortunately, all his gut had been saying for the past few years was 'For the love of God, more antacid.'

"What the evidence tells us," Gurrey continued, "is that this blackmailer's note and the homework note were written by the same person. The page came from an old scribbler that belonged to P. Jack and, therefore, P. Jack wrote the note and is our blackmailer."

"That's impossible," Grime said. He slammed his hand down on the table and hit a gutting knife with a vehemence that set it spinning, causing Gurrey to quickly duck aside as it flew across the room to finally impale itself between the breasts of the scantily-clad Miss July on the time-faded 1969 Weymouth Motors calendar that hung on the wall.

"Jack is long gone!" Grime said. "We both saw him disappear beneath the frigid waters of Grand Passage way back at the beginning of this book!"

"I can't dispute that," Gurrey replied with an icy calmness that his partner could only wish to attain. "But I have to follow the evidence, and it says that, as incredible and unlikely as it seems, somehow P. Jack is involved. It looks like we're going to have to set a trap for a dead man."

"It's a crazy idea," Lucy said.

"That's where we shine," Gurrey replied

The next day the two detectives were speeding toward Round Rock, a massive boulder known locally as the Mount Rushmore of the Tri-Island area because if you looked at it from just the right angle during a heavy fog it kind of resembled old Ezekiel Cudmore, past president of the Islands Chamber of Commerce.

As they passed over the ironically named Big Bridge, Gurrey suggested that a toll booth should be installed on the majestic ten-foot span to raise money for the village.

Grime disagreed. "It would hold up traffic during the morning commute. Anyway, let's get back to the case."

Gurrey scratched his head and a shower of dandruff fluttered downward. "How *do* you set a trap for a dead man, Grimesy?" The look on his face was not unlike that of a pole-axed mule. Suddenly his visage brightened momentarily as the remnants of what had once been a moderate intelligence flared briefly and then was gone. "Do we set a trap for him in the graveyard?"

Grime looked at his friend with a combination of pity and annoyance. "No, Gurrey. For one thing, his body has never been found, so he's not buried in a graveyard. What we have to do is work under the assumption that somehow he survived his plunge into the icy waters and is living locally."

"Ohhh," Gurrey said. A light bulb went on over his head, not the figurative one that gifted writers sometimes use, but a real one. The wiring in the ancient vehicle was badly in need of repair. The overhead light flickered briefly and went out. The analogy was perfect. "I don't see why he's mad at Lucy, though," he said. "It's not like she led him on or anything. Everyone knew that it was me she loved."

"Let me explain," Grime said patiently. "P was a frustrated musician. He played a satisfactory saxophone but was hard to get along with. He refused to accept any criticism of his technique. When they told him 'You suck and blow at the same time,' he took it as a compliment. Every band he tried out for eventually rejected him. The frustration boiled over when the Purple Candle Secret told him to take a hike. Figuring he had nothing to lose, he approached Black Spar, that legendary band fronted by a lead singer who was the Bobby Sherman of the Tri-Island area. Chris Thornton was one of those rock idols with groupies everywhere and questionable hygiene. His cover of *Jeremiah Was a Bullfrog* made the chickies weak in their knees and sometimes their stomachs. Whether they were playing the wharf in Tiverton, the wharf in Westport or even the sweetest venues of all—the three-wharf circuit in Freeport—they drew huge crowds. Chris decided to give P a chance. One August night in 1975, he was playing with the band at the government wharf around the point of land known locally as The Point."

"The Carnegie Hall of wharf venues," Gurrey said. "Of all the wharves, that one has a distinct aura about it, especially during lobster-bait season."

Unfortunately," Grime said, "that evening, P misunderstood something that Lucy said to him at the break. 'I love sax,' she said. 'I can't get enough sax. I especially love sax accompanied by a band. I would enjoy sax in the morning, sax at noon and sax all night long. Sax, sax, sax. I especially love your sax style and the way you move around. Who knew there were so many sax positions!? Whenever I see you I think of sax. And your tongue technique! That makes the sax so much more enjoyable!' It was obviously a very innocent series of comments about a popular musical instrument, but somehow he interpreted it as a come-on. His spirits, among other things, rose. In defence of P, it was an easy mistake to make. That's why saxophonists have unusually large families. It's what killed Clarence Clemons, truth be known. But you can see why P was so disappointed when she ended up with you at the school dance."

Growing weary of Grime's endless fascination with other people's sax lives, Gurrey attempted to change the subject. "Things might get physical from here on, I think we need to bring Owen in on this job." Grime, his mind preoccupied with trying to puzzle out whether 'saxophone' and 'phone sax' meant the same thing, merely nodded.

Owen Otley, Gurrey and Grime's detective-in-training, was sitting on his front porch having a post-breakfast pre-lunch snack when the Dickmobile roared, rattled and clattered into his driveway. "Hi guys!" he called out, Gesturing to a stack of bologna slices balanced on his knee. "Care for a bite to eat?"

"Some other time, Owen," Gurrey replied. "Right now we've got a case to solve and we need you to put on your wedding/funeral suit."

Owen Otley had a twin sister who, contrary to all known laws of genetics, was considered to be the most beautiful female—in fact, the most beautiful member of either sex—in the Tri-Island area. Ophelia Otley was a full foot taller than her brother and more than two hundred pounds lighter. Although she was constantly pursued by every breathing male within a three-day's drive, Ophelia was a pillar of moral rectitude and would not let a man touch her unless he put a ring on her finger. As a result, she was continuously inundated with offers of marriage and had in fact been married several times; tragically, each husband had expired within weeks of the nuptials. The autopsies invariably concluded 'death due to exhaustion'.

Otley had purchased a sturdy gray tweed suit to wear to his sister's first marriage and now, six marriages, six funerals, and six 'letting outs' later, he reckoned he had more than gotten his money's worth. Gurrey was formulating a clever plan to trap the evil P. Jack, and Otley's suit was to play a key role.

Carefully folding his last two bologna slices and tucking them into his shirt pocket 'for later', Otley went to put on the suit.

"I hope this plan works." Gurrey said.

His mind still on other things, Grime responded, "If a husband and wife both play the alto sax, is that considered a same-sax marriage? When I record my music, is that considered a sax tape?"

A few minutes later the three dicks had arrived at the designated drop-off spot. "Good. We're early." Gurrey said. "Everyone get in position."

While Grime and Otley took up their posts, Gurrey placed a bag containing the ransom on an outcropping of Round Rock, then quickly hid himself and waited.

Several minutes past the designated hour, the dicks were about to give up when some movement caught their attention. A strange-looking figure was making its way down the beach. Wearing white, unlaced sneakers, baggy oversized pants and a hoodie three sizes too large for him, the suspect shuffled up to the rock. Both Gurrey and Grime strained to recognize him, but with the hood covering his face and dark sunglasses shading his eyes, his identity was too well hidden.

The mystery man looked around, grabbed the bag with one hand, and holding his pants up with the other, started back up the beach.

Grime started to rise but Gurrey held him down, "Not yet!" he whispered. He waited until the blackmailer reached a certain spot, then stood and yelled out, "Now, Owen!"

At the sound of Gurrey's voice, the blackmailer briefly glanced over his shoulder, turning back just in time to see one of the boulders in front of him unfold itself, rise up and lock him in a suffocating embrace.

Huffing and puffing, Gurrey and Grime arrived on the scene where Owen Otley maintained a firm grasp on the mysterious blackmailer with one hand while fishing one of the bologna slices out of his shirt pocket with the other.

"Good work, Owen," Grime gasped. "The plan worked perfectly."

Given his shape, and dressed in his grey suit, Otley had blended in surprisingly well with the boulders that littered the beach.

"Now, let's see who we've got," Gurrey said. Reaching up, he grabbed the hood.

"Yo yo yo / Watch the 'fro," rhymed the blackmailer in a strangely familiar sing-song voice.

As Gurrey pulled down the hood and tore off the sunglasses, both he and Grime let out a gasp and exclaimed in unison, "P. Jack!"

"P. Jack's gone and I'm here to say
My rapper name is P Diddy J
I'm workin' at changin' my evil ways
By rappin' 'n' rhymin' to save the Bays."

"I think you owe us an explanation, P...er, Diddy," Grime said. "If you've changed your evil ways, why are you blackmailing Lucy?"

P Diddy hung his head. "I know it's not a good way to start, but I needed money and everyone knows that Lucy's husband is loaded. I thought she owed me something because of the way she treated me..."

"That's all well and good," Grime replied, "but blackmail is a serious offence—"

"Wait!" The voice came from Lucy who was running toward them, her ample breasts undulating provocatively. "I don't want to press charges," she gasped. "In fact, I'll give P some money to start his new career. I can see now how he misinterpreted my innocent words, lo those many years ago. I feel that I owe it to him to help turn his life around. I am a militant anti-fish farm advocate and if he can spread the word in song, more power to him. Of course, I was hoping that he'd start a Black Spar tribute band, but there are already six in the Tri-Island area so I guess he knows best. Besides, no one could possibly replace Chris Thornton."

Lucy dabbed her eyes with a hankie, remembering the bizarre details of Thornton's tragic death. Having previously ingested a near-lethal combination of toadstools and Golden Glow, he was choking on a ham sandwich when his limousine was struck by a plane full of music critics who were ironically flying in to review his show that very evening.

P Diddy was dumbstruck at the magnanimous gesture. He looked at the woman he had once loved and began to rap once again, pulling a saxophone out of his handy diddy-bag:

"Yo, yo, yo
Well I'm askin' you all to disarm
Cause I'm here to rap against fish farms
(Saxophone riff)
If my rappin' ain't up to par

I'll reform the group called Black Spar."

Later that evening, Gurrey and Grime were sitting around their office/fish house, drinking Ten Penny Old Stock Ale and reviewing their day. Suddenly Gurrey stood up and began to gyrate. He held a Ten Penny to his mouth as if it were a mic and intoned:

"Yoyo, yoyo
Well the case is closed, it's all wrapped up
Cause G & G always know wassup
Grimey is smarter and better lookin
But I'm the one who's really cookin
Break it down now!"

Figure 7: Hot on the trail of a cold case

10: The Case of the Cold Case

Gurrey and Grime were sitting across the desk/gutting table from each other. Each had a pen and was working intently on something.

Suddenly, Grime slapped his instrument down on the desk and said, "Done! That's the fastest I've ever finished the *New York Times* Crossword—eight minutes and twelve seconds. What's that you're working on, Gurrey?"

"That tic-tac-toe game we started yesterday Grimesey," Gurrey replied. "I went over the rules again last night but I'll be darned if I can understand it. I think I'll have to concede the game to you."

"Well, never mind," Grime said kindly. "Gurrey, my friend, I think it's time we opened up another cold case."

"It's only 8:30 in the morning, but why not? There's most of a 2-4 of Ten Penny left in the ice box next to the scallop rims." He started to get up.

"Not that kind of cold case. I'm talking about a case that goes back a hundred and fifty years—to the time when Joshua Slocum lived just down the street."

"Probably skunky by now," Gurrey said.

"It's a detective case," Grime said patiently. "A real mystery."

"I'm all ears."

"Nothing that some extensive plastic surgery can't repair, my friend. But back to the business at hand."

Grime reached into his ass pocket, pulled out his wallet and extracted a carefully folded and brittle-looking letter. He unfolded the yellowed parchment very carefully. "I found it in an old Bible at the Syst family estate sale yesterday. I bid twelve bucks and got it. Looks nice on the coffee table next to the *National Geographic*s I got at the Thurber yard sale. There isn't anything that shouts intelligence and sophistication to the girlies more than old Bibles, *People* magazines, and *National Geographic*s. I'll have to beat em off with a thole pin."

"So the widow Syst is selling up and moving away?"

"Yes. Ever since her husband, old Sebantianceous, died in that freak Gestetner accident at the school she hasn't been herself. She figures if she moves away it'll be easier to get on with life. Goin' to Halifax, nice place on Gottingen Street. As I'm sure you know, Sebantianceous was a Syst on his father's side, but he was also a relative of old Josh Slocum himself on his mother's side....anyway, I found this letter in the Bible. It's dated 1859. He would have been about 15 years old, still making boots with his father."

He carefully lay the letter out on his lap and read its contents:

> *Dear Mother,*
> *Sorry I run away.*
> *J S*

With Grime distracted by the note, Gurrey surreptitiously reached across the table and slid the newspaper over so he could see it. Just as he did every week, Grime had made a big deal to Gurrey about doing the *New York Times* crossword puzzle. And, just like every week, he claimed to have completed it in record time. *And*, just like every week, he refused to show the finished puzzle to Gurrey. But this week, distracted by his old letter, Grime had inadvertently left the puzzle lying on the table.

Just as he suspected. Gurrey could see that Grime had not completed the puzzle at all! He had simply filled in the spaces with the letters of the alphabet starting with an 'A' in the upper left-hand corner and continuing to 'Z', then repeating until all the boxes were filled. And, not surprisingly, he hadn't even done that right! Gurrey's finely-honed detective's mind, trained to pick up on any anomaly, no matter how small, immediately saw that Grime had repeated the same mistake over and over in each set of letters. He had consistently reversed two letters, placing the 'Q' before the 'P' and confirming for Gurrey what he had known for quite some time now, that Grime was utterly incapable of minding his Ps and Qs.

Pushing the bogus puzzle aside, Gurrey turned his attention to the note that Grime was so fascinated with. "Why are you so interested in that scrap of paper? Just because you spent most of your retirement fund on it doesn't make it valuable! You don't even know for sure that it was written by Joshua Slocum; 'J.S.' could be anybody, John Smith, Jane Seymour, Jake Snake, Junior Stanton; lots of people have those initials.

"True," Grime admitted, "but I compared the handwriting to samples from his diaries that were printed in a *National Geographic* story on him. Looks the same to me."

"If it's the real thing," Gurrey said, "we may have something of great historic value."

"That's true, Gurrey, and I think I have a clue about that. People used to record everything in their Bibles back in the day, and I found this notation on one of the blank pages at the back."

Grime opened the well-thumbed book and turned it around for Gurrey to read.

Josh was trying to run away again but the Rs caught him in time.

Has high notions for adventure. I fear for him.

With what appeared to be choreographed precision, but was in fact no more than well-timed happenstance, Gurrey and Grime both popped large chunks of chewing tobacco into their mouths from the supply that had been mouldering in the sun on the dusty window sill alongside a half-empty bottle of Resdan since early 1965. You could almost hear that movie-style flashback music as they lapsed into an Old-Chum-infused haze and drifted back, back, back to the time of their great-grandfathers:

Out of the swirling, tobacco-induced mists emerged an image of a sunny summer's morn in the year 1859. Along a rough dirt track that is Westport's main street, a yoke of oxen was straining against a heavy wagon load of salt fish just out of the pickle and on the way to be laid out for drying on the sunny fields up the New Lane.

As the team plodded along, it passed a dishevelled youth standing in the road in front of a nondescript building. He didn't notice the ox team passing closely behind him, so deeply absorbed was he in peeling the shell from a soft-boiled seagull egg.

The boy had a lot in common with the egg. In addition to the mottled, under-cooked physiognomy they shared, there were distinct similarities in their overall shape; although it must be said that the egg appeared to hold the edge in the physical fitness department.

Idly biting the top off the egg, the lad thought to himself, "That's a good egg, you can really taste the seagull." Then he looked up at the sign above the door:

Ye Islands Fish Evisceration Services and Detecting Agency
Rich'd Gurrey Esq. & Rich'd Grime Esq.
Proprietors

Although he could probably read the words if he worked at it long enough, he didn't bother; he already knew this was the right place.

Inside the building, the proprietors, Richard Grime and Richard Gurrey—who, in this more proper period in history, were known as Private Richards, the word dick being found offensive to polite sensibilities—were reviewing their notes on a recent scandalous case wherein a dastardly blackguard by the name of Pere Jacques had been filching the whalebone out of ladies' corsets while the ladies were still wearing them. Suddenly the light level in the office/fish eviscerating emporium dropped perceptibly, causing Grime to glance toward the fish-oil lantern hanging from a beam in the centre of the room. Seeing that the rancid-smelling flickering yellow flame was still lit, he then noticed that the brilliant sunlight which had been streaming through the open shop door was almost completely blocked by something struggling to fit through the opening.

Acting under the assumption that one of the oxen from the street was attempting to enter the building, Grime grabbed a pitchfork and advanced upon the grunting, thrashing intruder. As he drew closer, Grime suddenly stopped, tossed aside the pitchfork, nearly impaling Gurrey in the process, and called out, "Ah, young Otley. Come in, lad, come in."

Using some goose grease from his hair as lubricant, Oberon Otley finally squeezed his corpulent frame through the doorway, swallowed the last of his egg, wiped the brilliant orange yolk dribble from his chin with a deft swipe of his coat sleeve, pulled his cloth cap from his head, and respectfully greeted the two distinguished detectives. "Good morning to you, Mr. Grime, and also to you, Mr. Gurrey. I bring you a message from Mr. Slocomb the bootmaker. He desires to retain your services in the search for his son."

Gurrey stroked his long, luxuriantly flowing beard, his pride and joy and a source of contention between him and his partner who, try as he might, could raise no more than a few sparse hairs on his own chin, although that was still more than he had on his head. "Young Joshua has tried to run away to sea again, has he?"

"I'm sure I don't know, Sir. I only know that John Slocomb has spent the night looking for the lad on every vessel in the harbour; to no avail, I'm afraid."

The two private inspectors rose from their seats, grabbed their bowlers from the hand-carved hat-rack by the door, strode from their place of business, and mounted their recently-acquired company conveyance; a modern and sleek-looking tandem velocipede, better known in a recently popular song as a "bicycle built for two." Once astride their "wheel", with its wooden frame and solid wood tires, Gurrey shouted, "Put your mettle to the pedal!" and the Richard-mobile fish-tailed away, bumping and rattling along the rutted and puddle-pocked dirt road.

"S-s-s-smooth mode of transport-t-t-tation," Gurrey said as they clattered along.

"Y-y-y-yes," Grime replied. "Isn't modern technology w-w-w-wonderful? The complete l-l-l-lack of suspension really lets you g-g-g-get a g-g-g-good feel for the r-r-r-road."

As they made their way along the bustling waterfront they took in the sights of the village: the blacksmith shop, the cooper's, the cannery and the several fish plants were all alive with activity. They passed a cart loaded with heavy timbers on its way to the new copper mine at the back of the island, and another loaded with poles for the weir being constructed on Peter's Island, which was also home to a guano-processing factory.

The passage was filled with watercraft of every size and description, busily criss-crossing the harbour and passing in and out of Fundy Bay on the northern side and St. Mary's Bay to the south. As they watched, a large four-master came in past Dartmouth Point, yawed gracefully as it tacked around Peter's Island, then dropped anchor in Sweetcake Cove. In the clear morning air, Gurrey and Grime could easily see the crew scampering up the ratlines to stow the sails by lashing them to the yardarms. As they passed Central House, the main hotel in town, Gurrey noticed a young girl climbing into the stagecoach that now made twice-a-week trips to Digby.

"What an age we live in Grimey, old chap! Look how these islands have prospered from the generous bounty of the sea. We will never be able to deplete its rich resources! I predict that a hundred and fifty years from now, the population of our little town will have grown many-fold from its present 650. We will have four times as many fish processing plants, sailing ships will be twice as large, velocipedes will be able to carry up to four people, and the stagecoach will be making thrice weekly trips to Digby."

As they trundled along, the two Richards were constantly tipping their bowlers to friends and acquaintances on the busy street. Spying another cyclist approaching, Grime grew most effusive in his greeting, "Good morning, Miss Robichini, I hope you are feeling well this glorious morning, Miss Robichini!"

Rikiletta Robichini favoured Grime with a curt nod as she passed. The previous summer, Rikiletta had caused a village-wide scandal when she had had the temerity to be the first female to ride a bicycle in public.

"I'll never get used to the sight of a woman riding a cycle," Grime mused.

"Modern times, Grimey old chum, modern times! I believe it possible that at some point in the future, maybe one or two hundred years from now, women will be allowed to vote, and some may even run for public office; in fact, I believe that under the law, women will eventually be considered equal to men in every respect."

With a hint of pique in his voice Grime responded brusquely, "Really, Gurrey! I enjoy your fanciful prognostications upon what the future holds for us, but sometimes you go too far! What you predict is contrary to the order of the world, for a woman to vote is as unlikely and as unnatural as it would be for a fish to be raised in a cage!"

The duo rode on in silence over the small bridge that divided the town in half. As they crossed the stream flowing out of the Great Meadow, they left that part of Westport known to some as "Snobtown" and entered the more rough-and-tumble section known as "Irishtown". Presently they pulled up in front of the boot shop and dismounted their conveyance with an athletic grace that left some of the local maidens quite aflutter.

A tired and haggard-looking John Slocomb greeted them. "I am at my wits' end! I don't know what to do with that boy! He seems to think a life on the high seas will be more exciting than spending ten hours a day huddled in a dark and airless room pegging boots! I understand that he wants to make a name for himself, and I've tried to tell him that his assured path to fame lies in the Slocomb Water-tight Boot, whereas becoming a sailor is no path to acclaim and immortality. A century from now every man, woman and child will be wearing the Slocomb boot, the name will be on every lip, but who will know or care to remember the name of some obscure sailor named Joshua Slocomb—or Slocum, depending on if he decides to change the spelling for some reason."

Slocomb pulled a book off a shelf. "I even tried to discourage him by making him read this book of verse about people all over the planet who tried to follow their dreams but were unsuccessful; apparently it didn't leave any impression upon him at all."

He slammed the book down on the counter where Gurrey happened to notice the title: *Failing Around the World: A Poem.*

"You may rest your mind, sir." Gurrey stated with confidence. "We will find the young scalawag and return him to you posthaste."

Upon leaving the boot shop, Grime turned to Gurrey and, in that obtuse and pudden-headed way he was so well known for, asked, "How are we going to find him? His father spent all night searching and saw neither hair nor hide of the lad. Ships have been coming and going all morning. How do we know which one he's on?"

Gurrey was paying scant attention. "Something has been niggling at my brain, Grime. Something is not quite right."

Suddenly a wave of realization swept over his rugged yet intelligent face. "To the velocipede, Grime. We have not a moment to lose!"

As they rapidly re-traced their route through the village, Gurrey explained, "It occurred to me when we passed the Hotel earlier. A young girl was getting on the stagecoach, but it took me some time to realize that she was the only passenger! It would be exceedingly unseemly for a young girl, in fact, for a female of any age, to be travelling unescorted, would it not? I suspect that young Slocomb, having failed many times before at running away to sea, has tried a different tack this time and, disguised in women's clothing, is simply taking the stagecoach out of town. Faster, Grimey. We've got to catch that ferry!"

As the two furiously-pumping Richards approached the ferry wharf, Grime suddenly stopped pedalling. Despite Gurrey heroically redoubling his efforts, they arrived just in time to see the ferry, with the stagecoach aboard, slip past the end of the wharf.

"Sorry about that, old chum," Grime panted. "My gout started acting up something fierce and I was forced to cease my exertions."

"Not to worry, old friend. What we need now is a fast boat to transport us to the other side where we can overtake that stagecoach."

The only watercraft nearby seemed to be a small sailboat that, at first glance, appeared to be transporting a rather squat hogshead barrel. Upon closer inspection, Gurrey realized his mistake and shouted out, "Young Otley, may we conscript you and your craft to our cause?"

Within minutes the partners were safely ensconced aboard the boat. They were both surprised to see that young Oberon Otley, despite being somewhat lethargic and clumsy on land, was an able and competent sailor.

"This is a sea-worthy little vessel," Gurrey said. "Is it your own?"

"Yes," replied Otley. "I just turned sixteen, and in this modern age where transportation is King, any young man who hopes to draw the attention of the ladies has to have his own set of keels."

With obvious pride, he pointed out some of the custom work he had done to his ride, "It's got dual exhausts," he said, pointing out a matching set of bilge pumps, "and I just installed a stick-shift." He demonstrated the advantage of this feature by using a sturdy stick to shift the boom from port to starboard without having to get out of his seat.

"What's this contraption?" Grime asked, nudging with his foot a net bag attached to a long rope.

"Oh, that's a drag for catching scallops. You tow it along the bottom of the ocean. Sometimes a bunch of us go out of an evening and see who can catch the most scallops in the shortest time. Yes, we quite enjoy ourselves at the Saturday night drag races."

By this time the ferry, with its head start and combination of sails and long, sweeping oars, was almost to the Freeport dock and it was obvious that they were not going to catch it.

"Land us right on the beach in the cove,", Gurrey said. "The carriage follows the road along the shore and makes a stop at the bottom of Plunkett Street. We'll intercept it there."

Gurrey sprung easily from the sailboat onto the sandy shore, then turned to catch his arthritic and feeble partner as he was about to fall face-first into the surf.

"Sorry, old bean; inner ear problem," Grime explained sheepishly.

Running up the beach, the intrepid Inspectors reached the stage just as it pulled to a stop. Yanking open the door, they peered inside.

Grime then turned to Gurrey with a look even more stunned than usual and exclaimed, "Empty!"

"Not quite," Gurrey replied. "Look there."

On the floor lay a crumpled cotton dress and a length of hemp rope, frayed out to resemble long hair.

"The rascal has evaded us," Gurrey said with a tinge of grudging admiration.

Turning from the coach, he scanned the surrounding landscape. Obviously, the prosperity that Westport had been enjoying had not spread to the neighbouring island. Several ragged and emaciated inhabitants of the village had collected on the beach near Otley, who had stayed with his boat.

"Can we hurry this up?" he shouted. "These people are looking at me as if I were a giant pork chop."

Out of the corner of his eye, Gurrey caught a glimpse of someone entering a warehouse, one of the many tumble-down buildings that littered the Freeport waterfront. "This way," he said.

The two Richards arrived at the old warehouse at the end of the wharf and, with their magnifying glasses in hand, strode through the decrepit building looking for clues to the missing boy's whereabouts. Suddenly, they saw a slight movement behind an old crate and crept toward it. Seeing a tuft of hair sticking up, they deduced that it might be the lad in question

Gurrey reached down and plucked him up by his ear. "Okay, let's be havin' ya," he said jovially.

The two Richards recognized the lad immediately as young Josh Slocomb. They knew Josh to be a good boy, perhaps a bit too fanciful, but a good lad nonetheless.

"What's all this, young Josh?" Grime said kindly. "Your mother's worried about you."

The boy, snotty-nosed and dishevelled, blurted out his story. "I can't take it anymore. There are so many people in the house and father's always cross, and I hate makin' shoes and boots. I want to travel the world—beyond Westport, even beyond Freeport, Tiverton, and Mount Hanley. I want to sail the ocean."

The two seasoned Richards took him outside into the early morning sunlight where they sat him up on a hogshead and sat themselves on an old, upturned dory. "You ever been to see Billy?" Grime said, before correcting himself. "I mean, ever been to sea, Josh?"

"No."

"Listen, me bucko," Gurrey said. "Your day will come. But you're too young for all that now. I know your father is a tad stern, but he'd be lost without ya."

"Gurrey's right," Grime said. "Let me tell ya a story, me laddie, me buck. I was once a lad like you—wanted to travel and all that. My parents were convinced that the world ended just beyond Freeport, but I was havin' none of that. I knew somewhere there was a Central Grove and a Tiverton and even, God bless us all, a Digby."

The lad listened intently, his mouth slightly open to better catch Grime's words.

"One fine mornin' in June of '46, I set out to sea with my grandpa. We sailed on the sloop *John B*, my grandfather and me. 'Round Nassau Town we did roam."

As the two Richards spoke to the sad little boy, they couldn't help but notice that a small blond lad had approached quietly and was writing down on a slate what they said. They recognized him as Bartholomew Wilson, a lad who spent most of his time at the water's edge with the other beach boys. They looked at him quizzically.

He looked back shyly, and stammered, "Sssomeday maybe I—or my ancestors—will form a garage band and write a song about your adventure, Mr. Grime."

"What an odd thing to say," Gurrey whispered to his partner. "And what's a garage?"

"Never mind that now," Grime said. "The point is, we was drinkin' all night and got into a fight. I was so broke up I just wanted to go home. So we hoisted the *John B*'s sail. I saw how the mainsail set. Well Gurrey here was the first mate and he got drunk and broke in the captain's trunk and the constable had to come and take him away. Remember that, Gurrey?"

"Sure do," Gurrey replied. "Sheriff John Stone. He wouldn't leave me alone. I was broke up like Grimey here. I just wanted to go home."

"This stuff practically writes itself," young Wilson mumbled.

"Then what happened?" Slocomb said, completely spellbound by the tale that was being spun.

"Well, the poor cook, he caught the fits and threw away all my grits, and then—get this!—he ate up all of my corn! Can you believe that, laddie? My corn! Finally Gurrey and me just came back home and we've been here ever since. We're just two Richards trying to make a livin' now."

Gurrey looked the boy straight in the eye. "But let me tell you this, Josh, me lad, me bucko, me boy. If you have a dream to go to sea, you have to do it. And you will. I can see greatness in you, lad. Just don't ever go on the sloop *John B*."

He paused to let a stream of tobacco juice fly over the boy's left shoulder. Some landed on Grime. "Say it, don't spray it," Grime said angrily.

"That's it!" Josh Slocomb said. "If I ever have a boat, I'll call it *Spray* and I'll sail it around the world!"

Suddenly an easterly wind slammed the door to the fish shack/detective office open and a blast of cold air startled the two dicks from their tobacco-induced dream.

"Wow!" Gurrey said. "Was that real?"

"I don't know," Grime replied haltingly, "but I suggest we don't tell anyone about it."

11: In a Fog

Jim Grime entered the fish shack/detective agency with a flourish. He removed his oil-stained John Deere cap and slung it nonchalantly toward an ancient hat rack in the corner. It missed and landed on the wharf cat, which promptly curled up and fell asleep in it.

"I'm back, Gurrey, back from Saint John, New Brunswick. What have you been up to?"

His partner emerged from the small toilet that hung precariously out over the beach at the back of the shack, supported only by two rotting stilts. "Just finished up some paperwork," he said. "Jobs not done until you finish the paperwork, you know."

Grime sighed. "Back to reality I guess."

"How was your trip, Grimesey?" Gurrey said as he hoisted himself onto a hogshead and warmed his hands by the pot-bellied stove.

"I got there on a Friday and it was raining. It rained Saturday, Sunday, Monday, Tuesday, Wednesday and Thursday, and then the weather took a turn for the worse. I'll tell you, it was just like home."

"And how's your little grandson?"

"Little Sam's just like me," Grime said proudly.

"Incontinent is he?"

"NO! No!...I mean, yes...of course he's incontinent, he's a baby, for Pete's sake! I meant he's a good-looking kid, just like me."

"Dear God in heaven," Gurrey thought, but said out loud, "Oh, that's great, old friend. I confess that I missed you. It isn't the same trying to solve mysteries all by myself."

"Right you are. Sherlock had his Watson, Batman had his Robin, Superman had his Jimmy Olsen, the Lone Ranger had his Tonto, and—"

"And Charlie McCarthy had Mortimer Snerd."

"Yes...er, yes, that's right," Grime said, somewhat taken aback. "Tell me, what's been going on? Any crime on the go?"

Gurrey lit his corn cob pipe and took two deep draws to get it going. "To tell you the truth, Grimey, someone could have stole the whole village and I'd never have seen it. It's been solid fog for two weeks now. Hain't bin able to see across the Passage, or even across the street."

"Yup, she's thick out there all right," Grime said. "A real pea-souper. This is the kind of weather that criminals love. We'd better be on high alert."

Gurrey yawned and expelled a luxurious, forty-six second fart. "Right you are," he said contentedly.

Suddenly the shop door flew open with a bang, admitting several cold, grasping fingers of fog that clung tenaciously to the warm, stylish form of Dot Baker

She shook the heavy droplets from her clothes, looked around the detective office/fish-gutting parlour, wrinkled her cute little button nose and said, "I hope I'm not being rude, but this place really smells bad. You must have some rotting fish in here somewhere. Maybe it's time for a good cleaning."

With an uncomfortable and slightly embarrassed look, Gurrey replied while discreetly and vigorously fanning the air behind him, "Thanks for that house-keeping tip, Dot. We'll get right to it. In the meantime, what can we do for you?"

"Well, as you know, I recently opened a donut shop over in Freeport. —"

"Dot's Donuttery, we know it well," Grime said. "Your dulse donuts are my all-time favourites. You know, I've never been able to get them anywhere else, and I've tried all the way from here to East Ferry. I don't know why other people don't carry them. They're delicious, and full of iodine."

"Why, thank you, Grime. I'm pretty sure you're my biggest customer for that particular item. As a matter of fact, the bakery is the reason I'm here. We've been having some thefts recently. Every time the fog comes in, which is nearly all the time, someone goes around the neighbourhood stealing anything edible. I've tried to catch him myself, but all I've been able to do is snatch a brief glimpse of a vague form disappearing in the mist. Everyone in the area has been hit to some extent by this fellow who we call The Crocker's Hill Creeper, but I've been the worst affected because..."

After a pause, Dot continued quietly, "What I'm about to tell you is a trade secret. I'm assuming there is some code of client-dick confidentiality that prevents you from revealing this to anyone else?"

The two dicks nodded their heads—their couple of dick heads as it were—in confirmation of a code they had up to this point never known existed..

"My secret of success is that I cool my products in the fog, it makes everything nice and moist and imparts a slight flavour of the sea to all my baking. Because I have to put it all outside, I'm an easy target for The Creeper. He's stealing almost everything I make."

"Not the dulse donuts!" Grime was leaning forward with a look of alarm.

"No, that's about the only thing he hasn't taken so far."

With a sigh of relief, Grime settled back in his chair.

"Anyway, since I didn't have any luck trying to catch him myself, I decided it was time to bring in some able-bodied, highly competent professionals. Unfortunately, none of them were available, so here I am at your door. Do you think you can help me?"

"Hmmm," Gurrey said. "This reminds me of another case I read about —I can't remember where. It involved a guy named Simple Simon."

"That's a fairy tale character," Grime snapped.

"I don't care about his sexual orientation," Gurrey said. "If he's a crook, he's a crook."

Grime turned to question Ms. Baker in greater depth. "Pardon me for saying so, Dot, but you are much better known for your egg tarts than for your donuts. Whenever they see you walk by, everyone's first reaction is 'Tart!'"

Realizing that his comment could conceivably be interpreted negatively, he added, "Not me of course. I prefer your buns." Confident that he had cleverly covered up any imagined slight, Grime silently thanked his grade 11 teacher, Mrs. Hooper, for his diplomatic way with words. Little wonder that he was known as the Henry Kissinger of the Tri-Islands area.

He continued with the questioning as Gurrey took notes. "This person you saw sneak away into the fog…was he tall, short? Was there anything about him that was odd?"

"Now you come to mention it," Dot said, "the figure I saw approaching my store through the fog was very slow-moving, very lethargic. A few minutes later I saw an extremely animated, lively person walking away. I thought at first it was two different people, but after noticing some of my fish-bait fritters had been stolen, I realized it was the same person, before and after the robbery."

"Anything else?"

"As I said, visibility was not the best, and fog will often muffle and distort sound, but I could have sworn I heard him laughing. It was a very strange sound, like a seagull giving birth."

"I see," Grime said. "Well, thank you very much, Dot. You've given us a lot to go on. We'll be in touch when we have a result."

With a doubtful look back at the detectives, Dot left the building.

"This information is invaluable," Grime said, rubbing his hands together. "Let's meticulously review the evidence. Read me your notes Gurrey."

With a business-like nonchalance, Gurrey flicked open his notepad and began to read. "Always start by putting an 'X' or 'O' in the centre square. Don't let Grime make the first—" He stopped abruptly. "Sorry, those are my strategy notes on tic-tac-toe. I swear I'll master that game yet, Grimesey."

Grime gave him a withering look as Gurrey scrambled to find the right page in his notebook. "Stole fritters/slow coming/fast going/heard laughter." He stopped reading and looked at Grime.

"That's it?! Those are the only notes you made in a 20-minute interview?!"

"I have a mind like a steel trap," Gurrey said. "The rest is all up here!" He pointed toward his balding head, inadvertently poking himself in the eye with his Bic pen.

Tossing aside the offending pen and rubbing his eye, he rose from his chair and said, "Enough with the paperwork, it's time for some action! Let's roll!"

He was halfway out the door before realizing his partner was not behind him. Turning back, he saw Grime writhing about on the floor.

"What are you doing?"

"You said to roll, so I'm rolling."

"I didn't mean that literally, it's a figure of speech; what I meant was, 'Let's get in the car and drive off.'"

"Oh," Grime said, getting up. "Try to make your meaning a little clearer from now on. Now I've got fish guts all over my best suit."

A short while later the partners were sitting in the Dickmobile across from the Donuttery, watching customers come and go. Gurrey was getting eye-strain trying to spy anything suspicious through the dense fog, while Grime was preoccupied with flicking rancid fish entrails off his sleeve and muttering sulkily, "Nearly ruined my best suit...paid a lot of money for this suit...now I'll have to get it dry-cleaned...probably cost a lot to clean a nice suit like this."

"Look," Gurrey said at last, "that's a 1970s disco suit that you got out of the bargain bin at Frenchys for $1.25. If it's really ruined, buy another one. I'll gladly give you the $1.25. Just stop pouting about it!"

After an uncomfortable hour spent sitting in strained silence, Gurrey finally said, "Well, Dot was right about the fog. When it's this thick you can't see anything, and now it's getting dark. This is a waste of time. We might as well go back to the office and work on coming up with a plan."

"You go," Grime said, getting out of the car. "I'm going to take a closer look at the scene of the crime. I'll see you later."

Late the next morning, the Dickmobile was again in its usual spot across from the donut shop. Gurrey had been surprised the evening before when Grime arrived back at the office and announced that there was no need to bother with a plan, that in the morning, he would be able to pick out the guilty party in front of the store next to Dot's establishment.

As they sat waiting, Gurrey noticed a flurry of activity with people streaming in from all directions to enter the village's only store. Finally, the front door opened and a pale, anxious-looking fellow came out carrying a large bundle under his arm.

"There he is!" Grime cried. "That's him! That's our thief!"

"Are you sure?" Gurrey said. "That's Rev. McKinney. Why do you think he's the thief?"

"Yesterday while we were sitting here, I came up with a fool-proof plan to make The Creeper reveal himself. I didn't mention it to you at the time because I was still mad about the suit thing. After you left, I went in to talk to Dot, who was just about to put the chocolate icing on a batch of her irresistible breakfast donuts; everybody loves those, I figured if The Creeper is going to steal anything, he'll steal those. When she turned her back for a moment, I dumped a large package of ex-lax into the icing. It's a perfect plan, he'll steal the donuts, he'll eat the donuts, the ex-lax will do its stuff; and according to my calculations, just about now is when he will be running out of toilet paper...and there he is."

Grime concluded by pointing at the hapless Rev. who was struggling valiantly with an extremely large package of toilet tissue.

Gurrey was gob-smacked at this news. "Uh, Grimey, you do know that they don't put icing on hot donuts don't you? Those donuts were already cooled; they never went outside after they were iced, they probably went right out to be served to customers."

With a growing feeling of impending doom, Gurrey pointed out a fact that Grime already knew only too well. "Nearly everybody in town comes here first thing in the morning for a coffee and one of Dot's delicious breakfast donuts."

"No, no," Grime said with a rising note of panic, "It's a good plan! It's a good plan! That's our thief right there! I'm sure of it!"

Just then the door opened again and another customer emerged carrying a package of toilet paper; he was quickly followed by another, then another, and another.

"Oh, oh," Grime said.

"Oh, oh is right," Gurrey said, "Congratulations, Grimey, old pal. You've succeeded in singlehandedly giving the entire village of Freeport a case of the runs."

"Oh, no," Grime said, sinking down in the car seat. "What do we do now?"

"Well" replied Gurrey, "Under the circumstances, I think there is really only one viable course of action."

With that, he started the engine and the two dicks surreptitiously slunk away into the mercifully enveloping fog, cries of "Oh, the humanity," ringing in their ears.

Arriving at the office the next morning, Gurrey found Grime in surprisingly good spirits in spite of the previous day's events. He was sitting at the splitting table/desk, studying a large sheet of paper covered in circles and arrows and dozens of cryptic notations.

"I've been up all night working on a new plan," he said.

"I hope this one doesn't involve a laxative," Gurrey replied warily.

"No," Grime said with a wink. "Although I've never seen the citizens of Freeport looking so regular. This time I think I may really have an idea about who our donut thief is."

That evening, Gurrey and Grime were seated at the back of the room at the IOOF Hall, listening to the comic stylings of one Bertram "Chuckles" Allbrite, the finest stand-up comic in the Tri-Islands area. The crowd was in hysterics and had been since the show began some two hours earlier. The legendarily manic comic was constantly roaming the stage from end-to-end, improvising one-liners and knock-knock jokes that had the patrons howling, and "that's what she said" gambits that had them gasping for air.

To conclude his high-energy set, Albright had segued into a put-down argument with a tipsy member of the audience.

"Hey, yer not funny," slurred the clearly inebriated man in the second row.

"Yeah, so's your mother," Chuckles had retorted and his witticism was rewarded with gales of guffaws.

Encouraged by the response, Chuckles continued to attack his heckler. "You are short and ugly and I hope you die."

The put-down was classic Allbrite material and people were literally rolling in the aisles. He ended with the same catch phrase with which he began and ended every show. "Getting' any?"

This witty repartee left several people so helpless with laughter that they had to be assisted in leaving the hall.

Outside in their dick-mobile, the two dicks discussed what they had seen and heard.

"Notice anything about the way Chuckles tells jokes?" Grime said.

"Only that he's hi-larious," Gurrey responded.

Grime rolled his eyes. "I prefer the more sophisticated humour of Carrot Top. But never mind that now. Ever notice that he laughs at his own jokes?"

"Sure, that's his trademark. So what?"

"So, he has a very distinctive laugh," Grime said. "I think what we need is a laugh line-up. Round up five Joes off the street and our friend Chuckles and we'll see if Dot can identify who she heard laughing."

An hour later, Gurrey showed up at the bakery with five local loafers he had found loitering around the desolate streets of Freeport. "I couldn't find five guys named Joe", he whispered to Grime, "But I did get one Joe, a Jack, two Johns and a Jimmy."

"I guess that'll have to do," Grime said. "Put them in the back room with our suspect while I set up the interrogation equipment."

While Gurrey hustled the line-up participants into the storage room, Grime carefully unpacked his most prized possessions: his official Hey, Hey, We're The Monkees portable record player and his stack of classic comedy albums: Richard Pryor Live on the Sunset Strip, Stand-up Comic with Woody Allen, The Button Down Mind of Bob Newhart, Comedian with Eddie Murphy, Class Clown with George Carlin, A Wild and Crazy Guy with Steve Martin, and his secret weapon: an audio recording of the Canadian Parliament House of Commons session from the previous week.

"If these don't make 'em laugh, nothing will," he thought. Aloud he said,"Okay, Gurrey, bring them in one at a time."

Grime was merciless in his interrogation, blasting each suspect with the time-tested comedic stylings of some of the greatest humorists known to mankind. One by one they succumbed under the relentless barrage of jokes, gags, comic impersonations, and humorous stories, eventually finding themselves reduced to a state of helpless laughing, chuckling, guffawing, and one gentle tee-hee.

When it was all over, Grime turned to Dot and said, "I regret that you had to witness such a spectacle, but it was unfortunately necessary. Which laugh do you recognize?"

"I'm sorry," Dot said. "A couple sounded close, but none of them were exactly the same as the laugh of The Crocker's Hill Creeper."

Deflated, Grime leaned against a near-by donut rack, squashing several of Dot's freshly-glazed clam crunchies. "How could I be wrong again, Gurrey? I was so sure I had it figured out this time. Maybe what everyone says is true, that I'm too old, too senile, too stupid, too homely, too flatulent, too bald, too halitosis-ridden, too badly dressed for this job."

"Don't listen to that kind of talk, Grimey. They're mostly wrong about almost half of those things. Run that line-up through one more time. I've got a hunch you might be right about this after all."

This time, just as each candidate opened his mouth to laugh, Gurrey shoved a donut in it. As soon as "Chuckles" Allbrite emitted his first crumb-spewing belly-laugh, Dot yelled out, "That's it, that's it, that's the weird laugh I heard that night!"

Confronted with the testimony of an irrefutable ear-witness, Allbrite quickly folded and confessed to being The Creeper. "Believe it or not," he said, "being a comic at the Freeport IOOF Hall doesn't pay that well, and it takes a lot of energy to get up on a stage and perform. I was burning too many calories and started wasting away. I lost all my trademark stage energy, my audience started losing interest. The same jokes I'd told over and over to the same people for years were suddenly no longer getting the big laughs they used to. When I dropped below 98 pounds, I got desperate. I know an artist is supposed to suffer for his art, but I was about to die for mine. My whole family suffers from low blood sugar, we're kind of famous for it." he said with unwarranted pride. "I knew that Dot put her baking outside, so I started sneaking the odd jellyfish donut, or maybe a mussel muffin or lobster-bait brownie on the way to my next performance, just enough to give me the energy to get through another set. As you can see, it worked, I got my mojo back. My stage energy returned and with the addition of a few new jokes from that font of all things hilarious, *Barney's Big Book of Bathroom Humour*, I got my act back on track. The sugar boost worked; in fact it worked too well; her treats are so delectable that I couldn't restrain myself. I got addicted to the sugar-rush and became unable to perform without it. The white powder is a cruel mistress. That's how all the big comics went out you know! Lenny Bruce, John Belushi, Chris Farley, Sam Kinison, they all used too much of the good stuff. I'm afraid I'll be next ."

By the time Chuckles had finished his sad tale of woe, Gurrey, Grime and Dot were on the verge of tears.

"Isn't there anything we can do for him?" Dot asked with a sniffle and a dainty little snort, "Does he have to go to jail?"

"That's up to you," Gurrey said. "You were the main victim of his crimes. Do you want to press charges?"

A short while later, Gurrey and Grime were on their way to the ferry. Grime carefully selected another dulse donut from the large box on his lap, a gift from Dot in appreciation for solving the mystery of The Crocker's Hill Creeper.

"Well, that turned out all right. Everyone seemed happy enough with the way things were resolved." He mumbled around a mouthful.

After it was decided that there would be no charges, an appreciative and repentant Chuckles promised to do some benefit shows at the Donuttery to make up for what he had stolen; and Dot, being an expert on the subject and indirectly, the cause of his dilemma, offered to help Chuckles get his sweet-tooth under control and become his corporate sponsor and manager

"Yep" Gurrey said, "A good day for all involved and another case closed for Gurrey and Grime."

"Getting any?" Grime added, and the two collapsed in laughter.

Figure 8: Oceanside

12: Election Fever

Gurrey burst into the fish house/office, dragging the various medical apparatus that had kept him alive despite the dire predictions of doctors from Yarmouth to Cape North. He was barely able to contain his excitement.

His dashingly handsome partner Grime was sitting behind the desk/gutting table, talking on the phone. Gurrey sat down opposite him and impatiently began drumming his gnarled fingers on the gnarled surface.

The phone conversation continued, with Grime occasionally asking a question or making an observation. Finally, he said, "Well, it does interest me. I won't lie. Let me think it over."

He said a quick goodbye and hung up the phone.

"Grimey," Gurrey said, "you'll never guess what just happened."

Grime looked up from the notes he'd been taking and said, "I've got some news too Gurrey, but you go first."

"You'll never believe it!" The less attractive of the two dicks was bristling with excitement, two of his chins shaking violently and his good leg tapping uncontrollably on the floor like a crazed Stompin' Tom impersonator (which coincidentally had been his summer job in high school).

"Well?" Grime said. "What is it?!"

"I've been asked by the Literal Party to run in the bye-election next month!"

Grime jumped from his chair and his mouth fell open, revealing the beautiful pearly white teeth that were the pride of the Tri-Island area. He looked at Gurrey, then back at his notes, and then back at Gurrey. "B-b-but," he stammered, "but Gurrey, old friend, I've been approached by the Constipated Party to run for them!"

This time it was Gurrey's turn to struggle to his feet, his gaping mouth revealing a row of misshapen molars and bargain basement bicuspids.

The two old friends stared at each other in silence for a full minute. Grime was the first to speak. "Are you going to do it?"

"Well...I think I will, or at least I thought so until I heard your news. What about you?"

"Same thing. I've always had an interest in politics, but now..."

They again lapsed into silence. This time it was broken by Gurrey. "If this is going to hurt our friendship, then it's not worth it."

"I agree!" agreed Grime. "That's the most important thing."

"Still..."

"Yeah?"

Gurrey shrugged a Trudeau-style shrug. "Well, it's just that I've always thought I have a lot to offer politically, that's all."

"Me too, Gurrey. Me too. What the hell!! Let's do it—and may the best man win!"

"Great," Gurrey said, shaking his friend's hand with gusto. "But remember, if this begins to hurt our friendship, we call her quits, right? After all, we've led pampered lives here in the fish-gutting/detective business. We don't want to get our hands dirty."

"Absolutely! And we can't let it affect our job performance either."

Gurrey said. "Wow, this is exciting," Gurrey said. "I guess they asked us because we're so high profile. It's pretty unique though."

"What do you mean?"

"I bet it's the first time there's ever been a couple of dicks running for political office."

"True. Very true. Dicks in politics. Must be a first."

"Maybe we should test each other on some of the questions we're sure to get when we go knocking on doors," Gurrey said.

"Good idea! Let me start. Let's see...Okay, here's one. You knock on the desk and I'll pretend I'm a potential voter, okay?"

Gurrey rapped his arthritic knuckles on the weathered surface. Grime pretended to open the door and then said. "Oh, Mr. Ben, I heard you were running for office."

"Yes, I am. Can I count on your vote?"

"Well, that depends. What's your position on same sex marriage? I happen to be a big supporter of same sex marriage."

Gurrey smiled confidently. "I'm 100% for it!" he gleamed.

"That's good to know. Tell me, Mr. Ben, why do you feel so strongly on that issue?"

"Well, my third wife—or was it fourth?—anyways, she was always goin' on about how we had the same sex every Saturday night. So what'd I do? Only switched it to Friday night!"

"So you had the same sex but on a different night?"

"Yessir! Genius, right?"

"Yeah, that was clever," Grime said with a sly grin. "She left you anyway though, didn't she?"

"Yeah, there's no pleasin' some women."

The following morning found the sun slowly burning the sea smoke off the harbour as Gurrey and Grime gradually emerged from their own personal fog banks; the result of their respective nomination parties the previous evening. The two dicks, once again sitting across the desk/gutting table from each other, were trying out campaign slogans.

"How about this one? 'Now's the time, vote for Grime.'"

"Not bad, not bad at all, brief and to the point. What do you think of this one? 'Don't Worry, Vote Gurrey.'"

"I like it; it evokes an image people can identify with, and it rhymes!"

"You know," Grime continued, "this could work out very well for the area. With us running for the two major parties it's a foregone conclusion that one or the other has to win. It doesn't really matter who gets in, we both want the same things for our district."

"I had that exact thought," Gurrey said. "We've seen eye-to-eye for years working as partners, we're just the same two fish-gutting detectives expanding into the political arena, I guess you could say we've become a couple of poli-dicks. There's no reason why we can't continue to cooperate and work together for the benefit of the general public like we've always done."

The two old friends and partners sat in silence for a few moments, enveloped in an aura of good-will and anticipation. They were about to enter the political arena.

Their brief reverie was interrupted by a sharp rap on the office/fish house door and the abrupt entrance of a sullen-faced young man in an eighteen-hundred-dollar Armani suit.

Casting a disparaging look around the room, the stranger announced, "Those people outside must have been putting me on. They told me this was the Literal Party campaign office."

Gurrey rose and extended his hand across the well-used gutting table. "Pleased to meet you, I'm the candidate, just call me Gurrey."

"Why would I do that?"

"Because that's my name."

"Oh, right," the stranger said. "Well then, I guess we'll have to work with that. My name is Kickk Mout, I've been assigned to help you with your campaign strategy."

Taking care not to touch anything that might soil the fine Italian fabric of his suit, Mout said, "I guess the first order of business is to get you a decent campaign office. Maybe your assistant there can find out what's available."

It took Gurrey a moment or two to realize what Mout was getting at. "First of all", he explained when it finally sank in, "this *is* my campaign office. Secondly, that is *not* my assistant. That is Jim Grime, the Constipated candidate, and this is his campaign office, too!"

Across the table, Grime was preoccupied, trying to come up with another catchy campaign slogan. "'Elect Grimey, He's Not That Slimy', oh, that's a good one!"

Mout was so stunned by this development that he didn't notice that he had ruined his expensive Gucci loafers by splashing through a puddle of brine near the tanks of pickled fish. "You're not serious!" he gasped. "You can't campaign out of the same office as your opponent!"

"Why not?" Gurrey said. "For years we've operated a very successful fish-gutting service and a moderately successful detective agency out of this building. I don't see why running an election should be a problem."

"For starters," Mout said, "there are things we don't want the opposition to know. In fact," he suspiciously eyed an oblivious Grime, "we should probably continue this discussion in private."

Stepping out the back door onto the wharf, Gurrey settled comfortably into the rocking chair he had fashioned out of an old and still quite odorous lobster-bait barrel.

Mout looked around for a seat of his own, but after considering a lobster crate with a missing top, an old pile of mouldering dragger net containing several mummified dogfish, and an overturned trawl tub with a broken board in the bottom; he decided not to risk the Armani and remained standing. "This bye-election is an important one for the Literal Party. As you may be aware, the opposition has been running a non-stop campaign of dirty tricks for years now. We in the Literal Party refused to be drawn into this sleazy style of politics, preferring, as the party name implies, to rely on facts and information rather than plugging up the intestinal workings of the democratic process as the Constipated Party has done with their indigestible stew of innuendo, secrecy, misinformation and emotional rhetoric. We had hoped that the citizens would eventually rise up and get the democratic process moving again by inserting an electoral laxative into the figurative colon from which flows their cynical manipulation of the Canadian political system, but it seems that the putrid smell of their campaign has only discouraged people and turned them away from voting at all. The last election had one of the lowest turn-outs in history. There's great debate within our party as to how to proceed; some think we should just hold to our present course, while others are pushing to beat the Constipators at their own game. This bye-election will be our test case. For the first time, we're going to see if we can give the Cons a taste of their own medicine."

Gurrey had been carefully following Mout's impassioned presentation. "What exactly does that mean? What kind of things will we be doing?"

"I've already started. I arranged for an attack ad against your opponent to appear in the next issue of *Passages*. I've got a mock-up of it right here."

Mout placed his briefcase on the trawl tub and started to pull out a copy of the ad. On the sheet of paper Gurrey could make out the words, "Grime is soft".

"Now, just a minute," he said. "I'm willing to be tough in this election, but I think that's hitting kind of low. I don't see what a man's on-going, and so-far futile, battle with erectile dysfunction has to do with his suitability as a political representative. I think we should... I... uh...oh."

Mout had pulled the page completely out of the briefcase and Gurrey could now see that it in fact said, "Grime is soft on crime".

"Oh. But that's not really any better. and it's not true! Grime isn't soft on crime; in fact, in his own bumbling way he's done more than anyone to keep the crime rate down!"

"I know," Mout said with what Gurrey thought was inappropriate and excessive glee. "That's the great thing about these ads. You can't both be the law-and-order candidate. We have to make people think that's you. If there's anything we have learned from the Cons, it's that the truth doesn't matter! If Grime tries to ignore the lie, then that just makes people think it's true. If he denies it, then you can say he's trying to prevent the truth from coming out. Even if he eventually proves that what you said about him was untrue, by that time it's too late...The label will be stuck on him. Isn't this fun? We'll tear him to shreds!"

Gurrey thought back to his earlier conversation with Grime and could feel the aura of positivism dissipate.

Meanwhile, Jim Grime had begun canvassing the Greater Westport area, having convinced Owen Otley to drive him around in the back-up company car, a 1972 International half ton truck. Grime was in the truck bed, standing in a hogshead so he wouldn't tip over, and speaking into the small opening of a Javex bottle that he had painstakingly fashioned into a megaphone by cutting the bottom out.

"Citizens of Westport," he intoned. "I am your new candidate for the Constipated Party. I'm not some bandwagon jumper, no sirree. I've been Constipated all my adult life and my father and grandfather were Constipated before me. But despite my Constipated credentials, I'm still just a regular guy. Vote for me in the upcoming election. I know what the people of this island want: law and order. I think my record speaks for itself."

While he spoke, the occasional comment could be heard from the small groups of people along the route who looked up from their scratchin' and spittin' and whittlin' and such:

"A dose of Ex-Lax will fix that!"

"I always knew you were full of it!"

"I hear a feed of prunes will loosen things up!"

Grime either ignored the comments or had his hearing aid turned off. "Come to the rally tomorrow night on the ferry wharf. I'll be presenting my platform at that time. Remember, it's high time for Grime! Grime is tough on crime! Grime is sublime. Grime is in his prime. Vote Grime and watch your income climb!" He had decided to throw all the slogans out there to see what stuck.

The following day, back at the fish shack/detective office/party headquarters, Grime and Otley discussed strategy over a quart of Ten Penny Old Stock Ale which they passed back and forth.

"Then you'll be my campaign manager, Owen?"

"Sure," Otley wheezed. "It'd be an honour. My only concern is that I don't want to cause bad feelings with Gurrey."

"Not a problem. Gurrey and I discussed it and we've agreed that our friendship is too important to let politics ruin it. We're both tough on crime so it don't really matter who wins. Besides, he's got that feller from Halifax with the fancy Arm and Hammer suit and bottled sun tan."

Just then they heard the distinctive squeak of the rusty old mailbox outside. That meant the new issue of *Passages* had arrived, a major event in town.

Grime waited for Otley to volunteer to go to the mailbox, but he was busy consuming the final dozen of a crate of Joe Louis cakes that he had recently picked up for half price at the Digby Frenchy's because they were 2 1/2 years past their "Best By" date.

Grime retrieved the newspaper and resumed his seat behind the desk/gutting table. He perused the cover and riffled through the first few pages of the *New York Times* of the Tri-Island area.

Suddenly his mouth fell open and he began to shake violently, his face turning a deep crimson. Otley looked at him, concerned. "What's wrong, Mr. Grime? I'm no doctor but I have had twelve strokes and I'd wager my last cupcake that you're having one now."

Grime tossed the paper to Otley and said, "Read this!"

Otley's lips moved silently as he scanned the page. "Out loud!" Grime barked.

Otley swallowed hard and began to read.

> Two local men are vying to become the Digby Neck and Islands representative in the provincial legislature in Halifax. Ironically the two are partners in the well-known Digby Neck and Islands Fish-Gutting Service and Detective Agency. Jim Grime is running for the Constipated Party while Gurrey Ben will carry the Literal banner. Asked if this close association will be an issue in the campaign, Literal Party campaign strategist Kickk Mout chuckled. "I think we all know who made the DNIFGSDA the success story it is. I'm sure Grime is a good man and all that but Gurrey Ben is the brains behind that operation."
>
> Pressed on election strategy, Mout suggested that Grime's past would also be fair game. Candidate Gurrey himself was a no-show at the editorial board meeting. "He's helping feed orphans, cleaning up litter, and rescuing beached porpoises today," Mout explained.

Otley leafed from page to page, reading snippets from various articles about the election. "Look at this! Even Heather Crocker-Titus-Prime's column *Birds of a Heather* is against us: 'Saw a rare articulated Slovakian plover nesting the other day at the head of the cove. Jim Grime drove by in his campaign truck yelling loud anti-environmental slogans and the mother bird abandoned its nest, leaving its eggs behind, never to be hatched.'"

He flipped a page. "And here's the editorial by retired media mogul Randy Moyers:"

> *Passages* has decided to throw its editorial clout behind the candidacy of Gurrey Ben. We especially like his position on offshore oil drilling in Beautiful Cove at the end of Lover's Lane. Like his slogan says 'Don't take off for Fort McMurrey, Stay right here and vote for Gurrey.' Gurrey is the undisputed Winston Churchill of our own little island empire. As he said when watching men fill potholes on the road leading to Boar's Head. 'Never have so many done so little for so few.'

Otley continued to read as Grime sat in a stunned silence. "It says here that you're pro-fish farms and that you want to build a penile institution on Peter's Island!"

"That's strange. Randy obviously meant 'penal institution'," Grime said.

"You mean it's true?"

"Of course it's not true! But there's no excuse for bad English."

Otley shrugged. "Says you want to erect a nuclear power plant on Roney's Point. And listen to this: says here that you want to tear down the Joshua Slocum cairn and replace it with a statue of yourself."

"I think I know what's afoot!" Grime said.

"Twelve inches last time I checked," Otley said. "Although with that there new metric system I'm as confused as you."

Grime ignored him. "I know for a fact that Heather Crocker Titus-Prime-etcetera is every bit as Constipated as I am. And despite the fact that he once worked for the CBC and therefore had to pledge eternal allegiance to the Literal Party, Randy Moyers has too much integrity to write that tripe. He once met Peter Mansbridge, for Pete's sake! In fact I think I've heard some of that speech before somewhere. I think *Passages* has been taken over by the Literal Party and become—you should excuse the expression—their organ!"

"And they're holding Gurrey prisoner!" Otley cried.

"Obviously," Grime said, his razor-sharp mind once again several light years ahead of his assistant. "There's no doubt Gurrey and I have had our differences. Sure, we get a kick out of pointing out and exaggerating each other's eccentricities and mental and physical attributes, but I know he would never allow such blatant lies to be printed about me! My guess is he has once again become an unwitting tool, this time of the Literal Party. They've captured him and are possibly brainwashing him even as we speak, the poor, politically-naïve, incontinent, flatulent, flea-ridden, but strangely avuncular sap!"

"It probably serves him right," Otley said, to Grime's great surprise.

"Why do you say that?"

"He didn't do anything to stop Mout from firing me from his campaign staff."

"You were working on his campaign? When was this?"

"Yesterday afternoon."

"But you were working on *my* campaign yesterday! Are you telling me you were working for both of us at the same time?"

"Sure, I've always worked for both of you. Why would I stop now? In the morning I went around and put up your posters. Then in the afternoon I tore them down to put up his, then next morning tore those down to put up yours again. It's the perfect government job."

"Why did they fire you?"

"I'm not sure. That Mout guy said something about Gurrey not being happy with my public image. Can you imagine him saying that!"

"Well," Grime said, "all I know now is that there's a good chance our pal is in trouble. It's time to forget this political stuff and put our dick hats back on."

Later, Grime and Otley were staked out across from the imposing edifice that was home to the world-wide headquarters of *Passages*. It wasn't long before even the notoriously unobservant Grime could see that something was amiss. The broad granite stairway leading up to the impressive double doors of the Passages Building, normally abuzz with the constant comings and goings of reporters, notepads in hand, fountain pens at the ready, "PRESS" cards jauntily protruding from the hatband of their fedoras, was eerily empty.

"Something smells fishy," Otley astutely observed.

"Oh, sorry," Grime said. "I had to skip my weekly bath. Gurrey was using the tub to pickle some herring. I suppose I coulda taken a bucket-shower on the end of the wharf, but last time I did that Penny's whale-watch boat went by with a load of ladies from the Bear River Christian United All-Purpose Church. Penny said the sight of me naked holding a bucket above my head caused several of them to question the very existence of God. She had to stop three of them from jumping overboard."

"I mean in there," Otley said. "Something's fishy in there! We need to investigate."

The duo cautiously approached the building. As they reached the steps, they could feel a vibration and hear the low rumble of the mighty presses that produced the influential newsletter whose motto, written in Latin in gold leaf above the heavy oaken doors, translated to: *News is Merely Gossip Written Down*.

"You're right, Owen, something's definitely going on. This month's issue of *Passages* has already been printed. There's no reason for those presses to still be running."

As the two dicks surreptitiously slipped into the inner sanctum, they were greeted by a sight that only added to their apprehension. The desks nearest the door were normally occupied by the people at the very heart of the operation, the Community Correspondents. The area should have been a hive of activity with the reporters busily fielding calls from far and wide and recording for posterity all the comings and goings in the Tri-Island area.

Ominously, these desks now sat empty, save for a handful of Pulitzer Prizes and other prestigious journalism awards. Phones were ringing continuously, no doubt excited callers desperate to inform the reading public about the weekend visit of a distant relative, an outing to Digby, or the season's first sighting of a pussy willow, peeper, or purple finch.

Otley and Grime followed the rumble of the presses further into the eerily-empty edifice, eventually finding themselves deep in the bowels of the building. They cautiously approached the epicentre from which the now-deafening clamour emanated.

The enormous press room, normally a frenzy of activity with a crew of ink-stained pressmen attending the automatic staplers, collators and inkers of the massive press, was today occupied by one lone figure, standing with his back to the long corridor down which Grime and Otley now crept.

As they passed the doorway of the adjacent *Passages* Library, or, as it was known in Freeport, "Liberry", Grime glanced inside and was shocked to see not only Gurrey, but also Randy Moyers, his animal activist wife Christine, and the complete *Passages* staff tied to chairs and gagged with wads of wet newsprint.

Motioning for Otley to follow, Grime ducked into the press room.

Standing at the controls, Mout was focused on the rapidly increasing pile of hot-off-the-press newspapers coming off the conveyor belt.

Amid the deafening din, he was oblivious to the new arrivals until two ham-hock arms wrapped around him from behind and he found himself trapped in one of Owen Otley's patented bear hugs.

With Mout literally in the long arms of the law, Grime rushed to the library, quickly untying Gurrey and the other captives. He removed the gag from his friend's mouth.

Spitting out a few soggy scraps of last month's "Creatures of the Cove" column, Gurrey flashed one of his famous devil-may-care, 'danger-is-my-middle-name' grins and said, "Glad you could drop by, Grimey, old pal."

Otley appeared in the doorway, still holding Mout in a vice-like grip. Grime barely recognized the man. Mout's face was beet red, his hair in disarray, his eyes bulging with a fanatical fervour, the Windsor knot of his Louis Vuitton tie slightly askew.

"You fools," he shouted, the spittle from his lips showering Grime's shirtfront. "Let me go! You'll ruin everything!"

Grime, who could become completely lost trying to follow anything more complicated than the plot of a *Roadrunner* cartoon, turned to Gurrey and said, "What's he talking about? What does he mean?"

"He was trying to spread dissension," Gurrey said. "He even fired Owen, my right-hand man! I was so stunned that I couldn't speak for several minutes. I thought poor Owen was going to cry; in fact I'm sure I saw a tear fall, although it could have been the result of the onion, garlic and hot pepper sandwich he was eating."

"No, it was tears," Grime said. "He was still crying when he told me about it. He got his Montreal smoked meat sandwich all soggy."

"After he destroyed your reputation he was going to turn on me and do the same and then his radical new party would be in position for an upset victory."

"Ultimately, he was neither Constipated or Literal," intoned Randy Moyers, who had just been freed from his gag. "The strain of acting Constipated and then pretending to be Literal drove him mad. I've seen many such cases over the years. Mr. Mout tried to involve me in his sinister plot, but I worked for the CBC, dammit, and that means something to me. I have the CBC logo tattooed over my heart next to the Xed-out picture of the traitorous Rex Murphy. By the time I sat down for our editorial interview with Mout, his natural aversion to a free and balanced press started to kick in. By the end of the interview he was raving. At first he tried to dictate which questions would be asked; then, when I wouldn't comply, he refused to answer any at all. That's when he pulled a gun and tied us up. He dictated the editorials, he dictated the opinion pieces. That's when I suspected that he might be a dictator. He demanded that I help him. At first I refused, but then I saw an opportunity. So I dictated the quote about the penal institution, intentionally misspelling the word. I knew that Grime, wordsmith that he is, would smell a rat. Besides, we all know that Gurrey would never publicly say anything bad about his partner, even to win votes."

"Yes, that worked a treat," Grime said. "I ascertained immediately that only the direst of circumstances could compel you to express such derogatory and slanderous sentiments toward my personage."

Gurrey was glad to see that the thesaurus he had given Grime for Christmas was finally starting to have an effect.

"Well, you got here just in the nick of time, old friend, Mout stayed up all night writing an even more slanderous 'Election Day Special Edition' version of *Passages* about me. He had just about finished the press run;

another few minutes and every newsboy on every street corner from here to Little River would have been unknowingly spreading more lies."

"This seems like an unnecessarily complicated scheme," Grime said. "If it was in a book, no one would buy it."

"You mean the book or the lies?"

"The lies. They'd be fools not to buy the book. Did Mout really think it would work?"

"Of course it would have worked!" Mout said. He had calmed down enough to speak coherently. "I've worked my whole life as a fixer."

Oh, that's great," Grime said. "We've got lots that needs fixin' over at the guttin' shed/detective agency/campaign office."

"*Political* fixing. If a senator needs a do-nothing back-room government job for his lazy high school drop-out son-in-law, I can fix that. If a big political donor needs a little government contract money to get him through tough times, I can fix that too. I specialize in dirty tricks and under-the-table deals for whoever needs them. It's a dirty, ugly business and for the last little while I've been dreaming of creating a utopia where politics do not exist. When I arrived on these islands I thought this was my chance. I was going to ruin the election and amid the ensuing chaos, take over, maybe even separate us from the rest of the province. I could have done it! I could have had it all! I could have been King!"

Mout was slipping back into his former maniacal state. Otley picked him up, tucked him under his arm, and carried him down the hall.

As they watched the two figures recede to the sound of Mout screaming "No! No! Let me go! Dear Lord, please don't send me back to Ottawa!" Grime turned to Gurrey and said, "You know, I think I've just about had my fill of politics. What do you say to calling it quits?"

"I'd agree." Gurrey said, "but it's too late to pull out now. The election is tomorrow."

"What do we do, then?"

There was a thoughtful pause. Then, like Socrates, whom he had studied in junior high school, Grime answered his own well-aimed question. "We have to work our damnedest NOT to be elected. We have to get the third-party alternative, the Greenish Party, elected instead. I'll have to lie and cheat and make stupid, outrageous statements to show that I'm a complete buffoon. Gurrey, you can just behave as usual. If we play our cards right—that is to say, wrong—there's no way anyone will vote for either of us."

That very evening the two 'opponents' met at the Fire hall for an all-candidates debate. Approximately 50 people had shown up, mostly very elderly and wearing *Dief the Chief* or *I Like Mike* buttons. Retired newsman and local historian Johnny Thorborn was the moderator and questions were to come from the public as well as noted journalists from the Tri-Island area.

Representing the Greenish Party, currently a distant third in the polls, was Peg "Peggy" Thomtom-Farr, recently returned from a sojourn in the frozen north where she and her husband had made their fortune selling Frigidaires to Inuit.

Thomtom-Farr was a sultry beauty who had once been a heartthrob and pin-up girl for local Sea Scouts, Boy Scouts, the more mature members of the Cub Scout troop, and the Cornwallis Naval Base. After moving to the North, she had learned to hunt and fish and fix propane toilets, often at the same time.

After the introductions and other preliminaries had been taken care of each candidate was asked to sum up his or her platform in fifty words or less.

Peg Thomtom-Farr went first: "Having lived in the north, I've seen what can happen to our natural environment if we are not good stewards of the earth. I want to make sure that the Tri-Islands area develops in a sustainable and responsible way and that the jobs that are created are not at the expense of our beautiful islands and future generations."

"Thank you, Ms. Thomtom-Farr," the moderator said. "Jim Grime, you are next."

"Falderall and poppycock, Mr. Moderator! I'd like to point out that Ms. Thomtom-Farr just delivered a long-winded, 58-word speech, using all kinds of five dollar words! She's nothing but a come-from-away. My platform is simple, as am I. And speaking of platforms, I propose we move Balancing Rock to a more stable location before it tips over—downtown Digby, maybe, or Halifax. They will need something to replace that Cornwallis statue. And I wanna build a causeway to Meteghan. And turn Beautiful Cove into a fish farm for sculpin."

A high heel shoe flew by his head, followed by a rubber boot. If he had not ducked quickly, they would have hit him flat in the face.

"Er, thank you Mr. Grime," the moderator said. "Gurrey Ben, please give us your platform."

Gurrey straightened his toupee, adjusted his hearing aid, and spat his chaw of tobacco toward the pitcher of water, missing it by three feet. It landed on the moderator's Hush Puppies. He squinted at the assembly through his good eye and said, "I propose that we start our own Wharf Rat Rally. Why should Digby get all the tourists? Only we'll use real rats and train 'em up to ride little Harleys. Also, I'd allow recreational water skiing behind the Tiverton ferry." To his disappointment, there was little crowd reaction, save for a few nods of agreement. "Oh, and taxes, I'd raise taxes!"

The second high heel whizzed past his head, followed by the second rubber boot.

The debate raged on for hours as the three candidates fielded questions on everything from soup (two for, one against) to nuts (all three for). Gurrey and Grime did everything they could think of to disgust and alienate their political supporters. Gurrey came out in favour of longer waits at the ferry and Grime wanted whale watches banned from April to December.

There was a potentially-ugly scene when audience member Wilfred Prunetips asked each candidate how they would handle the always-contentious issue of Freeport-Westport relations. Grime was most eloquent on the subject until he remembered that he was supposed to sound stupid, so he added. "I've had relations with women on both sides of the Passage."

The two polidicks were pretty sure that the voting tide had turned against them, but just to be sure, Grime leaped to his feet again. "If one of us is elected, we've decided to amalgamate the two islands into one single jurisdiction and call it Longbrier Island."

Only the quick thinking of Owen Otley, who blocked the door after them, allowed Gurrey and Grime to escape the hall without being tarred and feathered.

[*Editor's note: For generations, tar and feathers have been available at all political meetings on the island. They have also been used at several Bingo games, two IOOF meetings, and at least one hymn sing.*]

The meeting broke up with the cheering crowd carrying Ms. Thomton-Farr out of the building on their shoulders. Gurrey and Grime gave each other a discreet "thumbs up".

The evening of election day, the two dicks were once again sitting with their feet up in the office/fish-gutting parlour chuckling over some vintage selections from their collection of old Mad magazines when the door opened and Owen Otley huffed and puffed his way in.

"The results are in and you guys did better than I expected. Between the two of you, you got almost four votes. Needless to say, Peggy Thomton-Farr is our new MLA."

Gurrey let out a long sigh of relief. "So things turned out okay after all. We got to experience a bit of the political life, and the Islands ended up with a good representative."

"You know," Grime said, "maybe that Mout feller weren't so crazy after all. Maybe getting rid of politics wouldn't be such a bad idea."

"Naw. Without politicians, who would we have to complain about and make fun of?"

"Good point, Gurrey, old chum. Good point, indeed."

Figure 9: A smooth crossing on the ferry

13: Gurrey and Grime's Last Case

Gurrey Ben and Jim Grime were once again sitting across from each other at the desk/gutting table that occupied the middle of their office/fish house. Grime was looking over some past-due bills while Gurrey had his head buried in the *Chronicle-Herald.*

"It's nothing short of amazing," he mumbled to no one in particular.

"What's that?" Grime said, not bothering to look up.

"Ever notice how people die in alphabetical order?"

"What are you talking about?" Grime said sharply, finally looking up from his chore.

"Right here: Abner, Andrews, Appleby, and so on. It boggles the mind."

Grime let out a deep sigh. "People don't die in alphabetical order. That's just the way they list the deaths. The real question is why hardly anyone dies on Sunday!"

Gurrey nodded. "That is strange. I've noticed that, too. Maybe God wants them to get one more chance before he pulls the plug."

Grime was impressed. "Not a bad theory, my flatulent friend. Not bad at all."

Settling back in his chair, Gurrey tossed the paper aside. "I guess it doesn't really matter. It all evens out, anyway."

"What do you mean?"

"According to the other notices in the paper, people are born in alphabetical order and get married in alphabetical order, so I guess it just makes sense that they die in alphabetical order, too."

"That's two good theories in a row, Gurrey. You're on a roll today! I wish we could put that agile brain of yours to work on a case or two."

The legend of Gurrey and Grime had spread far and wide, even to the United States of America, where the FBI was said to be "closely monitoring" their activities. And because of their expertise in solving fog-related crime, they had been called in to assist Scotland Yard with the Jack the Ripper cold case. After just three hours of investigation at a local London pub, they had determined that the so-called "murders" were just a series of unfortunate accidents. They were immediately driven to Heathrow and placed on the next flight home.

Despite the international fame, things had been slow lately at the offices of the Digby Neck & Islands Fish-Gutting Service & Detective Agency. Islanders and Neckers were taking them for granted. Familiarity breeds contempt and to them, they were just still just a couple of contemptible small town dicks. It seemed that there was very little need for their unique detecting skills these days. Even demand for their fish gutting services had fallen away to the point where it was hardly worth putting on the barvel.

They had tried to diversify the business by offering to split things other than fish, but except for old Mrs. Bailey dropping by with a coconut her grandson had brought back from his vacation in Jamaica, and a disastrous attempt by Grime to split the atom, the whole venture had been a bust.

Not that Gurrey and Grime needed the money, far from it. They were both quite comfortable financially, what with the nearly four hundred dollars a month they each pulled in from the C.P.P. No, it was more the intellectual stimulation and the physical challenge of a good criminal case that they were missing.

As Gurrey reflected on how much he missed the hustle-bustle of an active professional life, he leaned comfortably back in his chair, put his feet up on an overturned bucket, and closed his eyes. He was just about to drift off for his usual mid-morning nap, joining Grime, whose asthmatic snores had been vibrating the gutting knives for several minutes so they rattled intermittently where they rested together on the table beside the well-worn whetstone. He was teetering on the precipice of deep slumber when he was snatched back from the very edge by the sound of the draw-string latch on the shed door and a familiar footstep approaching across the creaking floor.

The clump, tap...clump, tap...clump, tap stopped in front of Gurrey's chair. Gurrey lazily opened one eye and confirmed what his brilliant detective's mind had already deduced.

Sure enough, standing before him was a familiar, barrel-chested figure with a peg-leg, a hook where his right hand should be, and a black eye-patch.

Ishmael (Awk) Welch was a long-time resident of Brier Island and the proprietor of Welch's Waterless Whale Watch. Welch had spent most of his early life at sea. His mother, Marion, was the first female captain in the Irving fleet, his father was the ship's cook and Awk had been conceived while their ship rode at anchor in the Bay of Fundy not far from the mouth of the Saint John River. Nine months later, in a magnificent feat of maternal multitasking, Marion gave birth in the wheelhouse of her tanker while simultaneously piloting the vessel through the eye of a hurricane forty miles off the coast of Venezuela.

Young Welch's mother was a great fan of the writer Herman Melville and, in a gesture that would later come to be seen as deeply ironic, named her son Ishmael after the wandering sailor in *Moby-Dick*. Ishmael was to spend practically his entire childhood aboard ship. In fact, he spent so much time at sea that he had difficulty getting his "land legs" during his occasional sojourns ashore, so he tended to stagger and stumble whenever he tried to walk on a surface that wasn't constantly rising and falling under him. This apparent clumsiness resulted in him being saddled with the nickname "Awk"; short for "Awkward".

By his mid-twenties, Awk Welch had been around the world several times. He'd sailed all seven of the seas and was a regular visitor to most of the great ports of the world, including Westport. The name his mother had given him seemed to have been prophetic indeed, but a singular event in Ishmael's life would soon change all that.

In early 1976, he was visiting relatives on Brier Island. After tossing and turning most of the night, unable to sleep without the sea beneath him, he crept from the house and bunked down in one of the waterfront sheds where the familiar and soothing sound of the ocean beneath the floorboards soon helped him nod off.

Suddenly, Welch was jolted awake by an eerily familiar sensation! For a few terrifying moments, he imagined he was back aboard ship, caught again in the August tsunami that had nearly shipwrecked him off the Zhongsha Islands in the South China Sea.

As he came fully awake he realized he wasn't in the China Sea at all. He was in the Bay of Fundy, and it wasn't August. It was the 2nd of February: Groundhog Day.

The first tidal wave of what would forever after be known as The Groundhog Day Storm had swept the fish house from its posts and was carrying it out into the harbour. Before Awk had a chance to gather his wits, the second wave thundered in, snatched up the old building, swept it along atop a towering, white-crested roller, and dashed it against the shore with a fury and a power that reduced it and everything in it to rubble. As the foamy tentacles slowly withdrew, they left behind a chaotic heap of splintered timbers, tangled fishing gear, crushed lobster traps, and the shattered and mangled body of Awk Welch.

The third and final wave would have surely pulled Awk's barely-breathing carcass to a deep and watery grave if not for the actions of two brave, handsome, and noble young future detectives, who dashed fearlessly into the seething maelstrom and, with no thought for their own safety—in fact, with pretty much no thought at all—wrested Awk's bruised and battered body from Poseidon's stubborn grasp.

Struggling valiantly against the elements, the two heroes fought their way back to shore, where they soon fetched up against the breastwork. Their strength sapped by the continuous pounding of the waves and the unrelenting cold, they found themselves too exhausted to climb the sheer wooden wall to safety, let alone pull Awk's unconscious and water-sodden body up with them.

Gurrey realized he was rapidly losing all feeling in his limbs; he could barely keep his head above water. Glancing over at his partner, he saw that Grime, the weaker and slightly less handsome of the two, had already given up and was starting to float away, resigned to his fate.

Even Gurrey, despite his impressive strength and legendary stamina, was starting to slip helplessly beneath the battering waves when suddenly a powerful and sinewy arm extended deep down into the surf and grabbed him by the collar.

Within seconds, all three men found themselves yanked over the breastwork like squid over a washboard. Lying in the grass coughing up salt water, the two limp dicks looked up and saw a slim but muscular, spandex-clad form standing over them.

As he wiped the seawater from his eyes, Gurrey realized that they had been saved from certain death by none other than Islands Consolidated School's star athlete and physical fitness fanatic, Owen Otley.

Awk's recovery was a slow and painful one. The loss of a lower limb resulted in the peg-leg he now sported, and a hopelessly crushed hand was replaced with a hook. The eye-patch had nothing to do with the storm. Both of Awk's eyes worked perfectly fine; he just thought it looked dashing and mysterious. He sometimes wore the patch over one eye and sometimes over the other, occasionally shocking strangers by switching sides in mid-conversation.

As bad as the physical damage was, it was the psychological toll that really affected Awk's life. Feeling betrayed in a very personal way by the vicious and unrelenting power of the ocean, Awk could not bring himself to return to a life on the sea. Even baths became traumatizing events. In fact, he was now so afraid and distrustful of the water that he could not even cross the harbour. As a result he had not been off the island in almost forty years.

Faced with the need to earn a living on dry land and on a relatively remote island, Awk had tried several different enterprises. The tap-dance studio had been a bit of a flop; the only real customer he had been able to attract was Grime, who with his background in ballet was a quick learner and an avid student, but due to his parsimonious ways was unwilling to pay enough for the lessons to make the project worthwhile. Next Awk tried a stenography service, typing up people's important papers and such. But, although he could type like blazes with his good hand on the left side of the keyboard, he could not develop any speed typing with his hook on the right side. Besides, the hook did so much damage to the keys that he spent most of what little money he did make on repairs.

Next, Awk opened a massage parlour. Unfortunately his customers left feeling totally relaxed and stress-free on one side but suffering from severe lacerations on the other. Finally, he hit upon an idea for a business that would prove profitable enough to provide him a modest income.

As he watched various whale watching businesses on the island develop and grow, Awk realized that there must be people out there who would like to see a whale but found themselves, like him, unable to venture out to sea. He commissioned the island's mechanical genius, Rick E. Gram, to build him a stretch ATV capable of carrying up to six passengers and started up Welch's Waterless Whale Watch or WWWW. (Note: Not to be confused with the Weight Watchers Waterless Whale Watch, or WWWWW, which would later shamelessly attempt to capture the slightly overweight aqua-phobic demographic.)

Awk was going after a very specific clientele, those who could summon up the courage to cross two ferries to get to the island but were not quite brave enough to venture out on the open ocean. The emphasis in this whale watching enterprise was more on the watching than on the whales; Awk would drive his customers to Northern Point or Seal Cove or other select look-offs around the island where they would spend hours peering out at the ocean from the safety of dry land in hopes of spotting a cetacean.

Along with a lot of misdirected excitement over distant wave crests and far-off seagull sightings, there was the occasional glimpse of an actual whale. Enough of his customers were satisfied with this that the business gradually built up a bit of a reputation among the aquatically averse and Awk was able to scratch out a meagre living.

This was the man who now stood in the office/gutting parlour of The Digby Neck & Islands Fishgutting Service & Detective Agency.

"Hey Awk, what's up?" Gurrey said.

"Call me Ishmael!" Welch responded: he had never liked the nickname as a child, and liked it even less now that his injuries had made it all the more appropriate.

"Of course; how can we help you, Ish?"

Welch balanced himself precariously on his peg-leg, scratched his stubbled cheek with the point of his hook and squinted at Gurrey with his one uncovered eye,

"Well shiver me timbers, matey, 'tis yer assistance I be seekin'. Some scurvy bilge rats be tryin' to scuttle me business; may the Devil take their landlubbin' souls, sez I. Yarrr!"

At this point Welch paused and gave his head a shake; then he continued, "Sorry guys, I've gotten into the habit of talking like that lately. The tourists seem to expect it of me for some reason."

By this time, Grime had roused himself from his stupor enough to contribute to the conversation. "No need to get your knickers in a knot, Ish. Just tell us in plain words what the problem is and we'll see what we can do about it."

After mulling this over for a moment, Welch said, "I think it will be easier if you see the problem for yourselves. C'mon."

Striding out the door with the two quizzical gumshoes trailing behind, Welch threw his peg-leg over the seat of his ATV. He quickly retrieved the leg, reattached it, and took up his position behind the handlebars. Gesturing to the seat behind him he announced, "You got the Captain's permission to come aboard, maties."

Gurrey and Grime eyed Welch's "vessel". Jutting out beneath the headlight at the "bow" was a hand-carved figurehead of a buxom mermaid and below that the name *H.M.S. Pequod* was painted on the front fender. Gurrey at first took the flag fluttering at the top of the "mast" rising from the stern of the bike to be a Jolly Roger, but upon closer inspection saw that the skull and crossbones had been replaced with the face of a smiling whale.

"Time to cast off!" Welch said impatiently, revving the engine.

A short time later the three "sailors" were bouncing along a rough trail, approaching the back shore of the island through a thicket of spindly alders and wind-blasted, salt-stunted spruce trees. As they drew closer to the shore, Gurrey and Grime both became aware that above the noise of the ATV engine they could hear a high-pitched screeching sound, a sound that was somehow vaguely familiar but at the same time unlike anything they had ever heard before.

As they progressed along the trail this curious noise got louder and louder. Finally, they burst out into a clearing atop a small hill where Welch brought his "ship" to an abrupt halt.

146

As the now-deafening cacophony swept over them, the two dicks sat stunned, slack-jawed and uncomprehending. This was not an unfamiliar position for them to be in, but this time it was caused by the incredible scene laid out before them. Just off-shore, a couple of hundred feet past the red and white wild rose bushes marking the division between the wind-swept field and the rocky beach, floated a line of cages. These cages followed the coastline far into the distance and reached high into the air.

This was where the sound was coming from and both Gurrey and Grime realized simultaneously why the racket was vaguely familiar. The cages were filled with seagulls, hundreds of thousands of screaming seagulls.

Waving his hook to indicate the wall of cages, Welch shouted over the din, "I guess my problem is pretty obvious! I can't subject my customers to this racket, and even if I did, the cages are so high they block the view."

"Where did all this come from?" Gurrey asked in amazement.

"Just showed up overnight. According to Hare Airquaculture, the company that runs this mess, they have provincial permission to operate an open-pen gull farm on what the government claims is an unused piece of coastline."

As they watched, a stubby, ungainly-looking craft that any self-respecting mariner would be hard-pressed to call a boat detached itself from the cages and slowly and awkwardly made its way toward the shore. At the wheel they could make out what appeared to be a giant vanilla ice-cream cone.

As the shipwreck-waiting-to-happen drew closer, they could see that the pilot was not an ice-cream cone at all, but was in fact a squat figure clad in tan oilskins and a large sou'wester. The sou'wester, normally black, was completely white with a several-inch-thick layer of seagull droppings, which flowed down onto the shoulders and made numerous dribbling trails down the front and back of the oilskins.

Grime, despite turning both hearing-aids up to maximum, was having trouble hearing over all the noise. He thought he heard Welch tell Gurrey that the figure on the boat was the owner of this offence against nature, Glen A. Hare.

As the clumsy craft nosed its way to shore, Gurrey started down the beach to see what he could find out. Grime, from his seat on the back of the Pequod, observed the massive operation and its effect on the environment. He noticed that as the captive gulls flew back and forth in the cages, they shed a constant cloud of feathers which drifted away in the on-shore breeze, creating a black-and-white coating on the water, the beach and the lower part of the field. Even the blossoms on the famous Brier Island wild rose bushes were hidden beneath this film of feathers.

As well, he could see that a greasy slick of uneaten feed pellets, seagull droppings and extraneous pesticide spray had spread out from the pens and drifted down along the shore, coating the rocks and sea-weed with a foul-smelling slippery scum. From his vantage point he could see down the coast as far as Seal Cove, where seals, ducks, herons, and a few free-range seagulls could usually be found. Today the cove was ominously empty.

As Grime swept his gaze over the coastline, he found he kept involuntarily returning to and fixing on the oil-skin-clad figure that Gurrey now appeared to be in conversation with. Gradually he realized that there was something about this person that he was finding attractive and, in fact, was causing a stirring in his lower regions that he hadn't felt in many a decade.

Although Grime had long considered himself a chick magnet, the truth of the matter was that the magnetism, if there had ever been any, had long since dissipated. Although he tried hard to resist the possibility, it now entered his mind that maybe the reason for his lack of success with women of the female persuasion was that all this time he had been attempting to practice what he considered to be his seductive powers on the wrong sex.

Looking back, he realized with a start that there had been many occasions when he had thrown an admiring glance in Gurrey's direction as his partner stretched his slim but athletic body across the keeler while reaching for another codfish. But, he told himself, that had been more in appreciation of the skilful and artistic way his partner handled the gutting knife than any physical attraction...or was it? Gurrey had certainly looked alluring when he dressed up in his yellow polypropylene wig and bait-bag breasts during a recent case. But when he continued to wear the outfit for the next three weeks and insisted on being called Misty, the attraction had turned to revulsion.

As Grime mulled over this confusing situation, he suddenly became aware that he had been staring steadily at the gull-guano covered figure for an uncomfortably long time, and most alarmingly, his gaze was being returned! Reluctantly accepting that there could be a definite mutual connection going on here, Grime began to consider the possibility that he had been living the first sixty-some years of his life under the mistaken illusion that he liked girls.

By this time Gurrey was making his way back up the beach. "Well, that was a waste of time!" he stated. "I couldn't get any information at all on what they are doing here."

"That's too bad," Grime said. "Er, by the way, did he say anything about me?"

"Did *who* say anything about you?"

"Why, him, of course, Glen A. Hare, did he mention me at all?"

"Oh. Well, yes, as a matter of fact, the subject of 'that cute hunk on the ATV' did come up during our brief conversation."

Grime felt a warm flush rise up his neck, turn his face a crimson red, wash over his bald head and disappear down his back. He was overcome with simultaneous feelings of flattery and a fast-accelerating emotional confusion about his own sexual identity.

Gurrey watched as Grime's face registered his less-than-successful attempt to adjust to the new reality he had unexpectedly learned about himself, then added, "And just so you know, the name is not Glen, its Glenna, Glenna Hare."

Grime's face now briefly registered total confusion, which was its normal state, then a large expression of relief, then maybe a small flash of regret with a hint of disappointment, and finally back to relief again. "So that's a woman down there?" he asked with barely contained glee as his life slipped back into its comfortable, familiar, if excruciatingly boring, groove.

"Yes, as far as I can tell, that's a woman. Why? What does it matter?"

"Oh, it's nothing, no big deal. I just misheard the name, is all."

"Okayyy! Well, I'm glad we got that all cleared up!" Gurrey said dubiously. "Now, what are we going to do about this monstrosity and how do we help Ish get his business back?"

"Well," Grime said, "I think we need to know more about this company. Why are they raising seagulls? How do they make money from this? What kind of a business are they really running here? To find this out, we need to get a man on the inside, and I know just the man."

Forty-eight hours later, the two partners were sitting around their office/gutting emporium feeling good about accomplishing the first part of their plan. It hadn't been all that hard to get Owen Otley, their 5'4", 365 pound apprentice detective, a position with Hare Airquaculture. Not surprisingly, Hare's wasn't exactly inundated with people looking for a job where they would constantly get crapped on. The people who want a job like that usually go into politics, as it pays better and although there is just as much squawking, at least occasionally some of it makes sense.

Grime was just commenting to Gurrey about how cleverly their undercover man had infiltrated the Hare enterprise and speculating on how much valuable information he might gain, when the door swung open and in sloshed a water-sodden and dejected-looking Otley.

"Owen," Gurrey and Grime exclaimed simultaneously. "What happened to you? Why aren't you at work?"

"I got fired," Owen said morosely. "They put me to work on the feed scow and I forgot to allow for my own weight when I filled it up with feed pellets. It overfilled and sank right beside the cages."

"Great," Grime said. "There goes our best chance to find out what that company's up to."

"Maybe not," Otley said. "I was thinking; maybe it's time we finally moved into the twentieth century. Undercover work is fun and all, but ten minutes at a computer keyboard will get you more information than ten days of hanging over that old scow's washboard would ever get you. All we need to do is hack into their computer system!"

"Great idea," Grime said dryly, "except I've got no use for computers and all I ever see you two do with yours is play Solitaire. Waste of money as far as I can see, would'a been a whole lot cheaper to just buy a deck of cards! 'Course, then you'd have to move your whole arm to play, instead of just clicking one little finger. Face it: we don't have the skills to hack into anything."

"No, *we* don't," Otley nodded. "But I know someone who does." And with that he heaved himself up from his chair and trudged out the door.

He was back in a flash (actually it was nearly forty-five minutes; but for Owen that was considered lightning speed), and was dragging with him a pouty-looking eleven-year-old girl.

"Who's this child?" Grime sputtered. "And why isn't she in school?"

"This is Pearline, and she's been suspended from school because she signed her teacher up on sixteen different internet dating sites."

"Okay, so she knows how to use a computer. That doesn't mean she has the ability to do what we need done."

"She paid the registration fees by hacking into sixteen other teachers' bank accounts."

"So maybe she *does* know what she's doing, but can we trust her? What did you say her name was?"

"Pearline, but everybody calls her Pearl. You know her family, she's a Bailey. Her grandfather was a policeman back in the old days when the town constable was called the beadle."

150

"Ah yes, Beadle Bailey, the name does sound familiar. I believe he also spent some time in the Army, didn't he?"

"That's right! And you must know her father George. He used to have that barber shop you liked, Bailey's Shavings and Foam."

"I loved going to that place! Things were so much better back when the Island had services like that. Oh, it was a wonderful life."

"As I recall," Gurrey said, "we went to her parents' wedding! Isn't her mother a Barnum from Little River?"

"That's right," Grime said. "The Barnum and Bailey wedding was a crazy time! They got married in a big tent! What a circus that was!"

"And of course you remember her Uncle Bill, the adventurer who left these islands to travel the world."

"Yes, that was big news. They begged and pleaded for him to return, but Bill Bailey never would come home."

At this point Grime paused to give his chin a severe rubbing, an indication that he was as deep in thought as he was able to go, which was barely below the surface. "So!" he finally said, "The name is Pearl Bailey, is it? I like that. It sounds kind of musical. Okay, put her to work, boys."

"Here you go, Pearl," Gurrey said. "You can get started on my laptop."

"Hold it right there!" Grime roared. "Gurrey! I'm surprised at you! There will be none of those shenanigans here! I won't have the good name of The Digby Neck & Islands Fish-Gutting Service & Detective Agency besmirched in this way."

"Grimey, you Luddite, I'm not talking about my lap top, I'm talking about my *laptop*, a portable computer."

"Oh, I see. Never mind, then. Carry on."

Casting an uncomfortable look over his shoulder, Owen ushered Pearl away from the two dicks, saying quietly, "Maybe you should sit way over here in the corner and use my computer."

Early the next morning Gurrey made his way down the stairs to put on the morning coffee. As he was standing in front of the stove in his bedroom rubber boots and his S.T.D.s (Stanfield's Trap Doors), he noticed a dull glow emanating from the corner of the detective office/gutting parlour. Approaching cautiously, he realized that the glow was from Owen's computer screen and that it was partially blocked by Pearl, who was fast asleep face-down on the keyboard.

Gurrey shook her gently, and when she raised her bleary eyes to meet his, Gurrey noticed she had several rows of little squares indented into her cheek. He thought he could make out the letters YTREWQ imprinted backwards just below her right eye.

"Were you here all night?"

"I sure was," Pearl replied excitedly. "And you'll never believe what I found out!"

"Tell me."

"Well, it was kind of confusing at first, but after a lot of digging around, I found out that Hare Airquaculture is just a tiny part of a much bigger company that supplies fresh and frozen food all over the world. After hunting around on the internet for most of the night, I came across something. I think we might be able to use it to get rid of the seagull farm."

"It would be great if we could get shut of that eye-sore on the seashore. What is this info? Do you really think it is powerful enough to force them to remove their operation?"

"I think it can."

"Don't keep me in suspense," Gurrey said. "What is this devastating secret that you have discovered?"

"Chicken Fingers©," Pearl said.

"Chicken fingers?" Gurrey felt deflated. "What does that mean? How are we going to bring down a multinational corporation with chicken fingers?"

"I discovered that they own the copyright to the words Chicken Fingers©."

"Mmmmm, chicken fingers!" Grime had just walked in on the last few words of the conversation. "I love chicken fingers! I must have eaten thousands of them over the years. They're my favourite meal. I wish I had some right now."

"You might want to rethink that," Pearl said. "You know how the Quarter Pounder© hamburger doesn't have to actually weigh a quarter of a pound because Quarter Pounder© is just the copyrighted name of the burger, not an actual description of it? The same thing applies to the copyrighted product name Chicken Fingers©."

"What are you getting at?" Grime said.

"When I saw that they had copyrighted the name Chicken Fingers© I looked deeper and found they had a production plant that was churning out hundreds of thousands of Chicken Fingers©, but nowhere could I find any mention of them owning any chicken farms or having any other source of chicken. I finally connected a lot of dots and found they have an 'interesting' source of raw materials. Chicken Fingers© are not only not made of fingers, they are not even made of chicken!"

Grime's stomach was starting to rebel at this unsettling news. With the memory of all those Chicken Fingers© he'd eaten over the years swirling in his memory, and despite a sinking feeling that he probably didn't want to know the answer to the question he was about to ask, he asked it anyway. "If they're not made of chicken, what *are* they made of?"

"I think the answer is obvious," Gurrey said. "It's floating a couple of hundred feet off our shore. The question we should be asking is, what can we do about it?"

By now Grime's stomach was staging a full-fledged rebellion and his face was a continually revolving palette of white, grey, green, blue, yellow and even a bit of orange. Suddenly he made a dash for the door leading out to the wharf.

To the accompaniment of some rather disturbing gagging and retching sounds, Pearl said to Gurrey, "I had an idea. I put all the information into a single document. All I have to do is push this button and every food quality agency, every animal cruelty society, every health standards organization, every food buyer and food reviewer with an Internet connection will receive all the evidence they need to understand that Chicken Fingers© are in fact made from seagulls."

"Give me a half hour before you push that button!" An ashen-faced Grime had staggered back inside.

Without stopping, he left through the front door, jumped into the Dickmobile, and after a bit of engine cranking and gas pedal pumping, roared off in the direction of the seagull farm.

Upon arrival, Grime was happy to see that the clumsy-looking farm boat was approaching the beach. As he walked across the rocks to meet it, his heart was doing flip-flops. His initial attraction to Glenna, the owner of this massive floating seagull farm, had only grown stronger over the past twenty-four hours. He hadn't yet acted on his feelings, and what he was about to do might forever remove any possibility that he would ever get the opportunity.

As Glenna alit from the boat, Grime launched into a confused and convoluted explanation of the farm's effect on Welch's whale watching business, his involvement in trying to help Welch by investigating the seagull business, what they had found out, what they intended to do about it, and why he felt it was only fair to warn her about what was going to happen. Jumbled in with all this, he managed to express to Glenna his feelings for her and the hope that these revelations would not ruin any chance for them to develop a relationship.

He eventually ran out of words and gradually sputtered to a stop, staring uncomfortably at Glenna, seeking desperately for some positive sign.

Without a word, she turned, climbed aboard her boat, and headed full-throttle back to the pens. Grime stood dejectedly amid the seaweed-covered boulders for a few minutes; then hopelessly started making his way up the beach.

Suddenly, a massive increase in the constant squawking of the gulls made him stop and turn.

Glenna was running from cage to cage, flinging open the doors and releasing thousands of birds. As he watched in amazement, she opened the last door, then tore off her guano-encrusted oilskins and threw them into the cage.

This done, she roared the boat back to shore, ran up the beach and to his utter astonishment, gave Grime a kiss so passionate that it almost short-circuited his pace-maker.

As Grime and Glenna strolled up the beach hand-in-hand, the soaring of his feeble heart was matched only by the soaring of the thousands of seagulls overhead. Enjoying their new-found freedom, they swept like a black-and-white cloud into the sky, dipping and wheeling with joy over the harbour. Then, turning as one, they swooped down and settled on every roof in the village; where they would sit, screeching and pooping, for months to come.

Two weeks later, Gurrey and Grime were sitting in their fish-gutting emporium/office, still trying to wrap their heads around the events that had taken place since Pearl had pushed that fateful button. Basically, they had achieved their objective. Once the details of the fraudulent chicken finger business went out, the conglomerate collapsed, the now-empty gull cages mysteriously disappeared overnight and Ishmael Welch was happy to be back at his land-based whale watching business.

But there had been unforeseen consequences, consequences that now appeared to be putting an end to the long and semi-successful history of The Digby Neck & Islands Fish-Gutting Service & Detective Agency.

It turned out that Glenna had been contracted to the now-defunct multinational corporation and had been under the impression that the seagulls she was raising were being used to replenish flocks around the world that had died off because of changes in food supply due to global warming. As soon as Grime informed her that her beloved birds were in fact being made into fraudulent food, she severed all ties with the company.

But now, unemployed, Glenna was returning to her home on the other side of the Bay to manage a blue jay sanctuary on Campobello Island. And Grime, finally having solid proof after all these years of proclaiming himself a "chick magnet", was going with her.

"I can't believe this is happening," Gurrey intoned morosely. "Don't get me wrong; I'm glad you finally found someone who can put up with you. But your leaving is going to have a huge effect on the whole Tri-Island area and all the people you've helped over the years."

"It's flattering of you to say so, but you exaggerate," Grime said. "I'll just slip out of here later today and no one will even notice I'm gone."

Gurrey glanced out the window, and a slight smile came across his face. "I wouldn't be too sure of that."

The words were no sooner out of his mouth than the door burst open and Owen Otley barged into the room. Once he had stepped aside, they could see that he was followed by a whole horde of people.

One of the first was a teary Rikilini Robichini. "We're really going to miss you. I wish you the best of luck, but if things don't work out, remember that there are certain people here who will always be happy to welcome you back."

Next in line was Dot Owdows, carrying a big box of Grimes's favourite dulse donuts. "Here's a little something to tide you over on your trip."

Then Ishmael Welch pushed his way to the fore. "Arr, matey, 'tis missing ye I'll be. C'mere, let's feel the bones of ye!" He followed this up with a ferocious hug and almost punctured Grime's clavicle with his hook in the process.

The well-wishers kept on coming. There was Pearl Bailey of course, and Grime's distant cousin several-times removed, Pearly Prime. Rubella Perry-Outhouse-Thurber-Cann, who had recently been released on parole, made an appearance to pay her respects. Even Grime's one-time arch-enemy, P. Jack, showed up to say a heart-felt farewell.

As Grime was reminiscing with Lucy the Floozy, he noticed Gurrey over in a corner deep in conversation with a familiar figure in an expensive suit and crocodile shoes.

After seeing the last of his well-wishers off, an emotional Grime turned to Gurrey and admitted that he hadn't considered what effect his leaving would have on others. "Especially on you," he said. "What are you going to do when I'm gone?"

"Don't worry about me," Gurrey said. "You might have noticed me talking with that guy from Ottawa, Kickk Mout. He was here to offer me a job. They need someone to look into the goings-on on Parliament Hill. He said they were looking for someone who could make a good display of investigating, but would have very little chance of actually finding anything out."

Gurrey stuck out his chest with a hint of pride. "I'm going to Ottawa! Mout said he thought I was perfect for the job."

And so ends the saga of Gurrey and Grime.

Well...not quite.

Owen and Pearl teamed up and created Digby Neck & Islands Computer Services. They got the contract to provide security services to the new tidal power operations flocking to take advantage of the strong currents around the islands and eventually built DN&ICS into a major player in the cyber security field.

Grime and Glenna became famous for their innovative work with blue jays, wrote several best-selling books on the subject and travelled the world giving lectures.

And Gurrey, in his own bumbling way, found out a few embarrassing secrets on Parliament Hill that inadvertently brought down the whole government and effected earth-shattering changes to the democracy of Canada.

But maybe that's a story best left for another day.

14: The Dicks Rise Again

Three years had passed since old friends Ben Gurrey and Jim Grime fought crime and gutted fish side by side at the Digby Neck and Islands Fish-Gutting Service and Detective Agency on Brier Island. They had recently returned from their separate off-island adventures and had both, coincidentally, chosen the Flat Ass Calm Home for Seniors, in Tiddville on Digby Neck, to retire to.

The two old pals and business partners were having breakfast and catching up in the Sit Down and Clam Up seafood restaurant that was one of the few perks at the modest retirement home.

"So what happened, Grimey? Last I heard you were shacked up with that chick Glenna, runnin' a bird sanctuary and had a big career writin' books about chickadees or somethin'."

"Blue jays, Gurrey! I wrote several books about blue jays. Thing is, it turned out I'm not a big fan of blue jays. Glenna was the expert; that woman was obsessed! I just wrote down what she told me. When I refused to write any more we had a big fight and things kind of fell apart between us. How about you? According to the papers you caused a lot of trouble in Ottawa, people resigning in disgrace, elections overturned, big financial scandals! What did you do up there?"

"Sorry. I can't talk about any of that or return to within fifty miles of the Federal Buildings on pain of what they call 'permanent incarceration.' Too bad things didn't work out with the bird lady. Must have been nice while it lasted."

"I've got to admit, after all those years of us living alone together, it didn't take me long to get used to the benefits of having a woman around. In fact, I'd really like to find some female companionship here, so I've decided to go off-island and online."

"What's wrong with the single women around here? Lots of good lookin' widows and divorcees."

"Too many hyphens, if you get my drift."

"I do not."

"They've all been married so many times. Can't fit their names on a wedding invitation." He hesitated. "Plus…if you wanna know the truth, I don't like to think of them making comparisons."

"Comparisons?"

"In the boudoir. Hard to make things interesting when a woman's been married to every Tom, Dick, and Harry in town."

"You mean the Patterson triplets, Tom, Dick and Harry?"

"Who else? Those boys get around. That's why I went online to find a new wife. I joined up with one of them dating agencies, called Single Yet Again. Had to fill in a questionnaire with all kinds of fool questions that's supposed to get rid of what they call undesirables."

"How's it going?"

"Not so good so far. One little spelling mistake and I was thrown outta the group without even a howdy-do."

"What was it?"

"Oh, they ask about your education and your personality and your looks and age and stuff. It's pretty thorough. Where I ran into trouble was with the personality part."

"You? Personality? But that's your thing. You've got personality, charm and sophistication up the old wazoo."

"I know! I was shocked, too, until I found out about the typo. I was talking about my modesty, how I was the most modest person on both islands and parts of Digby Neck. As you know, Gurrey, I'm famous for it."

"No question."

"Well I said I had a great self-deprecating sense of humour."

"What's wrong with that?"

"Apparently I spelled it self-defecating."

"Oh," Gurrey said. "If I had a dime for every time a little mistake like that messed up my love life, I'd have a quarter. One time I got home and the wife says, 'Where've you been?' Right suspicious like. Very jealous woman. Anyways, I says I've been down to Lavena's havin' a quickie. Well, you'da thought I'd spent the Family Allowance check on wacky tobaccy the way she went on. 'Quickie,' she says. 'You've been having a quickie at Lavena's?'

"'Yes,' I says, 'and I enjoyed every bit of it, and if there'd a bin time I woulda had two quickies,' and I walked out the door. When I come back two hours later she'd packed up and left. Never saw her again."

"Well, Gurrey, I can't really blame her. I mean…cheating on your wife just ain't right."

"There's what you call the irony, Grimey. Turns out I was pronouncing it wrong. Looked like quickie on the menu but turned out it's pronounced *keesh*."

"Easy mistake to make, my friend. Anyways, I joined another agency called Last Hope Discount Dating Service and I just heard back from them… got the letter right here in my back pocket. I gotta admit, I'm nervous to open it. Do me a favour and open it for me would ya, Gurrey, old pal?"

Gurrey grabbed the filleting knife he'd been using to butter his biscuit and expertly opened the envelope.

Dear Mr. Grime,

Based on the information that you have provided, we have found one potential match for you. She enjoys fishing and hunting. She likes being pampered and is old fashioned enough to let the man be the breadwinner. She's a big believer in life insurance, since three of her last four husbands died within a year of the marriage. The fourth has disappeared without a trace and the insurance company is still searching for the body.

"Sounds like a nice lady."

"Sure does, but I don't know if I want to get married again. Too much paperwork. Maybe I'll just play the field."

"I know what you mean. I was down to the Legion last Saturday night at a dance. Remember years ago when it was Lloyd's Hall? Lloyd used to tape music off WMEX and play it over the speakers. Sometimes you'd even hear a little bit of Larry Justice or Woo Woo Ginsberg introducing the record. Anyways, the dance was just finishing up and they were playing I Wanna Walk You Home, which, of course, is the signal to make your move and ask someone if they want to go parkin'."

"I wouldn't know. That's when I generally went out on the step to have a smoke and a good cry."

"Uh-huh. Anyways, I overheard Esrum Morehouse ask Janice Young if she wanted to go watch the submarine races up at Beautiful Cove. That sounded pretty good to me, so I got in my car and was pulling out of the parking lot and that pretty little Heather Mortell from Newfoundland sidles up to the car. You know the Mortell family, they come every summer and stay over at the Westcott place. Anyways, she asks what I'm doing and I say I'm going up to the Cove to watch the submarine races. She smiles and says, 'All by yourself?' and I says, 'Yeah, I like to watch sports by myself. I find I can concentrate better.'

"'Oh,' she says. 'II see'. Quite disappointed, she was. I'd really like to take her out some night but there's nothing to do around here, as you know, except going parking but there never seems to be an opening to ask her. Anyways, I drive up to Beautiful Cove and park at the bottom of Lover's Lane. Best view you can imagine. Full moon hanging over the water. No one else around, but I can just make out Esrum's Ford Falcon parked off to the side in a thicket of alder bushes. I don't know how him and Janice could see anything at all from there. Anyways, I sat there waiting for them races to start. I musta waited two hours or more. I was going to ask Esrum what happened but his windows was so durn fogged up I couldn't get his attention. Finally I just give up and went home."

"That's too bad," Grime said. "I heard tell from a feller that there was lots of action up the Neck at this here retirement home, so I moved right in. Feller told me people were comin' and goin' in big, black, limos all hours of the day and night. The bugger didn't tell me they were hearses! He said there was all kinds of seductive sirens only a phone call away. Turned out they was ambulance sirens. Why'd you come here, Gurrey?

"Are you kidding me? Who doesn't dream of retiring to Tiddville?"

While the two old pals were reminiscing, Gurrey's breakfast of fish cakes and baked beans had arrived. "Remember them good old days?" he said between bites. "Back when we gutted criminals and fought fish?"

Gurrey had once again forgotten to take his large regimen of pills but his kind-hearted, sharp-as-a-tack friend quickly came to his rescue. "You have it backward, old comrade," he said kindly, his silver hair glistening above his handsome, still-youthful face.

"Ah, yes, that was it," Gurrey mumbled as a flurry of half-chewed beans flew from his lips.

"You must remember to take your memory pills," Grime said. "And don't mix them up with the Viagra again. I never saw old Mrs. Cossabang so upset. And right in the middle of the Tuesday night hymn sing, too. 'Rock of Ages' took on a whole different meaning."

"Yes, Grimey," his friend replied, using his plastic fork to scratch his left ear.

Just then one of the home's senior employees, Florence Gidley, approached them carrying a cell phone. "It's David Hooter, councillor for Digby Neck and the Islands," she said, obviously impressed. "Oh my, we've never received a call from anyone of that stature before."

Her hand was shaking as she passed the phone to Grime, who accepted it with the kind of casual nonchalance that had made him a heartthrob among the hip, "haven't yet broken a hip" set.

"Yes, David, how are you?"

Gurrey was making loud noises as he scraped up the last of his beans and Grime motioned for him to be quiet.

"Well of course, Dave. If you think we can be of any assistance, we'd be happy to help."

Gurrey looked at him with a puzzled expression.

"Yes, yes, tomorrow will work. We'll be on the 10:00 crossing. See you on the wharf...What's that? Low key? Yes, of course, we'll be discreet. Undercover work was always our, what you call, fort. No one will even know we're back."

He pushed a button on the phone and handed it back to Florence, who was fanning herself with a ketchup-stained menu.

"Oh, I don't know how you do it, Mr. Grime. Talking to the power elite just like it's the feller at the gas station."

"He puts on his polyester plaid bell bottoms one leg at a time, just like the rest of us," Grime said, noting the admiring blush that spread across the woman's face as she glanced discreetly at his fashion choice *du jour*. "Excuse us, Flo, but Gurrey and I have business to discuss."

When she had left, Grime leaned across the table and spoke in a low voice. "Gurrey, this is our chance for a comeback. The councillor needs us. Brier Island is practically under siege by criminal elements. Even Long Island, which as you know is usually more prone to white-collar crime, has seen an upturn in thuggery. How would you like to resurrect the old DN&IFGS&DA?"

"Would I! But what about a car? We'd need a fast car. I'm not sure that the old Plymouth Fury 11 can be fixed. Engine's blown and it's more rust than car now."

"Have faith, my friend. Plymouth made fine automobiles in 1969. Built to last. I'll call Eddie Todd over at the junkyard. If anyone can bore her out and get 'er back in top shape it's Eddie! We'll bill it to the council."

"Great," Gurrey said. "I can be the wheelman again!"

~

The next morning at 8:00 sharp, Fast Eddie Todd met Gurrey and Grime in the Flat Ass Calm Retirement Home and proudly handed over the flathead screwdriver that doubled as the ignition key for the Digby Neck and Islands Fish-Gutting Service and Detective Agency company car. "Anything we need to know about her, Eddie?" Gurrey said.

Fast Eddie looked insulted. "You just got yourself a fine reconditioned automobile," he said."Practically like new."

The puke-green '69 Fury 11 had undergone a miraculous overnight transformation under the skilful hands of Fast Eddie. Where once the left tail fin was completely rusted off, there was now a brand new one, red in colour, from a 1972 Fury 111.

In actual fact, Fast Eddie had spent most of the night souping up the car's engine and had neglected many of its more superficial flaws. The tires were bald, the windshield had a diagonal crack that ran from the top of the driver's side to the bottom of the passenger's side. The back windows wouldn't go down, the front windows wouldn't go up, and the heater was stuck on high. The push-button radio worked but changed stations at random times. The gas tank couldn't be filled past the halfway mark or gas would pour from the seam. This was especially problematic since the gas gauge didn't work at all—always showing full—and the speedometer was stuck at 110 mph.

The rear view mirror had 16 little faded green pine tree deodorizers dangling from it, not nearly enough to mask the smell of...what *was* it the smell of? Something familiar but indefinable. A heady stew of odours from the past that caused the olfactory to work double overtime. The dash was decorated with more than three dozen gold anchors, souvenirs from a popular rye whisky of bygone days.

But to Gurrey and Grime's rheumy eyes, the decrepit old car and its haphazard, mismatched and downright dangerous collection of junkyard "improvements" was a thing of automotive beauty. As they cruised down the Neck toward the Islands, they continued to wonder at the amazing restoration.

"That Eddie sure is some clever feller!" Grime said. "Look at how he got our radio workin' agin'."

He gestured toward the front fender, where a straightened-out wire coat hanger was jammed into the stump of a long-ago broken-off antenna. "This radio ain't worked since the 60s. Now it's practically good as new!"

He frantically fiddled with the knob to locate 1510 WMEX in Boston, the top rock station of his youth that had gone off the air some twenty years ago. The vacated frequency emitted only a god-awful screech of static.

"Oh! This music the kids listen to today is just terrible!" Gurrey said. "Keep trying. See if you can find something by The Ruptured Duck Repair Service on CHSJ. Or maybe The Kingston Trio or The Dave Clark Five. They're still on Kasey Kasem's Top Forty, right?"

Despite having to stop twice, once because the car overheated and once due to car sickness from the exhaust fumes that rose from the floorboards, at exactly 10:05 the reinvigorated dicks were in East Ferry, first in line to board the ferry to Tiverton at the eastern tip of Long Island.

When the scow had disgorged its Digby-bound traffic, Gurrey dropped into dead low and eased the Fury 11 down the slip onto the ferry, wheezing to a stop at the far end. The rest of the vehicles followed suit until there was room for no more and the *Joe Casey* pulled away from the dock.

The 15-minute crossing was uneventful until they reached the other side and the ramps had been lowered. When Gurrey turned the key in the ignition, the engine resisted, creating a sound not unlike a snoring husband being slowly strangled by his wife.

He tried several times and each time the strangling sounds grew shorter and weaker until finally there was only a staccato clicking sound. The battery was dead.

"Damn Canadian Tire to Hell!" Gurrey said, striking the steering wheel repeatedly with the palm of his hand. "I bought that battery brand spankin' new in October of 1972 in Digby. I'm gonna write a letter, I swear to God I am. I can't stand a company what don't stand behind their products."

The drivers behind him were growing impatient with the delay, some beeping their horns. The two men got out of the car and Gurrey fumbled for the lever that opened the hood. A shower of rust rained down on him as he leaned in to examine the ancient battery.

"Well, there's your problem," Grime said, looking over his partner's shoulder. "Corrosion. Look at them terminals. We need a jump is all. I'll be right back."

Grime approached the pick-up truck behind them and motioned for the driver to roll down her window. She did so reluctantly. "Would you happen to have any jumper cables?" he intoned in the silky smooth baritone that had driven women crazy, some metaphorically and at least two clinically.

"Might have," she answered. "Check the back."

Grime spotted a frayed set of cables and asked the woman if she could nudge her vehicle alongside the Fury 11 to give him a jump. She rolled her eyes and sighed deeply but manoeuvred the shiny new GMC as far forward as space would allow. Grime popped her hood and carefully attached the cables to the two batteries before signalling for Gurrey to turn the ignition key.

The car roared to life with a deep-throated guttural growl that caused people on the wharf to scatter and seagulls to take flight.

Grime slammed the hood and hopped in the passenger seat. "That's what these islands are all about, Gurrey. People helping people. That lady don't expect nothing in return but a little wave of thanks."

Gurrey put the car in gear and started up the slip, forgetting that the jumper cables were still attached to the pickup. Seeing the imminent disaster unfold, the vehicles on the ferry laid on their horns, creating a coordinated cacophony.

"Hear that, Gurrey? That there is the sound of home." He looked in the rear view mirror and gave a small wave before shoving an 8-track cassette into the tape player that Fast Eddy had jerry-rigged for them.

"Is she wavin' back?" Grime said.

"She is indeed," Gurrey said, "and very enthusiastically, too, with both hands! Sorry babe, not today!" He stepped on the gas and the car shot forward.

There was a loud snapping noise, followed by the sound of shattering glass, a piercing scream and a string of expletives, but the dulcet tones of Boxcar Willie singing The Lord Made a Hobo Out of Me drowned out any exterior sounds.

They waved a final thank you to the good Samaritan and headed down the road at high speed to Freeport, 10 serpentine miles to the west, to catch the second ferry to Westport.

~

In his younger days, Gurrey had enjoyed somewhat of a reputation as a wheelman. He was known as one of the most skilful and daring drivers in the Tri-Island area, his reputation even extending off-island as far abroad as Whale Cove! From 1965 to 1967 he held the record for fastest times in the unofficial Ferry-to-Ferry Sprint, a highly illegal and ill-advised road race to see who could drive from the Tiverton ferry wharf to the Freeport ferry wharf in the shortest time.

As impressive as this was, Gurrey is to this day known far and wide for an automotive feat that has never been repeated or even attempted, the Telephone Pole Trifecta!

In a late Saturday night attempt to beat his own best time from ferry to ferry, Gurrey decided to keep the gas pedal to the floor instead of letting up as he usually did when approaching the combined dip, sharp bend, then rise in the road known locally as "Suicide." The result of this strategic decision was that his '57 Ford Fairlane rocketed off the road on the curve, tore along the ditch, took out a telephone pole, ricocheted off a boulder, broke off a second pole, ripped up several yards of Judson Cann's new wire fence, snapped off yet one more pole, and finally came to rest on the shoulder of the road just short of the next telephone pole.

Miraculously, Gurrey escaped with only minor injuries and later that evening could be seen regaling the locals with the story of his latest automotive adventure. His explanation was that he had at first kept his foot on the gas in an attempt to force the car back onto the road. But as the poles snapped one after another, he saw the possibility of another unofficial record. As he stated, "I was able to get three of 'em boys. I tried for four but I couldn't hold her!"

Since retirement, Gurrey had become somewhat less daring. True, he passed three cars on the inside and overtook and passed an ambulance with its siren blaring and lights flashing, but he did it with both hands on the wheel, a fact that would have forced him to question his own manhood back in his prime.

~

They arrived at the Westport ferry dock 15 minutes later, just as Boxcar Willie was polishing off yet another yodelling medley. They proceeded onto the waiting *Joshua Slocum* and once again were first in line to get off. A tractor trailing a loaded hay wagon pulled up on one side of them and an Esso Oil truck nudged in behind.

They were halfway across Grand Passage before a word was spoken. "Now remember, it's imperative that we slip into town quietly, unnoticed, completely anonymous," Grime said to Gurrey. "We had a small issue on the first ferry but I think we covered it smooth as silk. Just make sure you don't turn the engine off this time. Let 'er charge up a tad."

"It's making an awful racket," Grime shouted. "I think the muffler's come off of her."

Ten minutes later, the ferry nestled gently against the wharf and again Gurrey dropped it into dead low. He stepped on the gas and a cloud of black exhaust smoke immediately enveloped the vehicle. The noxious fumes rose up through the rusted out undercarriage, nauseating both men.

With little hesitation and even less thought, Gurrey acted. With only a rough idea where the waterside edge of the slip was, he floored the gas pedal, desperate to escape the black cloud of death. The tires squealed on the steel ferry deck and the car bolted forward, fishtailing up the incline trailing a shower of sparks from the dragging muffler.

When the newly-hopped-up Fury 11 made it to the top of the incline, Gurrey pulled over and slammed on the brakes. The worn-out shocks and springs caused the car to undulate like a dog shaking water out of its coat.

They desperately stuck their heads out the windows. Black smoke billowed past them and rose into the still air like a burnt offering to some vengeful god.

Still feeling the disorienting effects of the fumes, Gurrey said something that sounded like "Why do the elk pursue us?"

Without hesitation, Grime, who was now as pale as a sheet, replied, "Tuesday."

Behind them the sparks from the muffler had ignited the load of hay and the flames were lapping at the side of the Esso gas truck. Several volunteer firemen rushed past them to douse the flames.

Those who weren't busy extinguishing the fire were frantically running for cover. Several of them jumped from the opposite side of the wharf into the briny water.

Suddenly a large explosion rocked their car, sending a searing wave of molten metal and burning hay flying past them.

Somehow, despite Gurrey and Grime's complete discretion and monk-like circumspection about their new assignment, a large contingent of townsfolk had quickly gathered on the wharf.

"They haven't forgotten us," yelled Gurrey above the din from the muffler and shrill screams and explosions from the ferry. "Even with our strict code of silence, they haven't forgotten us." A single tear rolled down his left cheek.

Someone in the crowd yelled, "You two are total dicks!"

Grime could hardly contain himself. "Did you hear that? *Total.* That's why we do this job. Not for the money, not for the fame. We do it for that kind of respect from the public. To put it in nautical terms, we're the biggest dicks since Moby."

Gurrey and Grime waved to acknowledge the respect the crowd was paying them. "Look," Gurrey said excitedly. "Some of them are even giving us the #1 sign."

A tall, distinguished man approached the car and greeted the two battle-hardened dicks warmly. "Welcome, welcome!" counsellor David Hooter said, trying to ignore the chaos around him. "So glad to have you back. We're desperate, otherwise we wouldn't have called you. Er...that is, we desperately need your help."

"Got some crime goin' on, eh?" Gurrey said. "Whatcha got? Speedin'? Failure to stop at the stop sign? Loiterin'? Boot-leggin'? Peelin' out from the Sunday mornin' church service? Is that Kenny boy still pilferin' smokes from the general store?"

Hooter's face darkened and his voice dropped. "Something much worse, I'm afraid. Collusion!"

"What?" Gurrey said, shocked. "Well, have you called an ambulance?"

"Collusion, not collision," Grime explained. "Collusion by whom?" he said to Hooter.

"The Evil Empire itself!" Hooter said.

"Digby?" Gurrey said reasonably.

"Even worse. Russia."

The word hung in the air like a pair of your frozen-stiff long underwear on the clothesline on a Monday morning in February when the school bus passes your house on the lane leading up to the school and all the girls that you like look out the window and laugh…but I digress.

Gurrey and Grime's jaws had dropped, revealing the misshapen molars and brownish bicuspids of the former and the pearly-white, perfectly-aligned sparklers of the latter. The news had caught Gurrey as he was about to spit out a mouthful of tobacco juice. Instead he swallowed the entire plug and another spasm of nausea rippled through his frail body. Only the lightning-quick thinking of Grime saved him from toppling off the edge of the wharf.

"What?" Gurrey sputtered when he had regained his balance. "But who? Where? Why? How?"

"You'd have made a fine journalist," Grime said with the rapier wit that had made him the darling of the girlies from Bear River East to Bear River West.

"I'm certainly disconcerted by Hooter's news," Gurrey said, "but it's the glare from your teeth that really piques my journalistic interest. *Where* did you get those choppers, *why* are you wearing them, and *how* are they so excessively shiny? Last I heard, your dentures were firmly wedged into the sewer pipe of the Little River Bingo Hall's public toilet!"

"Here's a piece of free advice, Gurrey: don't ever sneeze while flushing. Took me the best part of a day to snake 'em back out, although it probably would 'a gone a lot faster if people didn't keep interrupting to use the facilities."

"They don't look any the worse for wear."

"No, they survived in pretty good shape, and the toilet bowl cleaner they use at the bingo hall shined 'em right up, so, overall, I'm calling it a win for me."

Grime belatedly noticed the look of horror and disgust on his client's face and, setting his denture adventures aside, reluctantly returned to the matter at hand. "Tell us more about this collusion."

Hooter spoke seriously. "As for who they're colluding with, that's what we need you to find out. We have our suspicions, of course. Obviously someone on the Islands, or possible up the Neck, who could gain monetarily from such treachery. Let's go to your old...er, office and I'll fill you in."

Two minutes later they were parked outside the office/fish house. Gurrey gave a subtle turn to the yellow Mastercraft flathead, switching off the ignition. The two old friends sat in silent contemplation for a few moments while the Fury continued to shake and shudder. Finally, the clapped-out V8 coughed, sputtered, and backfired a few times before falling into a resentful and uneasy silence.

They looked at each other and exchanged high fives, proud that they'd slipped into town without any undue attention.

"That's quite a feat, my friend," Grime said, "especially in this time of social media—CB radios and fax machines and such."

Somewhere in the distance they could hear the siren of the Westport Volunteer Fire Department's pumper truck as faint but frantic shouts of "Save me!" wafted on the wind.

"They only bring the fire truck out when big shots come to town," Gurrey said. "And those shouts! How can you not want to help people who put so much trust in you?"

Seeing Hooter pull up behind them, the two old, newly-un-retired dicks, accompanied by the squeaking and groaning of broken and sagging springs and other worn-out suspension parts, some the cars, some their own, extricated themselves from the vehicle.

They paused to observe before them a lop-sided, run-down, grey-shingled building. The door hung precariously on rusted hinges, the few intact windows were so thick with years of fish guts and grime as to be only slightly more transparent than the windows whose empty frames were covered with scraps of weathered plywood, tattered garbage bags, and, in one case, the remnants of an old oilskin jacket. The roof sported multiple missing shingles, an alarming sag in the middle, and a rusty stovepipe at one end that appeared to have been the subject of either enthusiastic target practice or a very determined but not very bright woodpecker.

Until they retired, this had been the illustrious headquarters of the Digby Neck and Islands Fish-Gutting Service and Detective Agency as well as the home of both Gurrey and Grime. The two fish-gutters / detectives now stood before it for the first time in three years, their jaws hanging open in amazement.

"Well, would you look at that!" Grime said.

"Amazing! I can't believe it," Gurrey replied. "Three years we've been gone, and it hasn't changed a bit. Still looks as good as it ever did. Look! Our old sign is still there!"

Over the entrance a misshapen piece of plywood advertised the existence of a detective agency at this unlikely location. Back in the mists of time, some unknown local wit had altered one letter so the faded banner read "DeFective Services Available". In a sad testimony to their powers of observation, as well as the accuracy of the sign, the two detectives had never noticed the change.

"Shall we go in?" Grime pulled a huge ring of keys from his pocket and approached the door. Squinting intensely, he fumbled with the ring, muttering mostly to himself as he painstakingly inspected each and every one of the variously-shaped keys. "Old apartment in Tiverton, old house in Freeport, room 8 of the Sea Shoal Motel in Digby, key to My First Diary, sardine can key, garage key, Room 10 of the Fundy Wind Motel and Cabins in Digby, shed key, suitcase key…"

Just as Gurrey was about to explode with impatience, Grime finally made what seemed to be a satisfactory selection and tried it in the rusty padlock. Several minutes later, he was sweating profusely and still struggling to open the door.

Gurrey heaved a sigh of exasperation and said, "I'll get the master key." He trudged back to the car, opened the trunk and pulled out a hacksaw.

Forty-five minutes later they had sawn through the padlock and were back in the headquarters of the most famous crime detection duo since Sherlock Holmes and Dr. Watson. Gurrey and Grime settled themselves behind their desk/gutting table on the familiar old chesterfield they had retrieved from the beach after the October blow of 1976.

Councillor Hooter, wearing the haunted look of someone who suspects he had made a terrible, terrible mistake, grabbed a clam bucket, turned it over and sat across from them, his head barely visible over the table. He looked up and addressed the dicks.

"It began when we started noticing strange lights offshore late at night. At first we thought it was just factory ships, but then one Saturday night after the Legion dance, Esrum Gidney and Squid Ossinger got all liquored up and decided to take a little trip to Grand Manan to see the Guptil twins, Rosatia and Tulip. They got out there a ways and saw them lights and decided to investigate. There was a huge vessel, made to look like one of them factory ships; but even drunk, Esrum and Squid knew better. Squid stayed in the boat and Esrum rowed over and went aboard, quiet as a mouse."

Gurrey and Grime were spellbound as Hooter spoke. The only noise was a slight rustle of paper as Gurrey rolled his makins and fired up a cigarette.

"He heard voices and tippy-toed over to where five shadowy figures were gathered on the deck. He crouched behind a pile of rope to listen. They were speakin' English. Kind of broken English, you know, like the kind they speak in Tiverton. But then one guy spoke up in perfect Brier Island English. They were talking about planting a mole on Long or Brier Island. That person's job would be to integrate into the community and become accepted by one and all. That's all he was able to hear before a sudden squall of rain forced the men to go below decks. That's when Esrum high-tailed it over the side and rowed like a scalded cat back to the boat."

Gurrey and Grime were dumbstruck, although somehow, no doubt due to their extensive two-week training session at the Bear River Police Academy and Storm Door Factory, it was impossible for Hooter to detect any change in their implacable visages.

Simplicity was the key to crime fighting, they had been told by the Academy's legendary Irish criminologist, Barry O'Leary. Gurrey and Grime hung on every word from Dr. B.O., as they affectionately called him, and their attention had paid off big-time. At the graduation ceremony, the professor had declared that Gurrey and Grime had mastered the art of feigning complete and utter ignorance and were, in fact, "the simplest, most ignorant students I've ever had." The two dicks still stuck their chests out proudly whenever their former mentor was mentioned.

"Are you saying there are spies among us?" Grime said.

"Not sure," Hooter said. "We think so, but they're obviously very clever at blending in with our diverse population here on the island. With a population of nearly 350 people, it's an almost-impossible task to find Russian spies, let alone moles. That's why we need your eagle eyes to reveal who they are. Obviously they'll be highly-trained operatives. They'll look just like you or me. And they'll be looking for recruits too, people they can mould, people that can help them gain a foothold."

"Are you saying what I think you're saying, Counsellor?" Gurrey said. "You want us to go undercover?"

"Exactly!"

"Well, we're not as young as we once were," Gurrey said. "We'll need our old, trusty legman Owen Otley. Is he still around?"

"He is and he's slimmed down to 325 pounds."

"Still 5' 4" though, is he?"

"Yes but he carries it well," Hooter replied.

~

All these years later, Gurrey's confidence in his skills as a wild man behind the wheel had barely diminished, so when he took the sharp turn off of Overcove Road onto Farm Road, he did it with such flair and panache that the worn passenger door latch on the old Fury flung open and it was only Gurrey's lightning reflexes and vise-like grip that kept a dozing and dozy Grime from rolling out onto the road.

Farm Road led, not surprisingly, to The Farm, an area of Long Island that had been settled two hundred years ago by a family determined to provide their fellow Islanders with the plentiful bounty of the soil. Unfortunately, they had selected the least productive piece of property on the island. It was said that alder bushes wouldn't grow there and that even dandelions struggled to survive. Eventually, after several successive generations of failed crops and futility, the family decided that no one could scratch a living from the stubborn dirt and the farm was sold. The new owners scraped off the quarter inch of topsoil and discovered that the farm stood atop a huge gravel ridge. They immediately put the land to productive use as a gravel pit, thus ensuring a reliable source of gravel and a parking place for every horny teenager from Boar's Head to Western Light.

Gurrey and Grime rolled cautiously across this now-barren landscape, heading toward a gate at the edge of the pit that faced the sea. From here a road led down to several cottages.

The Fury had snagged the remainder of its muffler on a rock, so they announced their arrival at a newly-built and fancy-looking cottage with a lot of un-muffled roaring and backfiring.

From the back step of the cottage one had an unobstructed view of the devastated landscape of the former Farm, its gravel ridge scraped down to solid bedrock, dotted with stagnant ponds and the rusted hulks of several abandoned cars.

"Why would anybody build such a nice place in such a dump?," Gurrey wondered out loud.

But upon walking around to the front, the two old dicks were greeted with what could only be called a magnificent vista. Two hundred feet of lush greenery, broken up by colourful banks of wild rose bushes, swept down to the shore. The blue waters of St. Mary's Bay sparkled in the sun. In the far distance the French Shore was just a green smear topped with fluffy white clouds drifting slowly across a startlingly blue sky.

"Wow!" Grime said. "What a view! Reminds me of a painting by Rockwell."

"Norman Rockwell?" Gurrey asked, seizing the opportunity to display the totality of his knowledge of the art world.

"No, Margaret Rockwell. Margaret Grime, as was. My sister. Moved to Dartmouth and married this Rockwell fella, Ray. Been putting on airs ever since. Big feelin', you know. Paints without the numbers now."

As the two stood contemplating the idyllic scene, they noticed an odd bubbling in the water just out past the columnar basalt rocks that stood like sentries along the coastline. Suddenly the roiling water was flung high into the air, accompanied by two massive, dark, hulking bodies. The two behemoths crashed back to the surface, sending glittering sheets of seawater flying, creating a sun-kissed rainbow-coloured halo around them.

Mesmerized by the majesty of this spectacle, Gurrey struggled to get out his words, "Grimey, did you see that? A double whale breach!"

"I sure did," Grime said in a disgusted tone. "Those damned whales, always showing off and raising a fuss! I'll bet the tourists that pay good money to go out on the tour boats don't appreciate that juvenile behaviour, if them whales don't soon smarten up they're going to ruin it for everyone."

Shaking his head, Gurrey guided his feeble partner over to a set of stairs that led to a large deck that stretched across the front of the cottage. The dynamic duo made their way slowly up the steps to the deck, stopping frequently to let Grime catch his breath.

Upon reaching the top they were greeted by the sight of a short, round, pale man lying on a sun cot, clad in nothing but a red Speedo and sunglasses. At his side sat a moribund bloodhound apparently too massive to lift his head to observe the newcomers.

Tipping his head, Otley, for it was he, looked over his sunglasses at the two detectives. "Hello boys. Heard you were back. You know my dog Lardy. We wondered when you'd show up."

"Hello, Owen."

Owen Otley had changed. Even though the local doctor had officially upgraded his condition from morbidly obese to merely dangerously obese, he looked larger than ever.

"I assume you need me for a case?" Owen said. "I'll need a steep-end."

"You mean a stipend?"

"No, steep-end, my prices have gone up with the cost of living." He pointed to his belly. "You know, inflation."

"Well, I guess we have no choice. You get what you pay for," Gurrey said.

"Glad you see it my way," Otley gasped, exhausted from the effort of uncrossing his legs.

They shook hands and the deal was struck. Otley was their trusty leg man once again.

During the drive back to the office, Grime was deep in thought. "What we need is an informant, someone who knows the mean streets of Westport and is willing to talk, for a price of course. But how do we find just the right person?"

"Well, there's Mitch the Snitch," Gurrey said

"It has to be someone with a complete lack of morals, a person who would sell out his own mother for the right price."

"Mitch the Snitch tipped the Mounties off about his mother's bootlegging operation. Got a twenty-dollar reward. She's doing 10 to 20 in Dorchester."

"It's got to be someone on the inside, someone familiar with the ugly underbelly of Westport society."

"Mitch the Snitch told the *Courier* about old Mrs. Ideson claiming she was 102 when she was only 101. She died shortly after from shame."

"Hmmm, this will require some thought. There has to be someone… someone low enough to sell out his own country."

"Mitch cheered for Russia in the last Canada Cup."

"I've got it!" Grime said. "Remember that guy who lived at the far end of Flour Cove Road? He was always in the know about everything…"

"Mitch the Snitch."

"Had a black beard and shifty eyes…Michael, Mark, Morty…"

"Mitch! Mitch the Snitch!," screamed Gurrey as they arrived at the office.

"Now I remember, Gurrey, old friend. It was Mitch! Some people called him Mitch the Snitch!"

A few phone calls later and Gurrey and Grime were sitting at a table with Mitch Mitchell, aka Mitch the Snitch, in a back booth at the Dingy Dinghy Pool Hall and Gentlemen's Club, a notorious Island hangout for layabouts, ruffians and malcontents. Mitch had a pencil-thin moustache, narrow sideburns that extended to his chin but didn't quite meet, and a wide, unruly unibrow that gave the impression that he was continually surprised at everything around him.

"So you'll do it?" Grime said. "You'll work with us to uncover the colluders?"

"Sure, what's the odds?" Mitch said, sneering around his toothpick. "Long's it pays, acourse."

"Oh, we'll pay well, never fear," Gurrey said.

"And as long as no one else knows," Mitch added. "The number one rule in being an effective informer is to appear trustworthy and above board at all times."

A man Grime recognized as the village minister walked by. He glanced at their table and waved. "How ya doin', Mitch the Snitch? Who ya snitchin on these days?"

"Hey Ray," Mitch replied absently.

Gurrey and Grime looked at each other.

The bartender approached the table. "Want another beer, gents?"

Gurrey and Grime shook their heads.

"How about you, Snitch? You wanna beer?"

"No thanks, Charlie."

The three men finished their drinks and Grime paid the tab. As they left the bar, there were shouts of recognition from every table:

"Hey Snitch, how's it hangin'?"

"Hey, Mitch the Snitch, ratted on anyone yet today?"

"Who ya squealin' on for these guys, Snitcher?"

By the time they'd reached the door, everyone in the bar was on their feet chanting in unison, "Mitch the Snitch, Mitch the Snitch..."

When they finally got outside, Gurrey spun the weasel-faced Mitch around. "What's goin' on? Everybody in town knows you're a snitch."

"Sure," Mitch said, deftly twirling the toothpick in a complete circle with his tongue. "It's the perfect cover, don't ya see? Everyone knows I'm a snitch, a rat, a traitor, a scumbag. You think them Ruskies are gonna wanna hang out with choir boys, of which we don't have any since the choir is all grey-haired women?"

Gurrey and Grime lapsed into deep thought, their faces contorted by the effort. Finally, Grime broke the silence. "Makes sense to me," he said.

"Absolutely," Gurrey said.

"Now we need you to infiltrate the colluders, Grime said. "Like you said, you have just the street crud needed to gain their trust."

"Cred," the Snitch said.

"Right," Grime said. "I'm sure that's what I must have meant. Find out who they are and what they're up to. Who they're colluding with. What lowdown, treacherous life form would help the enemy against his own people?"

"That'd be me," Mitch said. "I just do what they tell me and they pay real good."

"You…you mean that you're the go-between with the Russians? You're the Russian asset? You're the spy who's selling out his country? You're a mole?"

"Surprised you there, didn't I?"

"You're working for the Russians?"

"Well, now I'm working for you, too."

"Too?! You're working for us *too*?! Are you crazy?"

"Crazy like a mole," Mitch said.

"Are you proposing to be a double-agent?" Gurrey said.

"Unless a third person comes along with a better offer. Then I guess I'd be a triple-agent."

"You really are a horrible Canadian, aren't you?" Grime said in wonder.

"Oh contrary, may Sammy, as the Frenchies say. I'm the biggest patriot in the Tri-Island area. I'm bringing down an entire political philosophy."

"How did you figure that out?"

"Communism. I'm taking money from the Ruskies. Last I heard that was called capitalism. I'm introducing capitalism to the godless commies."

"Russia is no longer communist," Gurrey said.

"So it's working!" the Snitch said.

"It wasn't you, you tool. Happened years ago. Anyway, I guess we have no choice but to use you as our mole."

"Deal."

"Where are the Russians doing their colluding?"

"Their hideout."

"And where's that, exactly?"

"The abandoned lighthouse on Peter's Island. They row over at night."

"The third island, albeit less than a football field long and wide—CFL, not NFL—in the Tri-Island archipelago?" Gurrey said. "Well, I'll be...But why would they choose a lighthouse?"

"So's they can keep an eye out for their mother ship. Then they row me out and we collude like no one's business."

"Is it our culture they're trying to destroy? Replace our clean-cut hockey players with a bunch of ballet dancers? They are famous for their ballet, you know," Grime mused.

"Bolshoi," the Snitch said.

"No, they really are."

It was the Snitch's turn to roll his eyes. "No, they ain't trying to replace hockey with ballet. B'sides, if you're a Leafs fan, you wouldn't notice any difference."

"Vodka, then?" Gurrey said. "Are they smuggling Vodka? Russian dressing? Those little nesting dolls?"

"Nope."

"Then what?"

"They're smuggling sturgeon."

Gurrey was shocked. "You mean so's they can operate and put little gizmos in our brains to control us?"

"Sturgeons, Gurrey, not surgeons," Grime said. "The fish. Their eggs are a delicacy. And if my amazing powers of recollection are still intact from grade 12 science class, they are an endangered species."

"Exactly," the Snitch said. "They want to plant propaganda about raising sturgeon in fish farms. Right here on these islands."

The perfidity of the plot stunned Gurrey for a moment. "How many Russians are involved? Who are they?" he finally managed to say.

"Ivan Entrenchikov and Yuri Subversinski. But they go by the names Chuck and Phil. They're pretending to be tourists. Staying at the Bottom Feeder B and B, Room 6."

"Really? That's where Gurrey and I are staying," Grime said. "In room 7. Maybe we can listen in on them. We have the audio technology: there's a water glass in our room that's perfect for putting against the wall."

That evening found Gurrey, Grime, Owen Otley, his bloodhound Lardy, and Mitch the Snitch all huddled in room 7 of the Bottom Feeder Bed and Breakfast, awaiting the return of the alleged Russian colluders. It was a small room and the additional influx of bodies made it positively cramped.

Owen Otley sat on the small couch, leaving no room for anyone else. His constant wheezing and noisy intake of twin ham sandwiches were accompanied by Lardo's incessant howling.

Mitch the Snitch jabbered constantly. "Did you know Bert Finnigan is impotent? And the Hopper twins aren't twins at all, they just look alike. And McAdams General Store sells two-day old bread and calls it fresh—just put new heels at either end. And—"

Despite the TV being at full volume, Gurrey and Grime could barely hear Steve Murphy reading the six o'clock news.

Gurrey got up from his chair and peeked through the curtains just in time to see a car drive up to the unit next door. Two very hairy and extremely burly men got out and entered the room.

Gurrey turned off the TV and used hand signals to shush the others. The bloodhound continued to howl, but in a slightly lower key.

Grime took the water glass from his bedside table and carefully placed it against the wall. A stream of Ten Penny Old Stock Ale filled his right ear and dribbled down his face.

"First rule of audio detection, Grimey," Gurrey whispered. "Always empty the glass first. And use the other end."

Grime dried the glass with his shirttail and placed it correctly against the wall. Gurrey stood behind Grime, his right ear pressed against Grime's left, and the Snitch completed the sequence with Gurrey.

The bloodhound had somehow climbed onto the side table and was enthusiastically licking the beer from Grime's face. Owen Otley remained slouched across the couch, washing down his meal with a 2-litre bottle of Diet Seven-Up.

"Shhh," Grime said. "I think I'm hearing something."

The walls of the Bottom Feeder B and B were paper thin, so in fact no listening devices were needed. They all could hear every word loud and clear. The Russians were speaking English, possibly to perfect the language so that they would be accepted as the eccentric Newfoundland tourists they pretended to be.

"Lard tunderin, jazus comrade," Ivan, aka Chuck, said. "Dis is easier than I tot, me son."

"Yes me son," Yuri, aka Phil, agreed. "Dem dare people is some stupid. Stunned as me arse, the lot of em."

Having run short of Newfoundland colloquialisms, Chuck decided to continue in the Nova Scotia English they'd picked up while on the islands. "Tomorrow night the mother ship's gonna release the first school of young sturgeons into the fish farm we've placed off Peter's Island.

Fifteen hundred of them little buggers. You know what this means, Phil? Soon there'll be sturgeon fish farms in every cove and bay in Nova Scotia. Once they're in place, and the fish have grown, we'll release them. They'll migrate down the eastern seaboard of the US and soon the entire North American continent will be ours."

"How does that work again, exactly?" Phil conveniently asked..

"Caviar, my friend. The Americans will eat the caviar as they do all things, in large quantities. They will gorge on it. Fast food caviar shops will dot the landscape. Little will they know that the caviar is laced with the special drug developed in our secret labs back in Mother Russia by our great leader. They will eat the caviar on a cracker and soon they will be like zombies, drinking Budweiser and listening only to Fox News all day. The code name for our evil scheme is Putin on the Ritz. Now all we have to do is wait until dark, go to our Peter's Island hideout and send our nightly report back to the general who's waiting aboard the mother ship."

"You mean the sturgeon-general's report?" Phil said.

"Yes," his countryman said. "The sturgeon-general's report."

That was all the intrepid crime-fighters needed to hear. This was incontrovertible proof of collusion.

With an assist from Gurrey, Grime, and Mitch the Snitch, the islands' top legman Owen Otley sprang to his feet and waddled from the room with Lardy nipping encouragingly at his ample buttocks. The others followed close behind.

Otley crashed through the door into the adjoining room and was face to face with the shocked Russians.

"Lard tunderin' I want me a geezily lawyer," Ivan Entrenchikov said.

"G'wan with ya, me too, me son," Yuri Subversinski added.

"Might I suggest the finest law firm in the Tri-Island area," Owen Otley wheezed. "Outhouse, Outhouse, Outhouse and Pugh, conveniently located in the basement of the decommissioned IOOF Hall in downtown Tiverton."

Otley had been an Outhouse but changed his name for "professional reasons," following the example of his older brother Ivan, the Realtor Note: Other famous Outhouses who have changed their names for professional reasons include Elton John, Olivia Newton-John, Edith Head, WC Fields, and—oddly—John Crapper. The unfortunate Olivia Outhouse, of Central Grove, married an Italian gentleman and became Olivia Outhouse-Lavatori.

Next morning, back at the office/fish shack, Gurrey and Grime were eating caviar and washing it down with Ten Penny Old Stock Ale.

"Well, the guilty parties are safe behind bars," Grime said with satisfaction.

"Yup. If we hadn't stopped 'em quick, the people of these islands woulda been up to their whatnots in caviar. It'd be caviar for breakfast, caviar for lunch, caviar for supper. You'd be watchin' Hockey Night in Caviar and instead of ketchup potato chips, it'd be caviar chips. Soon, we'd be known as the caviar capital of Canada. Can you imagine?"

"I see what you mean," Gurrey said. "We'd all be eating caviar. Then the tourists would expect us to have them expensive $10.00 wines from up the Valley. Then we'd be what they call elites. I ain't ready for that. How about you, Grimey?"

Grime smacked his lips loudly. "I have to admit this stuff does have a certain, what the Frenchies call jenny c. qwaws. In fact the Grime family is part of the elite of the favoured isle to the east...But, naw, I like my ketchup chips."

They sat back on the tattered and stained chesterfield. Gurrey and Grime were back. They had solved the collusion case in record time and the islands had been saved from the Russian caviar cabal.

"You know," Gurrey said. "I always thought Peter's Island would be a great place to put prisoners like they did with that Napoleon fella."

"Dynamite?" Grime said.

"You like my idea!?"

"No, I mean you're talking about *Napoleon Dynamite*, like in the movie?"

"No," Gurrey said. "Bonyparte, like in the part of the mackerel you don't eat. Napoleon Bonyparte, you know, like when they put him on Elba?"

"Oh!" Grime said, finally catching on. "You mean you wanna make Peter's Island a penal colony?"

"Not at all! Women criminals could go there too."

"It's a brilliant idea, my friend! Absolutely brilliant!"

They lapsed into a prolonged silence, drinking their beer and savouring their breakthrough plan for prison reform.

Finally, Gurrey turned to Grime and grinned. "Let's face it, Grimey, retirement ain't for us. We're too young and virile, and, let's face it, irreplaceable. Fact is, we've just wrapped up another successful case, slick as a smelt. Our faces are plastered all over the *Digby Courier's* Crime and Punishment section. It don't get much bigger'n that, unless..."

"You're not thinkin' of the *Chronicle Herald*, are you, Gurrey?" There was childlike wonder in Grime's good eye. "You think that MacKinnon fella might scratch out a cartoon of us?!"

"The world is our oyster," Gurrey replied. "We're back, baby!"

"Just goes to show, old friend," Grime said sagely. "You can't keep a couple of good dicks down."

About the authors

Jim Prime is the author of over 20 books, mostly on the subject of sports. He co-authored *Ted Williams' Hit List* with the legendary Boston Red Sox hitter and *How Hockey Explains Canada* with Canadian hockey icon Paul Henderson. He has also collaborated with baseball eccentric Bill "Spaceman" Lee on two books. He has contributed articles to various magazines including *Baseball Digest*, *Atlantic Insight*, *Atlantic Advocate*, *The Ring*, *Boxing Illustrated*,  and the *Acadia Alumni Bulletin*, where he briefly served as editor. He's a five-time winner of the People's Choice award at the Kings Shorts Festival of Ten Minute Plays in Annapolis Royal.

Jim grew up in Freeport on Long Island and will always consider himself an islander. He lives in New Minas in the Annapolis Valley with his wife Glenna.

Ben Robicheau is a recreational writer. He has contributed a series of autobiographical stories about growing up on Brier Island to *Passages*, the monthly Digby Neck and Islands newsletter. In collaboration with Jim Prime he created the Gurrey and Grime characters and for two years they wrote monthly episodes which appeared in *Passages*. He also collaborated with Jim on two award-winning plays which were performed at  King's Theatre in Annapolis Royal as part of their King's Shorts Ten Minute Play competition.

Ben lives with his wife, Randi, in Hamilton, Ontario, close to his children Sarah and Michael and grandchildren Felix, Charlie and Lyla. He is working on a collection of short stories about growing up on Brier Island.

Jim Prime books

(an incomplete list)

Ted Williams Hit List (with Ted Williams)
Tales from the Boston Red Sox Dugout
More Tales from the Boston Red Sox Dugout
The Little Red (Sox) Book (with Bill Lee)
Red Sox Essentials
Baseball Eccentrics (with Bill Lee)
How Hockey Explains Canada (with Paul Henderson)
The Goal that United Canada
Amazing Tales from the 2004 Boston Red Sox Dugout
Ted Williams: a Tribute
Ted Williams: a Splendid Life
Fenway Park at 100
Fenway Saved
Tales from the Toronto Blue Jays Dugout
The Boston Red Sox World Series Encyclopedia
From the Babe to the Beards
Ted Williams, the Pursuit of Perfection
The Barber of Mud Creek
Boston Red Sox Killer Bs: Baseball's Best Outfield

About the artist

Currently living in Poway, California, Catherine Prime is Nova Scotia born and bred and is very proud of her home province. She graduated from NSCAD in Halifax with a fine arts degree in Ceramics before earning her B.Ed from the University of Western Ontario.

Her artistic tastes are eclectic and she works in a variety of mediums, including textiles, clay and graphic art. Her household consists of her bio-chemist husband Dave, sons Fin and Sam, Sundae the cat, and Bagheera the dog.

Her online shop is at **etsy.com/shop/catherinejane**